Augathella Short and Sweets Books 1-3

An Augathella Surprise

An Augathella Baby

An Augathella Spring

ANNIE SEATON

AUGATHELLA SHORT AND SWEETS

An Augathella Surprise

An Augathella Baby

An Augathella Spring

An Augathella Wedding

An Augathella Christmas

An Augathella Easter

An Augathella Masquerade Ball

Following on from:

THE AUGATHELLA GIRLS

Book 1: Outback Roads –The Nanny
Book 2: Outback Sky – The Pilot
Book 3: Outback Escape – The Sister
Book 4: Outback Winds – The Jillaroo
Book 5: Outback Dawn – The Visitor
Book 6: Outback Moonlight – The Rogue
Book 7: Outback Dust – The Drifter
Book 8: Outback Hope – The Farmer

An Augathella Surprise

ANNIE SEATON

Augathella Short and Sweets: 1

Chapter 1

Gold Coast Weddings -Chapel of Love

'Move away. Give her some space.' Jenna Wilson stepped forward as the bride dissolved into a fresh round of gasping sobs. 'Listen up, everyone, how about we all step out for a minute and let Rina compose herself?'

'Don't you friggin' tell me what to do. She's *my* friend and my sister-in-law-to-be.' A tall woman with dark hair shoved Jenna, and she had to grab for the counter of the vanity as she tottered on her high heels. It didn't help that the floor was wet and slippery from a leaking tap at the end of the row of basins. This wedding venue was nowhere near as upmarket as Jenna had expected when she'd been invited to her boss's wedding.

'Excuse me!' Jenna's best friend, Alana Rickman, pushed through the melee of women filling the small restroom. 'You almost knocked my friend over.'

'I don't give a flying fig what I did. She doesn't tell us what to do. Rina, sweetie, come here.' The dark-haired woman tried to put her arms around the sobbing bride. 'Jock'll be okay in a minute. They're pouring coffee into him now.'

'Leave me alone, Diane.' The bride stepped away from the bossy woman. 'I'm not marrying your brother. Not today, not *ever*.'

'Come on, sweetie. He's only had a couple of beers.'

From what Jenna had seen as the groom lurched out of the gents' restroom in the foyer of the wedding venue, he had a lot more than two beers under his belt.

Alana, who'd agreed to come to the wedding with her, had

nudged Jenna as they crossed the foyer towards the chapel. 'Get a load of that,' she'd whispered.

Jenna's eyes widened as she turned.

A man with a bare chest, his pants around his knees, seemed unaware that a trail of toilet paper hung from the back of his Calvin Kleins as he lurched towards the chapel. He was muttering, but his words were slurred and impossible to understand. Two guys in suits hurried after him.

'Jocko, stop!' A burly guy with tattoos circling his neck and on the back of his shaved head grabbed for the man.

A couple of the female guests tried to distract the bride when she came through the main door with her two bridesmaids. Jenna's mouth fell open in shock as her elegant boss spotted him before he fell to the floor, a happy grin gracing his face.

It hadn't been until Rina screamed and ran for the ladies' room, followed by most of the women who were in the foyer, that Jenna had realised the comatose guy on the floor was the groom.

She couldn't believe her eyes. Rina, the bride and her work supervisor at the premier real estate agency at Surfers Paradise, was always stylish and cultured. Word was she'd moved to the Gold Coast from Double Bay in Sydney and had been part of the social set in the city.

Jenna had expected Sydney socialites at the wedding, but the group of wedding guests—to put it politely—were a tad rough around the edges. The venue had surprised her, too; it was tired and tatty, and she'd noticed a mouldy smell in the foyer as she and Alana waited to go into the chapel before the ruckus started.

'Next time you ask me to come and keep you company at a wedding, I'll think twice,' Alana said, shaking her head as the tattooed man crouched over the groom.

'I don't believe you,' Jenna said. 'You're a serial wedding

guest. Nothing keeps you away from weddings. You love them. That's why when it said "plus guest" on my invite, I thought of you straight away.'

'You need to find yourself a man. I keep telling you that.' Jenna nudged her with a grin.

The two girls had been friends since the first year of high school, and now they caught up at least once a week since Alana had moved to Burleigh Heads. They were polar opposites; Jenna was career-oriented, and Alana flitted from one job to another in her perpetual search for Mr Right, but Alana had been good for her. She'd taught Jenna to chill and not focus so much on trying to climb the career ladder. If Jenna was honest, she hadn't been getting as much satisfaction out of her job lately.

'Although this is almost enough to turn a girl off getting married.' Alana's grin was cheeky. 'But you know me, Jen, I'm always on the hunt for my perfect groom.'

'I do know you.' Jenna had tried not to chuckle. 'I'd say the guy on the floor is far from perfect. Come on, I'll go and check that Rina's okay, and then we might head to the pub. What do you think?'

'We're too dressed up for the pub. How about we go to the Sheraton? My shout.'

'Sounds like a plan.' Alana followed her across to the ladies' room. 'By the look of the groom, I don't think there's going to be a wedding this afternoon.'

When they entered the ladies' restroom, Jenna couldn't believe the scene that greeted them. Rina was hanging onto the side of the vanity, her head over the basin. Another friend had come in with two glasses of champagne and was trying to push one into the bride's face.

'No,' Rina yelled. 'I don't want it. Just everybody, get out of here. Let me catch my breath, and then I'm going home.'

'You can't go home, sweetie. You're getting married,' one

of the fuchsia-pink-clad bridesmaids piped up.

Rina straightened, her eyes widening. 'You're right, I can't. I'm not going home because I'm never going to go back to his apartment again.'

'Aw, come on, sweetie. You've got to get married. Jock is waiting for you.'

'Waiting for me? Prostrate drunk with no pants on, out in the foyer? You must be joking,' Rina said. The culture had come back into her voice a little bit as the immediate shock wore off. 'I'm a laughing stock already.'

Jenna stepped forward. 'If you're serious, Rina, I can give you a lift back to wherever you want to go,' she said quietly.

The pushy woman stepped in front of Jenna. 'No, you piss off, bitch. Rina is marrying my brother. He'll get himself together in a minute. Rina honey, scull your champers. Come on, pull yourself together, and wash your face.' She waved a huge hairbrush in front of the bride's face. 'I'll help you get your hair tidy again.'

'Diane, I am not marrying your brother. In fact, if that's what the thought of getting married can do to someone they're supposed to love, I'm not ever marrying anyone. He needed a skinful of grog to go through with the wedding. So, get out of my way. I'm leaving. Now.'

Jenna didn't see the punch coming as she stepped closer to Rina. The next thing she knew, her face was aching against the cold tiles of the restroom floor. Her ears were ringing, and Rina was screaming, 'Diane, you're as bad as your stupid brother! Just look at what you've done to poor Jenna!'

Alana crouched next to her. 'Oh my God, Jen, are you okay? Do I need to call an ambulance? Did you hit your head?'

Jenna's face was aching, and her right wrist was throbbing. She'd managed to break her fall with her right arm, and for a moment, she thought she'd broken it. She flexed her wrist gingerly. 'No, I'm fine. Let's just get the hell out of here.'

As Alana helped her to her feet, Jenna leaned against the wall. Her head was spinning, and she put one hand on her cheek. 'I'm not bleeding, am I? I hope I don't have any broken teeth.'

Voices were rising, and there was a lot of pushing and shoving as the groom's family tried to persuade Rina to stay and her friends tried to get her to leave.

'No, there's just a red mark there. Come on, let's get out of here before this turns into a brawl.'

Rina screamed from behind, 'Jen, wait! I'm so sorry! Don't go.'

'It's okay, Rina. It wasn't you.' Jenna glared at the woman who apparently was going to be the sister-in-law-no-more. She shook her head. 'I might even go to the police station and press charges,' she said as the woman made a rude gesture.

Alana held her arm as they walked across the car park. 'Well, that was fun. Do you want to go to the pub or home?'

'Do I look okay? I'd love a drink.'

'You look fine. As long as you feel okay.'

'Good. Let's go.' Alana's eyebrows rose in question. 'The police station first?'

'No, I was just trying to wind her up. Besides, poor Rina was wound up enough without the police arriving. Let's get out of this place.'

Chapter 2

Callie Cartwright leaned back on the soft cushions of the new sofa she and Braden had bought in Charleville a couple of weeks ago. She sighed with pleasure as her husband's strong fingers massaged her bare feet. The room was warm from the crackling fire in the slow-combustion stove, and she closed her eyes and murmured, 'I didn't think those three boys were ever going to go to sleep tonight.'

'It's all your fault,' Braden said, grinning at her. 'You brought up the choice of the baby's name over dinner.'

'It did lead to a bit of a discussion,' she said with a grin.

'It sure did. I quite like "Muesli".' Braden chuckled.

'Our child is *not* going to be called "Muesli", no matter how much Petie wants it.' Callie sat up straight but she couldn't help giggling. 'Although he was really cross when we said no. First time I've ever seen him storm off to his room.'

'It was more like a Nigel tantrum than Petie's usual behaviour, but he did come back when the ice cream came out,' Braden replied. 'I think he's been a bit spoiled and we've let him have his own way too much since he came home from hospital.'

'Maybe. But oh, sweetheart, how wonderful is it to see him running around with the other pair as though he never had that awful accident.'

'It is, despite all the new grey hairs I gained in those weeks.' Braden moved up the sofa next to Callie and rested his chin on top of her head. 'But there's no way he's getting his way this time. "Muesli" Cartwright? Not a chance.' His chest rumbled against her as he laughed.

'Nigel was closer to the mark with Malachi. What is it with all the M words anyway? Rory wanted Michael.'

'I could live with Michael,' Braden said.

'Fifty-fifty chance it's a girl. How about Megan? I quite like that.'

'How about Melody?' Braden asked.

'No, not a fan.'

'Anyway, I'm sure there's a big boy growing in there.' Braden put his hand on Callie's huge stomach and shook his head. 'If it's a girl she'll be playing for the Augathella Meat Ants, my sweet.'

Callie shook her head. 'It's a girl, and I don't know about her playing football.'

'Will we have a bet?' Braden's grin was wide and Callie snuggled closer—as best as she could—and her heart filled with love for this strong, wonderful man.

If anyone had told her eighteen months ago where she would be now, and how happy she would be, she would never have believed them. Living on a cattle station in the western outback, far away from all that was familiar to her, with a gorgeous husband and three adorable stepsons, and back in the classroom part-time, she would have laughed. Even going worldwide on TikTok with that embarrassing incident on the weather network had been worth it, because it had sent her fleeing to the outback and she had been rescued by Braden.

'Your appointment in Charleville is next week, isn't it?' he said, interrupting her musing. 'Tell me again what the obstetrician said when you went down to see him last month.'

Callie opened her eyes and lifted her head. Braden was looking at her with a concerned look on his face.

'Stop worrying. He told me everything is fine. All those minor issues that I've had have all sorted themselves out. My blood pressure is perfect. The baby is the right size, and the heartbeat is nice and strong.'

'It's a bugger that we're mustering next week. Do you really think you should be driving?' Braden asked.

'Of course I can drive,' Callie reassured him, reaching out and pushing a loose strand of hair back from his forehead. 'You need a haircut.'

'I know I do, but we've just been so busy with the mustering, there's been little time for anything. It's nice to be home with you tonight. I'm just glad Jon's here to help us this month. Once he takes over his own property after the sale goes through, he's going to be pretty busy down there. And Fallon's busy with little Ryan, so she won't be flying helicopters for a while. I know Kent's got onto a new helicopter pilot from down in the Channel Country, and he's coming up to see us next week, but we're on horseback and our bikes until we see if he can help out. It's been such a great season. I still can't believe how healthy the cattle are,' Braden said.

'That's good. Healthy cattle, better prices?'

'You're turning into a station wife, Cal. And yes, it's going to be a good year financially.'

'That's good to hear. Did I tell you I looked at prams when I was down in Charleville last month?' she asked.

'No, you didn't. Did you order one?'

'No, I didn't. They were too expensive.' Callie shook her head. 'I was going to look online.'

'So, what are you going to do? Carry the new bub around all the time and not have a pram? Don't be silly,' Braden said.

'Yeah, but the one I liked was over a thousand dollars!'

'Less than the price of a beast,' Braden stated matter-of-factly. 'Order it.'

'Are you sure?'

'Of course I'm sure. If you order it tomorrow, you can pick it up when you go down next week. How often do you have to go down after the next visit?'

'I'm on weekly visits after that, so five weeks to go. Five weeks and our baby will be here,' Callie calculated.

Braden chuckled. 'You know what I'm thinking?'

'What?' she asked with a frown.

'Muesli Sylvia Cartwright does have a nice ring to it, don't you think?'

'If you want "Muesli" I'll buy the two-thousand-dollar pram!' Callie reached across and tickled him.

'Okay, time we went to bed, Mrs Cartwright. I've got an early start tomorrow,' Braden said, standing up and holding out his hand to help her to her feet. 'I haven't told you today how much I love you, have I, Callie Cartwright?'

'No, you haven't, Braden, but I'm happy for you to tell me again,' Callie said with a smile.

Chapter 3

Jenna came out of the ladies' powder room of the Sheraton restroom feeling a lot better. She'd washed her face, examined the red mark on her cheek and camouflaged it with more makeup, fluffed her hair up, and if you hadn't known she'd just face-planted onto the tiles at the wedding centre, you'd never have guessed it had happened.

Alana passed her a glass of bubbles when she climbed onto the barstool beside her. 'Cheers, girlfriend! That was the shortest wedding I've ever been to.'

Jenna shook her head. 'I still can't believe what happened.'

'I thought you said your boss was elegant.'

'Well, she's always very well-spoken and often speaks about her time in Sydney when we have morning tea in the office. She was so different today.'

'I'm sure I've seen some of those guys before. The ones who were hovering outside when we came out. Those guys belong to a motorcycle club,' Alana said. 'They used to come to the Burleigh pub where I worked.'

'Oh well, it was nothing like I imagined, but what an experience.' Jenna sighed. 'It'll be interesting to see what happens in a couple of weeks when Rina comes back from her two weeks off. They were supposed to be going to the Cook Islands for the honeymoon. I wonder if she'll change her mind and marry him.'

'You know, once he sobers up, they'll probably make up, run away somewhere and get married, and then have the honeymoon. Love's a strange thing.' Alana rolled her eyes. 'Not that I know.'

Jenna sipped from her glass and the bubbles tickled her nose. 'You try too hard, Alana. You're happy in your new job, aren't you?'

Alana pulled a face. 'Not really. I've got a bit bored down here on the Gold Coast. I'm thinking about moving west.'

'Moving west? Why would you do that?'

Alana grinned. 'I thought I could set my sights on some rich cow cocky.'

Jenna widened her eyes, and she couldn't help the laughter spilling from her lips. 'You marry a cow cocky? Have you ever even been to the country, girl?'

'I went there once when I was a kid. Mum and Dad took me out to Toowoomba.'

Jenna shook her head. 'Alana, that's not the country. Toowoomba is a city.'

'Well, I'm thinking about looking for a job out that way. Anyway, I'll get to one of those B and S balls. They seem to have lots of single blokes there.'

'You try too hard, Alana. Marriage isn't the be-all and end-all. We've got a life to live before all that happens. Go overseas, have great holidays, and have no responsibility.'

'It's all right for you with your swanky real estate office job and your degree behind you. Being a waitress doesn't pay that much. I'm hardly saving, and I don't like the new job much.'

Jenna looked at her friend over the rim of her glass. She knew that Alana was speaking from her heart. She might change jobs and find another one on the coast and she'd be happy again for a few weeks. It was sad that she felt as though she needed to have an engagement ring on her finger.

'Don't get offended, but I think you come on a bit heavy talking about the future on your first couple of dates.'

'I know, but I want to make it clear that's what I'm after.'

'And they run a mile?'

Alana nodded sadly. 'They do.'

'I rest my case. Have you been back on that dating app lately?' Jenna asked.

'Don't talk about it. Let's have another drink.'

Chapter 4

The two weeks that Rina had been away from work had increased Jenna's workload considerably. The day Rina was due back, Jenna arrived in the office early so that she could get everything up to date and have the new files moved across to the shared folder that Rina would access. Three contracts needed to be finalised today, and Jenna made sure that they were printed out, slipped into plastic sleeves labelled with the clients' names and placed on Rina's desk.

Jenna had closed on a particularly good sale, one of the units at the new complex on the Isle of Capri. They were so hard to come by, and when she had been the agent who had finalised the sale, she knew that the commission would go towards the holiday she'd been talking to Alana about last weekend.

Alana had left her job as Jenna had known she would, and now she was working in a small fish and chip shop at Broadbeach and was already saying how much she hated it.

Jenna understood Alana had a tremendous work ethic and was really smart, but she didn't seem to have the confidence to go for the bigger jobs.

Jenna focused on her work as she heard a lift ding outside her office. Rina pushed the door open; she was dressed immaculately in a red silk suit with her signature Jimmy Choos making her about ten centimetres taller.

Alana stood to greet her, and Rina glanced across at her with a brittle smile. 'I'd like to meet with you in my office at nine o'clock, please, Miss Wilson.'

That was a bit strange. Jenna pulled a face and glanced at her watch; it was fifteen minutes away.

She'd just have time to make a quick cup of coffee, touch up her lipstick, and be on time for the appointment. She felt unsettled; the woman who had just walked into the office was very different from the devastated bride she had left at the wedding centre two weeks ago.

There had been no news in the office as to what had happened, and Jenna had been the only one from the real estate agency invited to the wedding. She'd been surprised when she received the invitation but had been keen to go along. However, it had been such a fiasco, she pushed it out of her mind. Alana hadn't mentioned it again either. She'd been too caught up in her own woes.

Right on the dot of nine o'clock, Jenna stood. She walked across to the other side of the office. Rina's receptionist, Cathy, gave her a cool glance. 'Miss Wilson, please take a seat.'

Jenna went to say something; she knew Cathy quite well, but when Cathy turned back to her computer she shrugged and sat down.

A moment later, the phone on Cathy's desk buzzed. 'Rina is ready now, go in, please.'

Jenna walked into Rina's office and waited to be asked to sit down. This was obviously a formal meeting, so she treated it as such.

Rina walked around the side of her desk, the glass wall behind her providing a panoramic vista of the beach at Surfers Paradise. 'Jenna,' she said.

For a moment, Jenna wondered if she should ask how she was, but no, Rina wasn't very receptive this morning. As she stood there waiting to be invited to sit down, her boss reached over for an envelope and passed it across to her as she stood there. 'This is a statement of employment for any future employer, Jenna. Unfortunately, we have to terminate your services.'

Jenna's stomach sank like a lead balloon, and she stood there in disbelief, looking at Rina.

'Your performance hasn't been up to what we wanted at this agency, Jenna.'

'But my figures have—'

'Please don't interrupt me. You haven't reached your marketing target for the year.'

'We're only three months into the financial year,' Jenna protested. 'And I—' The unfairness of what Rina was saying burned in Jenna's chest.

Rina waved a dismissive hand. 'Please don't argue. I've discussed this with Bob, and we've decided to let you go. Your final payment, your severance payment, has already been paid into your account. An email of how it's been worked out has been sent to your personal account. Your business email account has been terminated. If you have any problems, you know the accountant's number. Please call our accountant, and he'll talk you through it. I'll also remind you that you signed an agreement not to contact any of your former clients should you leave the agency.'

'You can't do that,' Jenna said. 'I *have* met my marketing targets.'

Suddenly, the penny dropped. 'This is because I saw what happened at your wedding!'

'We won't go there, Jenna, and I'd appreciate it if you don't share what occurred on that afternoon. I've moved on now, and I'm sorry, but as I said, your marketing achievements are not up to what we want.'

Anger bubbled in Jenna's stomach, and she stepped forward, gripping the chair in front of her so tightly it moved forward and scraped on the white tiles. 'So that's it?' she ground out.

Rina's eyebrows raised, and her stare was glacial. 'Yes, that's it. Welcome to the world of big business, Jenna.'

'No, I won't accept this. I have worked my butt off for this agency for the last three years. In the last two weeks while you were away, I—'

Rina had the upper hand. 'I've seen what you've done in the last two weeks, and that was a little bit better. Well done. I ensured that the commission has been added to your payout, as you'll see when you check your email. Your personal email. Please clear out your desk and leave immediately.'

Chapter 5

Three weeks later, after Jenna had given a lot of thought to what had happened at the wedding that never was and the subsequent meeting with Rina, she walked out of her solicitor's office.

The new paralegal at her regular solicitors had been a cute guy, and he'd asked her for a date on the way out from her appointment. She shook her head. 'No, thank you. I'm moving away.'

He shrugged. 'Fair enough.'

She did feel bad about being a bit too dismissive. Alana was the one with the burning desire to partner up and get married. Jenna had visions of living in her new home and having a happy life by herself.

It wasn't just the wedding and being laid off that had woken her up to where she really wanted to be. It was the whole city thing on the Gold Coast. The crowds, the crime, the tourists and the false glitziness of the social scene. Not to mention the business environment that had let her down.

She and Alana had caught up for coffee a week after the wedding when Jenna's black eye had faded, and she felt like she could go out in public again. She had taken a couple of sick leave days, and it had given her a lot of time to think about her future. Maybe she'd look for something else, the cutthroat workplace environment in the world of real estate was wearing thin. She had Granny's inheritance carefully invested, and as she'd walked out of Rina's office, an idea began to form.

A total change of scene and she could start the business she'd always dreamed of.

Definitely not on the Gold Coast. Maybe she could start her vintage tea room in the hinterland of the Sunshine Coast?

Jenna spent the first week of being unemployed looking for cottages on land in the country. After seeing the price of real estate on the coast, her search took her further west. She could imagine a cute little country cottage on an acre of gardens, and maybe if she went further west, she could afford what she was looking for. By the end of the second week of searching, her search had taken her way out west. Seven hundred kilometres to be exact.

She hadn't mentioned it to Alana when they'd caught up for coffee the other day, but they were meeting for a drink tonight, and she was going to break the news that she'd been sacked—because that was the only word for the way she'd been treated—and that she'd found the perfect location for her new venture.

Excitement trickled through her. Maybe Alana would come with her. It would be great if she had company to start up her business, but if not, she would make the most of it. She was sure there were people out there looking for a job.

##

'Hey Jen, how's it going?' Alana stood as Jenna walked across the bar. She ignored the few interested looks thrown her way.

'I'm good. How are you?' Jen greeted her friend.

'The usual.' Alana pulled a face. 'Not good.'

Jenna raised her eyebrows. 'How come? Not enough business at the fish and chip shop?'

'No, I left there last week and started a new job. Didn't I tell you? A swanky restaurant.'

'And you don't like it?'

'I *loved* it! But I got the sack.'

'They sacked you? Why?'

'Yep. The excuse was that they had enough staff already,

but I overheard a conversation on my second night. The boss said I wasn't elegant enough and that hurt. I took the next day off sick, but I decided to stick it out, and then he told me he was overstaffed.'

'Have you been sick?'

'No, I just didn't want to work there after what I heard, but then I changed my mind. I'm totally over the Gold Coast. I'm thinking about going back to Gympie.'

'Do you really want to go home?' Jenna stared at Alana, hope flaring. 'I've got some news. I'm moving too,' she said.

'You sold your apartment?'

'No, I was only renting.'

'Oh, I thought it was yours,' Alana said. 'You're moving to a new one?'

'No. Not only did I get the sack too, I've bought a house, and I'm going to start the business I've always wanted.'

'Hang on, let's rewind here. You got the sack too?'

'Yes, apparently Rina didn't like me witnessing her wedding fiasco.'

'So, she sacked you?' Alana's voice was full of indignation. 'What a bitch. She can't do that.'

'Probably not, but I'm really pleased. It's forced me to do what I've always wanted to. Buy a cottage and start a vintage tea room.'

'My God, Jenna! Did you win the lottery?'

'No, I got a good payout from the company and I added it to some money I inherited from my gran, and I've found the place I want to buy. I've been to see the solicitor today, and I signed the contract.'

'Lucky you. I'd like to move too, but if I go back to Gympie, which I probably will, I'll have to stay at Mum and Dad's.'

'Why do you want to go back there?'

'I'm over the busyness of this place,' Alana said. 'I'm

over working for dickheads, and I'd like to go back to where I grew up. Life is slower there, less hectic, and you don't have to try to measure up all the time. It's just that I don't suit this place, and I know I've been slack taking sickies, but this last time did me a favour. It made me decide.'

'So you've given up your apartment too?'

Alana nodded. 'I have. I'll be going home in a couple of weeks. I'll miss you, Jen. Can you take me and show me your new house after we have a coffee?'

Jenna chuckled. 'Not really. It's a little way away.'

'How far?'

'Well, about two and a half days' drive west.'

'What? Where the heck are you going?' Alana said.

'I'm starting my own business. I bought a cottage on an acre on the highway at Augathella, and I'm going to start a vintage tea shop.'

'Get out of it! Are you for real?'

'I am.' Jenna looked at her best friend, who had supported her for three years on the coast. 'I'll be looking for staff, and it would help to have someone to help me fix up the place. What do you reckon?'

'It's in the country?'

'It's in the country, that's for sure,' Jenna said.

'And you want staff, and you want someone to help you fix up the place.'

'I do.'

'Where would I live?'

'It's quite a big cottage. The tearoom will go into the current living room and dining room, and there's still room to live at the back. It does need some work before I can open the business. I'll definitely have to add a small powder room for the customers, but from the pictures...'

Alana interrupted. 'What do you mean, from the pictures? You haven't seen it? You haven't been out there?'

'No, I bought it on spec,' she said. 'I looked at the pictures and the surrounding area. It's on the highway. It's going to have a captive audience of grey nomads as they go past. I've looked at the tourism figures, and I've done a feasibility study and a business plan, and I reckon I can build a really successful business in a cute little town. I need a hand, though. What do you reckon?'

'When do we move? Alana's features spread into a wide grin.

'Two weeks.'

'Count me in, girlfriend.' She high-fived Jenna. 'Hang on, where are we moving to?'

'Augathella,' Jenna said with a big smile.

Chapter 6

Reg closed the door of his house and sat down on the rickety chair on the veranda before setting off on his morning walk to the pub. Like he had every morning since he'd come home from his job out in the bush a few years back. He'd moved back into the house that had been in his family for almost a hundred years. Reg looked down at the floor. It needed a bit of work these days. The chair leg of the other chair had gone through the timber at the end of the veranda last week, and he stayed away from that end. The last thing he wanted to do was fall over and break something looking like an old codger.

He couldn't believe it when someone from Charleville Real Estate called and said they had an offer on his house. Who the heck would want to come and buy this old place? It was falling down around him. He thought someone would buy it and bulldoze it to run cattle. He always hoped that Polly Jones, who owned the land next door, would take the hint and buy the extra bit of land, but no matter how much he hinted, she'd never been interested.

Some woman had bought it, and he had to go down and sign the papers at the real estate agent tomorrow. When Callie Cartwright heard he was looking for a lift down and back, she'd offered to drive him to Charleville because she had a doctor's appointment there. She and Braden and the three little boys had been there for dinner last night, and she always talked to him. When he told her he had to find a way to Charleville tomorrow, she'd offered straight away.

He looked at her, his forehead wrinkled in a frown. 'You won't pop that baby out on the way, will you?'

'No, Reg. I still have four weeks to go.'

'Should you be driving that great big Land Cruiser of yours?'

Callie laughed, and he thought again what a lovely smile she had. It reminded him of Margie's smile. He had a soft spot for Callie since she moved to town a couple of years back, for that very reason.

'I will give you one thing. It's getting a bit hard to climb up into. I've got to pull myself up like an old lady,' she said. 'But don't worry, there is an alternative.'

'Well, love, if you're offering to take me down, I wouldn't mind a bit of company on the way. That would be really good.'

'Where do you have to go to?' she asked.

'I have to go to the lawyer's office, and I have to do a bit of shopping.' He didn't tell her what for, but if he was going to the aged care place, he'd have to get some pyjamas.

Callie looked at him curiously but didn't ask, and he appreciated that. He was a private bloke, and he didn't want everyone to know his business. He'd been into what he'd once called "the old people's home" when the lawyer fellow sent him a letter saying the sale was going through. These days he reckoned "aged care" had a nicer ring to it.

Matron Ramsay, who he'd known since she was a whipper snapper had looked at him with a nod. 'Well, Reg, you must've known something. We've got two places. We've got a room where you can go to the dining room and be totally looked after. Or we've got an independent living unit where you look after yourself.'

'I'll take the room,' he said. 'Who carked it?'

'Carked it?' Matron looked horrified. 'Oh no, Reg. Nobody's passed away. Mr and Mrs Fuller have decided to move to the aged care facility in Charleville to be closer to their children, and Bonnie Dwyer has gone to Newcastle in New South Wales to be closer to her sister. We just happened to have some rooms come available all at once.'

'Where do I sign up?' he said.

'Well, we have to fill out an application form.'

Reg waved a dismissive hand. 'Just do whatever needs to be done. Can you post it down to my solicitor in Charleville? I've got to go down there. He can organise the payment or whatever it is.'

'It's going to be a significant amount, Reg.' The whole town thought he was as poor as a church mouse and that he drank his pension every week.

But they didn't know anything about old Reg MacGilvray.

Chapter 7

'Yes, I let Dad drive my car.' Callie smiled and answered Nigel's question as the three boys sat in the back seat of the Land Cruiser. She soon lost sight of Braden because he was going a lot faster than she was; the red dust billowing out from underneath the wheels of her car was the only sign that he was ahead of them.

When she'd suggested taking her little red sports car down to Charleville this afternoon because it was easier to get into than the Toyota, Braden had readily agreed.

'But you're not driving into town over the corrugated roads. It's too bumpy. At least the Cruiser's suspension gives you a smooth ride. You can take it in with the boys while I drive your car in, and then when we get to town, we'll swap over, and I'll drop them off at school.'

'And you can help me down out of the car. I can't see Reg doing that.'

'Reg looked like all his Christmases had come at once when he found out you were driving the sports car to Charleville. When you went to round up the boys, he said to me, "Not only am I getting a lift to Charleville with the best-looking woman in Augathella, but we're going in her flash red sports car".'

Callie laughed and couldn't wait to see the look on Reg's face when she pulled up at the pub to pick him up.

It was only a short time before Braden turned onto the main highway and headed into Augathella. She followed him to the school at a sedate pace until he pulled up in the back street, where there was enough room to park both cars.

'Mum, will you stay parked out here for a while so we can

show all our friends your red car?' Rory asked.

'They are going to think it is so way cool.' Nigel grabbed his bag and opened the door of the four-wheel drive. 'Come on, Rory, we'll bring them to the back fence before she can go.'

'Will you wait in it out here for a while so we can get them all to come to the fence and have a look?' Rory begged.

'It's just a car,' Callie replied.

'No, Mum,' said Nigel. 'It's not just a car. Like I said, it's way cool.'

'Can you park it outside kindy too?' Petie asked.

'You stay right there, Peter Cartwright, Braden said through the window. 'I'm dropping you at kindy.'

'I have to leave now to get Reg because we both have appointments, but when Dad picks you up this afternoon, if some of your friends want to see it, we'll wait. But like I said, it's only a car,' Callie said.

Each of the boys leaned forward and kissed her cheek before they climbed out, and a warm glow suffused her.

Braden came to the passenger window after Rory and Nigel had run through the school gate. 'Come on, Callie. I'll help you out.'

Callie picked up her handbag and waited for him to come to the driver's side. She seemed to have doubled in size this week, and it was impossible to get in and out of the high car without Braden's help. So, when he'd suggested taking her sports car to Charleville, she jumped at it.

As long as he could put her seat back, she'd be right.

She hoped.

Callie put a hand on her stomach as she waited for Braden. She'd been up all night with heartburn and had thought twice about going down for her obstetrician appointment, but she'd felt better when she woke up. Now, her indigestion had come back. She put her hand to her mouth as she let out a small burp.

'Pardon you, Mum,' Petie said from the back seat.

'Yes, pardon me.'

Braden looked at her with concern as he opened the door and held out both hands.

'Are you okay, love?'

'I shouldn't have had that lamb last night,' she said. 'I know exactly what caused it. I don't think your next child likes lamb.'

'That's good. I'm hoping he or she is a beef eater to support the family,' he said with a smile. She swung her legs around to the side and slid down slowly from the driver's seat. Braden supported her as her feet reached the ground, but her stomach was in the way. He leaned over and kissed her on the neck.

'You drive safely,' he said. 'Don't be tempted to speed.'

'Reg will keep me in line.'

'What's he going to Charleville for?'

Callie shrugged. 'I don't know why, but he has to see his solicitor and do some shopping.'

'He'll be good company for you.'

'It'll be quiet at the pub without him there today,' she said.

'It will, but I'm sure he'll pick up some gossip in Charleville.'

'Bye, Mummy. Drive safe,' Petie parroted his father.

'Bye, sweetie. You be a good boy at kindy.' Callie kissed her fingers and blew the kiss to Petie, and he pretended to catch it and throw it back.

'Love you, Mummy.'

'Love you too, Petie.'

Braden waited until Callie put the seat back and was safely in the sports car before he leaned down and kissed her goodbye. 'You ring me if there are any problems. I'll try to get away from the muster in time to get back here, but if I can't, Jon said Fallon will meet you here at three. Ruth's at their place and can look after Ryan.'

'Bye, sweetheart. You be careful too.' Braden kissed her again and hurried over to the four-wheel drive.

The sports car started with its familiar purr, and Callie smiled as she drove down the street from the school to the pub. She pulled up in the side street and her smile widened as she spotted Reg. Instead of his usual navy-blue King Gee pants and shirt, he was wearing a suit. His white shirt had seen better days, and as he climbed into the front of the car with her, she noticed the yellow, threadbare cuffs, and a wave of sympathy ran through her.

Reg was a very private man, and Callie had asked Braden about him, but even though he was a local from way back, no one seemed to know a lot about him.

'I remember first seeing him at the pub when my dad was alive,' Braden said. 'I would've been in primary school, maybe even before then. I remember Mum and Dad talking about him when he first came back to town. Apparently, he was born here and was a shearer, working around the country, and he was pretty good at it. He won some championships. Anyway, he moved back to town and did some farm stock work out in the bush until he retired.'

'How old is he?' Callie asked.

'I've got no idea, love. I imagine he'd be heading to eighty if he's not there already. Not a bad innings for someone who sits and drinks beer all day outside the pub.'

'Does he live in town?'

'No, out on the highway. I probably should've pointed his house out to you.'

'On the highway?'

'Yes, just south of town on the way to Charleville.'

'Not that real old place on the western side of the road.'

'That's it.'

'I thought that property was abandoned. Surely, he can't live there?'

Braden nodded. 'He does.'

'But how does he get into town? He hasn't got a car. I mean, he might have a car, but he can't drive into town and drink all day and then drive home.'

'He walks in and out. Gets the occasional lift, I guess.'

'Really? Oh no, the poor old thing. It must be about five kilometres each way.'

'Probably how he keeps himself fit.'

Callie stared at Reg as he walked across to the car. He was a wiry and fit-looking man for his age.

'Morning, love,' Reg said as he clicked the seatbelt.

'Good morning, Reg. You're looking very swish today,' she said.

Reg looked down at his suit and brushed his hands over the shiny suit trousers. 'Long time since I've been to the big smoke.'

'The big smoke? Are you flying to Brisbane?'

He chuckled, and as she glanced over, Callie noticed he'd even shaved this morning.

'No, down to Charleville, love. I don't think I've been down there for a couple of years.'

Callie put the indicator on, shifted the sports car into gear, and pulled out into the main street. It was quite busy this morning. Sue Watts had a cake stall near the butcher's shop, and a group of Augathella Primary School kids were walking to the library. They certainly hadn't taken much time to get the kids out and about.

She kept a close eye on the group because it was Nigel's class and frowned when she didn't spot him.

'What are you looking so worried about?' Reg asked.

'I think that's Nigel's class, but I can't seem to spot him.'

Reg turned to look and said, 'Yeah, there he is, love. He's bringing up the rear with the teacher. They're still waiting to cross the road.'

As they drove, they took the southern exit out of town and turned right onto the Matilda Highway. Callie glanced across at Reg again.

'I could've picked you up at your house,' she said.

Reg's voice was gruff. 'You know where I live, do you?'

'Braden told me the other day. I could have saved you a walk.'

'No,' he said. 'I had to go into town and have a haircut and a shave. The barber's got to make a living. Seems there aren't many blokes in town who go to him anymore. All the young blokes these days go to the hairdresser. Talk about pansies.'

Callie made a non-committal noise.

'What about Braden? Where does he get his hair cut?' Reg persisted with the thread of conversation.

She felt guilty. 'I cut it for him. He finds it hard to get into town. He's so busy at the moment.'

'That's fair enough, love,' Reg said.

They drove on, and Callie tried not to look at the house on the right as they cruised down the hill.

'You can look if you want to,' he said.

'I didn't want to seem to be a stickybeak,' she said.

Reg looked sad as he stared ahead.

Chapter 8

'We're like Thelma and Louise,' Alana said with a grin as they exited the ramp onto the westbound highway. Jenna had had an early appointment at the local solicitor's office. Alana had come in and waited in the foyer.

'Thelma and Louise who?' Jenna asked.

'That's right, I forgot you don't watch movies.'

'Oh, I think I've heard about it. Didn't they both die in the end? That's not how I want to start this trip, hearing stuff like that.'

'No, it's a new adventure,' she said. 'Maybe we'll meet Brad Pitt on the way.'

'I told you the other day I don't need a man in my life.'

Alana shook her head and wagged her finger at Jenna. 'Famous last words, love. Famous last words.'

'No, I'm putting all of my energy into my new business.' She flashed a grin at Alana. 'Our new business. I'm so pleased you've come in with me. It's going to make such a difference having someone to help me.'

'How much "doing up" is there for us to do? I can wield a paintbrush.'

'The photos of it don't look too bad. It's an old place. I think maybe a coat of paint and some new furniture. It shouldn't take us too long.'

'And have you applied for all the proper permits to run a business out there where it is?'

Jenna nodded. 'I have. I've got all the necessary certificates and permits from the local shire. The only funny thing was that the guy at the council said he'll have to send the building inspector up after we do it all up. I didn't think a building inspector would want to see that a place had been painted.'

'Sounds a bit strange. Are you sure the photos were okay?'

'Yeah, it looked spacious. I've got the floor plan, too. As well as the coffee machine, I'll need to buy a couple of new appliances for the kitchen, probably a dishwasher and maybe a new stove. We'll see what the other ones are like. And some appliances.'

'And you've got a unit for us to live in while we're doing the place up? Did you need to?'

'Yeah, a unit came up. I thought it was wise just in case the place needed more work than I thought, and when the agent told me about this unit, I agreed to take a three-month lease. One of the primary school teachers has moved to Brisbane; there are two bedrooms, and the rent's not too bad. I think I told you what it was the other day, didn't I?'

'Yep, all good. Now we've got to sort out how I'm going to be doing this business with you.'

Jenna nodded. 'I thought we'd agreed that I'll pay you a wage.'

'Have you ever thought about me putting some money in and going into the business with you?' Alana sounded hesitant.

Jenna preferred to go it alone, but didn't want to hurt her friend's feelings or have her think that she might have thought Alana was unreliable. Which, she had to admit to herself, Alana didn't have a good track record with any job.

'Don't take it the wrong way, but I have to go into this by myself; it was a condition of the loan from the bank. Don't worry, I'll pay you well, the going rate plus ten percent.'

Alana laughed. 'That's not what I meant. I just thought

it'd be nice to have a finger in the pie, so to speak.'

'You will. You'll be baking the pies.'

'I'm looking forward to it,' Alana said with a chuckle. 'I love the sound of a vintage tea room.'

Relief filled Jenna; she hadn't wanted to put Alana offside. 'Did I tell you I went to the op shop at Southport the other day, and I got the best clothes? And when I got my hair trimmed before we decided when to leave, my hairdresser showed me how to do that 1940s tight roll.'

Alana nodded. 'And you should see the absolutely gorgeous red lipstick I've got. We're gonna slay them in the aisles, kiddo.'

'I can't wait. I've got all Gran's recipes. I've been practising baking scones, and I reckon this is going to be fantastic. And we're coming into the green season. The highway should be busy. Who knows, we might make a fortune in the first month.'

The three days of travel passed quickly, and they spent their last night in Charleville, hoping they could get an early start the next morning for the very short trip up the highway to Augathella. While they were there, they had a look at the World War II airbase, and Jenna had a chat with the lady at the counter about their new venture up the highway.

'Sounds great,' the woman said. 'If you get some advertising material done, I'd be happy to put up flyers here in the cabinet. We get lots of tourists coming through in the winter—actually all year—but winter is when the grey nomads hit the highway. And if you get flyers done, make sure you put them in the tourist information centre and the caravan parks.'

Jenna nodded. 'Yes, my mum and dad have been travelling like that for about ten years, and I know how many people they meet on the road and what they like. So, fingers crossed, we're hoping it will be a success.'

'I think it's a great idea,' the woman said.

After dinner at the Corones Hotel and the luxury of staying overnight in one of the fabulous suites there, the next morning, Jenna and Alana picked up the keys to the unit in Augathella as soon as Jenna had finished at the solicitor's office.

Even though it was winter, the sun promised a warm day. As they drove out of Charleville just before eleven, mist still lingered in the paddocks, creating an eerie image as black cattle loomed out of the trees.

'It's certainly different from what I imagined,' Alana said. 'I thought it would be the outback with red dirt and dust. I must say I'm a little bit surprised.'

'It really is quite a pretty place. Look at the silvery leaves on those trees.'

'Do you think you'll stay out here long?' Alana asked.

Jenna shrugged. 'Well, I want to find somewhere new to live. There's nothing for me on the coast anymore, and I've got to hate how crowded it was. Mum and Dad are on the road, so I'm sure I'll see them every year or so as they come through. What about you?'

'I'll probably stay for a year, maybe longer. If you're happy to have me, you might need a whole heap more staff if this takes off.'

Jenna grinned at her friend. 'But it would be nice. If I do, you can be the manager of the floor.'

'What did you think of all those photos of the 1940s clothes we saw in the museum at Charleville? I can't wait to see what you bought.'

Jenna glanced at her watch. 'Settlement is at one o'clock. It's almost mine.'

'It was a good idea of yours, getting a local solicitor to do all the stuff for you and having it settled as soon as we arrived. He seemed like a nice guy when he came out of his office with you.'

'He was pretty cute, actually.'

'I didn't think you were interested in dating?'

'I'm out here to work. It doesn't hurt to look at the local scenery, though. He seemed a bit surprised that two city girls were coming out to Augathella to start a new business. He asked me if I'd seen the house yet, and when I said no, he frowned. And then he asked me if I'd ever been to Augathella, and when I said no, he looked shocked.'

'The receptionist chatted to me a bit while I was waiting for you. She asked me if I knew what a small town Augathella was, and I said we're not targeting the town.'

'Although, if we get a good reputation, we might find a lot of the locals will come in for coffee.'

'Jenna, did you see that beautiful girl walking through the foyer when we walked in?'

'Yes, I did. She was really pretty. She looked familiar to me, but I don't know anyone out this way.'

'And she was very friendly. Lovely smile she gave us. I do like country folk.'

'Country folk, Alana? It's starting to sound like you're a yokel yourself.'

'A local yokel, that's what I'll be,' Alana said with a grin.

Jenna glanced at the navigation screen, and her excitement rose. 'We're only ten kilometres out of Augathella, and the place is two kilometres south of the turnoff. So, keep your eye out another eight kilometres, and you should see a little cottage on the left.'

'Is it going to be out here by itself?' Alana asked. 'I haven't seen any other houses since we left Charleville. Just the occasional farmhouse set back from the road. Is it just on a normal suburban block?'

'No, it's on an acre. I've even been thinking that once we get the inside of the place done and the business up and going, we can start doing some garden settings, maybe have some little grottos and things like that.'

'You're full of plans,' Alana said as she kept her eyes to the left.

'I am. I'm really excited about this.'

'Are you going to be able to afford it all?'

'I am. My gran left me quite a nice little sum. But I still have to be careful and make sure I get a good return on investment. I've got to work out prices and what it'll cost me to bake everything.'

'And milk and tea and coffee, and crockery and stuff.'

'Did you see that big timber crate in the back underneath our suitcases?'

Alana nodded. 'I thought that was a toolbox.'

'No.' Jenna shook her head. 'It's full of my Gran's collectible china. That's what gave me the idea in the first place. She used to love her tea in a Shelley teacup, and it was a real treat for me when I was little. Mum and Dad used to take us around to Gran's place in Morningside, and she would always have a high tea ready for us. She used to make me go and wash my face and hands when I'd been playing outside with the neighbour's kids. I had to comb my hair, take off my shorts and T-shirt, and put on a pretty dress. Then we'd sit up at her high dining room table and have a high tea. The pouring of the tea was a ritual.'

'Sounds like fun,' Alana said. 'The most my grandparents ever did was send me to the shops to buy milk. Although I did get a couple of dollars for lollies.'

'I miss Gran so much.'

'What about your grandfather?'

'Never had one. Gran was a single mum, and she brought Mum up by herself. It was a really big thing to have a child out of wedlock in those days, as Mum used to call it, but Gran was always happy.'

'Was her boyfriend killed in the war?'

'I don't know what happened to him. Gran was always very quiet about that. It's a family mystery.'

'Maybe you could do the genetic stuff with the DNA tests and all that. What do they call it? Ancestry.com?'

'I'm not really interested,' Jenna said. 'I don't know what happened to him, and I doubt if he'd be alive anymore.'

'What about your mum?'

'Mum was always quite closed about it. I think it bothered her, not having a dad when she grew up.'

'Two kilometres to go,' Alana said, looking at the Google map on her phone. 'Maybe go a little bit slower so I can spot it.'

A small hill appeared on the left, and as they began to climb, Alana rolled her eyes. 'Gosh, I hope it doesn't look like that place.'

An overgrown paddock with falling-down fences met their eyes about fifty metres back from the road. A rutted dirt driveway led to an old, tumbledown cottage that sat on the crest of the hill. Even with the bright morning sun, it looked dark and uninviting. A crooked milk can was painted with the number RMB 182.

'I hope seeing that place doesn't turn the tourists off when they see it before they get to our place.'

Jenna kept driving slowly, and they travelled another three kilometres.

'There are no more houses on the left,' Alana said. 'Does your house have a number?'

'I don't know. It's before the turnoff, and we passed that about two kilometres ago. I'm sure he said south of town. Maybe I misheard the instructions. Maybe it's north of the turnoff.' Jenna pulled over and parked on the side of the road. She reached for her bag on the back seat and pulled out the paperwork the solicitor had given her.

'It's RMB 182.'

They looked at each other.

'It can't be that place,' Alana said quietly.

'No, it won't be. It's nothing like the photos in the ad. I'll do a U-turn, and we'll go back and have a look.'

'Where's your phone? Can I open it and have a look at the ad?'

Jenna pointed to the console behind the gearshift, and Alana reached for her phone. 'What's the password?'

'It's my birthday,' Jenna said.

'That's not very secure.'

'Doesn't matter. There's nothing private on the phone. The ad's in the photos. It's about two weeks old.'

Jenna scrolled through Alana's phone, paused, and stared at the screen. She turned to Alana as the old cottage on the hill appeared ahead of them. Alana looked at the phone again and then glanced across at Jenna.

'RMB 182,' she said.

Jenna widened her eyes as she slowed right down and stared at the cottage on the hill.

'Oh my God, Alana, what have I done?'

Chapter 9

Callie walked out of the obstetrician's office, feeling comfortable and relaxed. The doctor reassured her that everything was on track. The baby was growing well, and his or her heartbeat was strong and steady. Her blood pressure was spot on, and all of the other tests that he had run had come back satisfactory. The only thing that he'd commented on was the size of the baby and he had booked her in for a scan at next week's visit.

She walked across to the pub opposite where she'd parked her car near the town hall. The street was busy today, and she had to wait while caravans drove past, heading out towards the World War II Centre. Reg was sitting in the sun with an empty beer glass in front of him. His appointment with the solicitor had been a little bit earlier than her doctor's appointment. She'd waited with him in the office until he went in and then went to see the doctor in the same building. Callie knew if he came out first, he'd have a beer while he waited for her.

'How did it go, Reg?' she asked. 'All done?'

'I am. I even got my bit of shopping done.' He pointed to a plastic bag on the floor beside him. 'So, did the doc say you're still allowed to drive that flash sports car home?'

'I surely am. Unless you want to drive?' she said.

He harrumphed. 'Me? I haven't driven for years.'

Callie was determined to find out something about Reg's past, so she looked at him with her head tilted to the side. 'Would you like to grab an early lunch before we head back?'

'Your shout, love,' he said, his grin cheeky. 'Maybe we could have an early bite to eat. I think I could stretch to a sandwich and a cup of tea. Does that suit you, lass?'

'It does. I'm starving,' she replied.

They walked along the street and found a new coffee shop around the corner, near the council chambers. Callie ordered a salami baguette while Reg went for the roast beef and pickle sandwich. She knew she would regret it later, but she was starving and hadn't had a gourmet baguette since she left Brisbane two years ago. When they'd been there with Petie a few months back, they'd lived on plastic-wrapped sandwiches from the hospital café.

As they waited for the meals to be brought to the table, she looked at Reg. 'I've known you for well over eighteen months now, and I'm curious. Tell me, how long have you lived in Augathella?'

He stared at her steadily. 'I've lived in Augathella for over sixty years.'

'So, you weren't born here?' she asked, but he remained silent for a few minutes.

'I went away, and I got on the shearing circuit when I was a young lad. Then I came back to town,' he finally replied.

'And what did you do when you came back to town?'

'I drove a truck for quite a few years. I used to actually take stuff out to Braden's place when his parents were still alive. He was just a young whippersnapper. He probably wouldn't remember.'

'He's never mentioned it, so he probably doesn't,' she said.

The young waitress put their sandwiches on the table, and they thanked her. 'So, Reg, you've always been a loner. You've never had a wife or a family?'

He tapped his finger on the side of his nose. 'That would be telling, wouldn't it?'

Her curiosity was piqued. 'Oh, so you've never had a wife?'

He sighed. 'I never took myself a wife. There was someone once, a long, long time ago, who I would have married.'

'What happened, Reg?'

'One day when we've got a lot of time, I'll tell you, love. But for now, we've got lunch, and then we've got an hour's drive back home.'

'I'm not being a stickybeak. I sometimes worry about you being lonely.'

'Me lonely? I'm not lonely, love, and I'll be less lonely from next week.'

'Next week. Is that why you went to the solicitors?' she asked.

'I've sold my house, love. I'm moving into the aged care home in town.'

'Wow, that's a big move.'

'I figured I might as well get someone to cook meals for me and someone to have a yarn with, and it's a lot less distance to walk to the pub every day.'

Callie grinned. 'It sure is. Who bought your house?'

'Some girl from Brisbane. Don't know why she'd want to come and move out here,' he said apologetically.

'I did.'

'But you had a reason too, didn't you?'

'Best move, best decision I ever made in my whole life,' she said. 'So, when do you move into town?'

'Well, I can move in any time now that we've signed on the bottom line. Apparently, this woman is coming in the next few days, and she just has to come into the solicitors and sign. It's all organised. I'll have the money this afternoon at one o'clock, I can pay the home fees, and I can move into my new room when it's all sorted.' Reg looked down at the big old gold watch on his wrist. 'Actually, that's only an hour away. Maybe we could go via the bank on the way out.'

'Of course, we can. We have plenty of time. I don't have to be back until school comes out.'

'Thank you, love.'

Callie sat back and put her hands on her stomach. She could feel the effects of that salami already. 'Well, that's certainly big news.' She picked up her cup of tea. 'Now, we have time. Tell me about this person that you loved once.'

'Oh, it's not much of a story, love. I met Meggie back in the sixties. We spent some time together, and she decided I wasn't good enough for her family. I was a shearer back then. I'd planned to marry her, but it wasn't meant to be. I was heartbroken and a bit lonely for a while, but I learned to live with it.' When Reg's eyes met Callie's, they were sad. 'I never got over her, ya know. There's not a day goes by when I don't think about her. Wonder where she is, whether she had a happy life, that sort of thing.'

Callie blinked to clear the moisture from her eyes. She reached over the table and held Reg's hand. 'Would you like to talk about her?'

For a moment he hesitated and she thought she might have overstepped the mark.

'That's the first time I've said her name for many years.' Reg's voice was a bit husky and he cleared his throat. 'You're a good girl, Callie. You care about people, not just what they can do for you. I see so many types in the pub every day, and I'm a pretty damn good judge of character, and let me tell you, Braden Cartwright was damn lucky when you put your bags in that drain.'

'How on earth did you know about that?' she exclaimed. 'Braden promised he wouldn't tell anyone.'

'But did the boys promise?' Reg's thin shoulders shook underneath the shiny suit jacket as he laughed.

She was pleased to see the sadness had gone from his eyes.

'I know everything that happens within a hundred miles of Augathella.'

Callie grinned back at him. 'So, tell me about your Meggie and what happened a long time ago.'

'She was the prettiest girl I ever laid eyes on. She was working at the local bakery. I was shearing out on the remote stations in the sixties, and I didn't see many girls, but she stopped me in my tracks that day I went in to buy a pie.

'Back then, they used to have dances in the hall on Saturday nights, and after I went in there three days in a row to buy a pie—just so I could look at her—I got up the courage to ask her out.'

'And?' Callie prompted.

'And I've never eaten so many pies in my life.'

'No, I meant what did she say?'

'She said yes. We went to lots of dances whenever I was close by, and then I got a job driving trucks with Horrie, Jim Andersen's dad, so I could stay in town. We used to go for picnics on the river, and we saw a lot of each other in those six months.'

'What happened?'

'One month, I had a big trip to do for Horrie, and when I came back after three weeks away, she was gone.'

'Gone? Do you know why? Or where?'

Reg slipped his hand into his jacket and pulled out his wallet. His hands shook as he pulled out a piece of paper. The paper was so flimsy it was almost transparent. 'I'll let you read it as long as you don't tell a soul. Not even Braden.' He held it out to Callie and looked away from her as she took it.

'If you're sure, Reg?'

'I am. You've been kind to me, Callie.'

The writing was loopy, and the ink faded, but Callie could easily read the words. She glanced across at Reg, but he was looking away from her, his lips were pressed together, and she would swear he had tears in his eyes. As she swallowed, the baby gave a ferocious kick, first on one side of her ribs and then there was a big roll, and then a kick on the opposite side. Maybe Braden was right, and it was a boy.

She put one hand on her stomach, but the kicking eased as she began to read.

Dearest Reg,

I know I'm a coward but I couldn't tell you this to your face. I'm moving to Brisbane. Augathella is not enough for me. I want more out of life. I don't want to live in the bush, and I know how much you love it. I want a house in the city. Where it rains and where flowers will grow all year. I want a life where I can go to the pictures and go shopping when I want to. Not have to wait until there is a bus to Charleville.

The bush feeds your soul as you told me so romantically that night we lay under the stars. I will never forget that night, and I will never forget you.

Thank you for the loveliest six months of my life. You are a very lovely man. I wish you a happy and successful life.

Warmest regards
Margaret Hope

Callie blinked back tears as she carefully folded the letter and passed it back to Reg. She sensed that he didn't want to say any more so she looked down at the half-eaten baguette and pushed her plate towards him.

'I can't eat the rest of this. Would you like the rest of my sandwich?'

'With that wog food on it? Not bloody likely, lassie. Give me roast beef and pickles any day,' he replied, his voice still a bit shaky despite his gruff words.

'Do you want another cup of tea?'

'No, let's go home.'

Chapter 10

Jenna and Alana stood on the front porch of the ramshackle cottage, looking over the long grass and the gardens full of weeds. Two large chimneys flanked the eastern side, and a brick outside toilet was on the other side.

Alana looked at Jenna. 'How much did you say you paid for this place?'

'Not much,' Jenna replied slowly. 'No wonder it was so cheap, and now I know why the solicitor guy was looking doubtful.'

'Look on the bright side.' Alana spread her arms wide.

'Is there one?' Jenna kicked at the rotten floorboards on the veranda where they stood.

'There is!' Alana's eyes were shining. 'I love a challenge, don't you? That's what's been missing in my life for so long. Working for greedy people who just want to make money. You've got a dream, and you want to create something special here. And look!' Alana pointed to the road. Caravan after caravan passed by, pulled by large four-wheel drive vehicles heading north.

A surge of enthusiasm raced through Jenna as she counted seven caravans going past. 'Look at them all!'

'And not one of them turned into Augathella,' Alana said.

'They are my market. We have to get working, and tidying, and cleaning and scrubbing.'

'We do.' Alana carefully stepped across the broken floorboard. 'It's the beginning of the tourist season. We can have this place up and running by the time they all head back south to wherever they come from.'

'We can! Let's be positive. What's it really going to take

besides some timber and paint and a lot of hard work? Are you sure you want to put that much work in, Alana?'

Alana looked at the holes in the front door and the three-legged chair. 'It's gonna take a hell of a lot of work, but count me in.' She laughed. 'And we haven't even seen inside yet!'

'You really think we can do it? Close your eyes and imagine. Imagine a big circular driveway coming in over there.' Jenna pointed to the front yard. 'With lots of space to park caravans. And even buses.'

'You've got a good imagination. It could be a circle, but it's full of potholes, red dirt, long grass, and lumps of rock. A little bit of elbow grease on a mower, and yes, we can fix it.'

'I'll have to buy a ride-on mower with an acre.'

'According to Google there's a hardware store in Augathella, and we can go get some new timber and make a new floor. Come on, let's go and look inside. Are you really sure you want to stay?'

'I am. Are we supposed to go inside before it's yours?'

'I signed the final papers this morning at the solicitors, and my money is going over at one o'clock.' Jenna pulled out her phone and checked the time. 'I'm sure no one is going to complain about me being here fifteen minutes before it becomes mine. Just don't fall through the floorboards until after one.'

Alana laughed. 'You do have insurance?'

'I do, and I took out public liability for the business as well.'

Alana shook her head slowly from side to side. 'I don't believe we're here. Give us a month, and you won't recognise this place.'

'I'm really excited about it,' Jenna followed Alana to the front door. She'd expected her friend to be horrified when they'd pulled up and realised that this old, falling-down shack was what she'd bought. But as she watched the caravans and cars on the highway, she knew that when she fixed it up, she could make a success of it.

I will.

'Look, here's my first customer now,' Jenna said, her eyes lighting up as a red sports car turned off the road and into the overgrown driveway.

'It can't be your first customer. We're not ready, and it's not legally yours yet,' Alana protested.

'Close enough.' Jenna widened her eyes as she recognised the pretty woman she had seen in the solicitor's office. The elderly guy was helping her out of the sports car. 'That's the lady we saw in Charleville.'

'I wonder what they're doing,' Alana said.

The pair walked across the end of the driveway and up the two steps onto the veranda. The woman was smiling, but she kept shooting worried glances at the old man walking beside her.

'Hello,' Jenna called out. 'How can I help you? I can't help with any directions, I'm sorry. We've just arrived here.'

The old man looked up at her and grabbed the rickety stair rail. His face went white, and his mouth opened and closed as he stared up at her.

The woman with him grabbed his arm. 'Reg, are you okay? What's wrong?'

The man stared at Jenna, his eyes huge and one hand on his chest. She worried that he was having a heart attack or a turn of some kind. He looked quite old. He lifted his hand to his throat, and for a moment, she thought he was going to pass out and fall to the ground. 'Would you like to come up and sit down?' she offered. 'There's a chair here.'

'I know there's a bloody chair there. It's my chair, at least it will be for another ten minutes,' Jenna realised at the same time as Alana looked at her, wide-eyed.

'Are you Mr MacGilvray? Are you the owner?' Jenna

asked. The man was still pale.

'I am. Who are you?' he asked, still looking at her with wide eyes and an open mouth.

Chapter 11

Callie was worried that Reg was having some sort of episode; she had never seen him so pale and shaky. He hadn't taken his eyes off the two young women above them on the front veranda.

'Reg, what do you want to do? Do you want to go back to the pub or stay here?' she asked. Then she looked at the two young women. 'You've just stopped in here to see the place, right?' she asked hesitantly. 'Or did you come to see Reg?'

'I don't know them,' Reg said. A little bit of colour had come back into his face, but he was still staring at the young woman with the long, dark, curly hair.

'No, we've just stopped to have a look for now. I've actually bought this place,' the taller woman said.

'Oh, you're the new owners. Reg told me he's sold it.' Callie thought about what a pretty young woman she was, but she still kept shooting worried glances at Reg. He was sitting on the chair now, his arms dangling between his legs, looking at the rot in the floorboards. Perhaps he felt guilty about the state the house was in.

He lifted his head. 'You can stay here. I'll just grab my gear, and I'll stay at the pub tonight if you want to move in.'

'Oh, there's no need to do that, Mr MacGilvray. We're staying in town for a couple of months. We've actually rented a place there.'

'We haven't made any introductions. I'm Callie Cartwright, and I live about thirty kilometres out of town. I just gave Reg a lift down to Charleville this morning.'

'I'm Jenna Wilson,' the tall woman said.

'And I'm Alana Rickman,' the other woman said. 'I've

come out to help my friend Jenna with her new venture.'

'Your new venture?' Callie asked, her eyebrows raised.

'Yes, we're turning this into a cafe.'

'A bloody cafe! You gotta be bloody joking,' Reg burst out, and Callie tried to catch his eye.

'I think that sounds like a wonderful idea,' Callie turned to the two young women. 'Welcome to town. You'll love living in Augathella. It's the best place to live and work. Where have you come from?'

'We spent the last three days driving from Brisbane.'

Callie chuckled. 'As I did two years ago.' She sensed the girls' eyes on her pregnant stomach. 'I met somebody here, and I live here now. And we're about to have our first baby. That'll make it four.' Callie smiled when the young woman frowned.

'You've been here two years, and you've got four children?' Jenna asked.

'I have three stepsons, and this is our first baby together. My husband and I, that is.'

'Enough of that,' Reg interrupted. 'Come on, I'll soon find out enough about this idea.'

'Please don't rush. We can go. We just called to have a quick look at the place. Don't let us impose,' Jenna said. She and her friend turned towards the steps. 'It was good to meet you. I'm sure we'll catch up.'

'We're going into town as well. Are you sure you want to come in to town, Reg?'

'Well, it'll save me the bloody walk. And it means I won't have to carry my gear.'

'Please Mr MacGilvray, you don't have to do it this afternoon. There's no rush.'

'I'll do it now,' he said. 'It won't take long.'

'Do you want me to help you pack anything?' Callie noticed that Reg was looking anywhere except at the woman called Jenna.

***

Jenna looked at Mr MacGilvray when he walked out of the house with a bag over one shoulder and a small box in his hand. He put the bag on the floor and then placed the box carefully on the chair near the rotten floorboards.

A small clock and a fine china tea cup rested on a stained tea towel. The way he placed the box gently on the chair it was as though it held a whole lifetime's worth of his precious things.

'Come on, Callie, it's time we got going. You take this bag and the box and I'll go back for my suitcase.' He went back into the house. Jenna felt as though they were intruding in his last time in his home.

'Can I help?' Jenna offered, meeting Callie's eyes. She looked sad too.

'Thank you. Perhaps if you take the small bag and the box,' Callie said. 'I'd like to have two hands to hang on going down the steps.'

'When are you due?' Jenna asked as she reached down to pick up the box.

'Four weeks.'

Jenna stared at her and a niggle of memory tugged. 'I feel as though I know you. What did you do in Brisbane?'

Callie's cheeks reddened. 'I . . .um . . .worked in weather.'

Jenna smiled. 'You were that wonderful weather girl in the clip that went viral. I knew I recognised your face in the solicitor's office.'

Callie nodded and her smile was rueful. 'I don't know if I'd say wonderful.'

'You were.' Jenna followed her down the steps to the red sports car. 'And you moved from the city to here and you love it? That encourages me. I've been having doubts about the move already.'

'Don't,' Callie said. 'It's the most wonderful community. I've made so many friends and our social calendar is always full. My husband' — she smiled '—I still can't get quite used to saying that, is busy with the cattle muster at the moment, otherwise I'd invite you out to *Kilcoy Station*. There are many young people in the district now and since the drought broke, there's been a huge influx of young couples.'

'It sounds good.'

'We usually come into the pub for dinner once a fortnight or so. They do good meals, and you'll meet lots of locals there.'

Alana had followed them down the steps. 'Only couples? Are there many single guys around?'

Callie's smile widened. 'A few. There's a get-together to welcome the new arrivals in town in a couple of weeks. I'll get the details to you when I know when it's on. Where are you staying?'

When Jenna told her the address of the unit, Callie nodded.

'That's Jacinta's apartment. She's moved back to Brisbane. So, would you like to come to the get-together?'

'Sounds good,' Jenna said.

Callie looked up and Jenna turned to follow her gaze. 'Here's Reg now.'

'Where's he moving to?'

'He's going into aged care,' Callie whispered.

Reg clomped down the steps. 'I've got all my gear. Look after the old place, girl. She's been good to me.' Before Jenna could answer, he hoisted a suitcase into the small back seat of the car, and held the door open for Callie as she climbed in awkwardly. He got into the passenger street and didn't look up again.

'See you both later. Good luck,' Callie said as she started the engine. 'And if you need anything just ask in town.

Someone will help you.'

Jenna and Alana watched as the cute little red car turned onto the highway.

'That was interesting,' Alana said.

'It was. I felt sad for him, and mean that we were in his house.'

'He didn't have much, did he?'

'Maybe he'd moved it earlier and that was the last of it.'

'I hope so. Come on. Let's go and see what I've bought, and see how much work we've got ahead.'

Chapter 12

'Did you see the way that Reg guy looked at you, Jen?' Alana asked as they drove into town.

'I did. He made me feel really uncomfortable. I thought he was going to pass out there for a while. Maybe he was upset to see someone had actually bought his house.'

'He must've been in the solicitor's office when we passed Callie in the foyer. Wasn't she lovely?'

'She was. The solicitor didn't mention that the vendor was there before me. I didn't notice him come out of the office though, did you?'

'No, I didn't.'

'Callie was very welcoming. It was lovely of her to invite us to that get-together she mentioned. Will we go, Alana?'

'Of course.'

'I didn't think I'd be able to keep you away.' Jenna nudged her. 'An opportunity to scope out the local talent.'

'You've got me interested.' Alana smiled. Seriously though, can I ask you one thing, Jen? I'm a bit curious. Especially now that we've seen this place. Why did you choose it? Surely you could've got something better way closer to the city?'

Jenna glanced across at Alana. 'The first reason was, it was really cheap. Really, really cheap. It fit all my requirements. On the highway, close to a town, and on some land but I guess I should've known that it was going to need a lot of work. I was in real estate, for goodness' sake! I think it was the other reason that I wanted to come this far out that put blinkers on my reasoning.'

'The other reason?' Alana asked curiously.

'I wanted to come out here because this is where Gran grew up.' When she talked about the place her face lit up.

'What about your mum? Did she grow up here too?'

'No, Gran left here when she was in her teens. I often wondered why she stayed in Brisbane, but I guess it was to give Mum the chance of a good education, and more opportunities as she grew up.'

'When she passed, I invested what she left me, and I vowed I'd come out here one day and check out where she grew up. When the cottage came on the market, I thought there was no better way to spend her inheritance than to come out where Gran grew up.'

'It's funny, you know, this landscape really appeals to me. It's very different to the coastal landscape, but I like it,' Alana said.

'It is. Anyway, let's head into town and hope that where we're staying is a little bit more upmarket than my cottage. The fourth street on the left is Nelson Street. Then on the right, the agent said we'll see three brick units and a large carport.'

'I'll tell you when to turn.'

As they drove along the old Charleville Road, Jenna was thoughtful. She felt guilty that she'd bought the house from old Mr MacGilvray. He'd looked absolutely stricken to see that there were actually new owners, and she knew that the amount of money that she paid for it would barely fund his retirement.

Maybe after a couple of days, she'd go and visit him and check he was okay.

***

Callie was sad, but she tried to hide it from Reg. Seeing the old house he'd lived in and his few belongings had really shocked her. But it was his reaction to the new owner that had worried her; she'd even considered calling the ambulance for a few minutes until the colour had come back to his face.

It must have been the realisation that he was leaving the house that he'd lived in for many years. She was glad that they were close to town.

'So, where should I drop you off?' she asked as they passed the rural store. 'Do you want me to drop you at the . . . at your new home . . . or take you straight to the pub?'

'The pub. I'll sleep there until my room is ready next week.'

'What about your stuff?'

'It can stay with me. I've already brought the rest of my things. I carried a bit when I walked in each day. Sean let me put it all in the back storeroom at the pub.'

Callie wondered about the contents of the box. The small clock was ornate, and the teacup looked like a Shelley vintage cup. Her heart broke. Reg had walked the five kilometres every day with some of his belongings. Why didn't anyone in town know what he was doing and that he needed help? She promised herself she'd go and see Maisie Ramsay at the home and check he had everything he needed. If he didn't, she'd buy what he needed next time she went to Charleville. It was time someone looked out for him.

'This was just the last of it that I needed last night,' he said.

'Are you feeling okay now?' she asked carefully.

'I am,' he said.

'I might come in with you and have a cold drink.'

'Suit yourself.'

'I will. I've got plenty of time. We can keep yarning.'

Reg was such a strange fellow. Who knew what was going through his mind? Everything seemed guarded, but he didn't reveal much about himself. He knew everything there was to know about Augathella, the history and settlement, the families and who belonged where, but who knew anything about him? Even Braden who'd known him all his life knew little.

Sure, he had opened up to her today but now he was closed as tight as a clam shell.

She turned right at Biddenham Street and drove around the back of the pub and parked there. The car could stay there until Braden or Fallon came into town at three. She glanced down at her watch. It was just after two, another hour and school would be out.

'Do you mind if I come in and have a lemon squash with you?' she asked.

Reg shrugged. 'Suit yourself.'

This closed-down man was totally out of character for the usual friendly Reg. He'd gone inside himself when he'd seen Jenna and Alana on the veranda of his house. For a moment, he looked as though he had seen a ghost. His eyes widened, and then his mouth dropped open in shock. Callie suspected it had more to do with her, rather than her being the new owner of his house. She was going to get to the bottom of this even if it took all afternoon.

'I'm going to have to ask you a favour again,' she said, pulling a face as he climbed out of the passenger seat of the low-slung sports car.

'Yes,' he said, turning to face her.

'Can you come around and help me get out of the car again, please?'

His face softened, and the old Reg resurfaced as he walked around the back of the car and opened her door.

He smiled as he held out both hands 'Sorry, I've been a bit cranky, love.'

His skin was rough and papery but his grip was surprisingly firm. He held her elbow firmly as she pushed herself up to her feet. 'Thank you, Reg. You're a true gentleman. And strong!'

'Now, let me buy you a beer for driving me all the way down to Charleville.' Her stomach gurgled.

'Are you hungry, lass?' He laughed and Callie relaxed as he held her elbow as they walked into the pub together.

'Actually, I am, but I know they won't be serving this time of the day. I'll see if Sean's around. He might have a bowl of fruit salad or something in the cool room. If not, I'll have a bag of chips.' She chuckled. 'I've given up worrying about my weight.'

'Damn,' Reg said. 'I forgot my box.' He led Callie over to his usual table. 'You sit here while I get it, and when I come back, I'll find Sean.' He made sure she was settled comfortably.

'Thank you. Like I said before, Reg, you're a true gentleman.' Callie leaned back in the chair and looked along the street. There was not a soul to be seen, and the coffee shop down the road had already closed for the day. Someone came out of the butcher's as she watched, and a sole caravan rumbled slowly down the road, heading towards the free camp near the river.

It was a peaceful country scene after all the rain. The footpath in the park was green, the sky was a brilliant blue, and she put her head back and closed her eyes. The warm afternoon sun relaxed her.

She must've drifted off briefly. When she opened her eyes again, Reg was sitting there, staring into the distance. A glass of lemon squash was on a coaster in front of her, and a bowl of fruit salad with a fork and spoon sat on a place mat in front of her.

'You're an absolute gem, Reg. Thank you so much,' she said, fighting back tears. 'I just caught forty winks. I'll be glad when this baby's born. I've never needed so much sleep in the afternoon.'

'You were snoring.'

'I was not,' Callie said indignantly. 'Ladies don't snore.'

'It was a pretty little snore. Not like old Jim Andersen when he nods off at the bar. You can hear him from out here.' Reg laughed and Callie smiled. He'd come right out of his mood.

'Won't hurt you. I like my little naps out here. And this is the time to have it, between two and three in the afternoon. The town's dead until school comes out. Then all the mums and school buses break the peace and quiet and soon after that, all the local cockies come in for their beer, and the fun begins.'

'The town does come alive then.'

'Best time of day in the pub. Did I tell you what I heard last week?' he said.

'You might have. You've told me a lot about what happens here, Reg,' Callie said. She glanced down and noticed the box on the third chair on the other side of Reg.

Reg lifted his middy of beer, took a deep draft, and Callie smiled. Froth stuck to his whiskers.

'Craig Wilson was in here, and apparently, he and Mandy had a blue before he left home. Something to do with their young bloke, Rusty.'

Callie shook her head. Reg's knowledge of the local community amazed her.

'Never did find out the upshot of what it was all about. Rusty came in to pick him up and told him that a bunch of flowers would do the trick at home. Jim Andersen told him there was some pretty stuff that had just come up behind his garage, so Craig went and picked a big bunch of it. And then he took a whole bunch of flowers home.'

'Oh, that was nice of him. It would have cheered Mandy up.'

Reg started cackling. 'It was bloody lantana. A noxious weed. It's only just appeared out here in the west and he thought it was a flower. After Craig left, Jim had us all falling about laughing.'

Callie laughed, and after a while, Reg's shoulders shook as he laughed silently.

'Apparently, she threw them out and he got the dirts with her until Rusty told him he'd picked her a bunch of weeds. He brought Mandy in here for dinner the next night.'

Callie shook her head. 'You don't miss a trick, Reg.'

'You know what, love? I'll be glad to be in town all the time,' he said. 'Doesn't matter about that old house. Just a house, isn't it, love? Bits of timber, bits of dirt, it'll be there long after I'm gone.'

Callie chose her words carefully. 'It will be nice to see it renovated a little bit, and I think the idea that those girls have got sounds like a plan. Sometimes it can be hard to get a coffee in town, and the caravans soon hear that and keep going on the highway. If they see the new cafe, they come into town and stay. We might get some more people in town. It's always good for business, isn't it, Reg?'

He dropped his gaze to his beer glass instead. 'I was rude to that girl. It was because of what we were talking about in Charleville.'

'What do you mean?'

'I reckon I've forgotten what my Meggie looked like. I never had a photo of her. Only thing I've got to remind me is that letter and my cup and clock.' He gestured to the box on the chair. 'That's why I left them at home until my last night. Meggie liked to drink her tea out of fine china, so she left one of her cups at my place. I always drink my tea out of it. Might look like a bit of a pansy, but it reminds me of her.'

'What about the clock?' Callie asked gently.

'She gave it to me for my birthday, the first three months we were going out. I was always late and I didn't wear a watch back then, so she bought me that clock.'

'She liked fine old things.'

'She did.' Reg's laugh was bitter. 'Maybe if she'd hung around, she would have liked me more. I'm an old thing now.'

'A fine, old thing,' Callie said putting her hand on his.

'I was rude to that girl because it's a problem with an old mind, pulling out dreams, instead of reality.'

'What do you mean?'

'When I saw her standing there on my veranda. I thought it was my Meggie come back. I thought she looked just like her. Same dark, curly hair, same eyes, same pretty mouth. She came out of my dreams. It wasn't her, was it?'

'No, it wasn't. But I think your house has a lovely new owner. When they get up and going, I'll take you out there for a cup of tea one day.'

Reg nodded slowly. 'I'd like that. A man can dream.'

Callie couldn't help herself. She held the table, stood and walked around to the other side of the table where Reg was sitting. She leaned down and brushed her lips across his cheek. 'You take care of yourself,' she said softly. 'Braden just turned down towards the school. I'll walk down and meet him. I'll get him to drop your bag and suitcase here before he drives my car out to *Kilcoy*. It'll give him the opportunity to have a beer, I guess,' she added cheekily.

Chapter 13

Jenna stood on the newly-sanded floorboards on the front veranda and looked out over her acre. It was amazing what a difference three weeks made. She had spent a fortune at the local hardware store, and the truck had come out to '*Margie's Cottage Café*', as she started to think of her new venture, at least a dozen times delivering timber, paint, sandpaper, roller brushes, paint trays, nails, and, with one big splurge, she'd even bought a ready-made Kaboodle kitchen.

The new stove, dishwasher, and coffee machine were in boxes stored in the back bedroom. As they'd stripped rooms and pulled out cupboards, she'd found quite a few of Mr MacGilvray's possessions and had packed them carefully into a box to take to him when he'd moved into the aged care facility.

A local handyman had called in to see if she had any work going; Kirk had proved a godsend. Not only had he provided a third set of hands with the inside work; he had been a fabulous help in the garden. He had all the tools needed for clearing and a huge mower, and the acre was already looking like a picture with the freshly mowed lawns. He also had plumbing skills and the customer powder room was almost complete. Jenna had decided to convert the sleepout on the side veranda. It was coming together quickly, and she was really happy with their progress.

She smiled as she watched Kirk talking to Alana down near the mulch heap. Alana had been *very* happy when she'd hired the good-looking young man.

Callie had called in a few times to see how they were going, and now Jenna walked to the stairs as she spotted the four-wheel drive come up the newly surfaced driveway. Another woman was driving, and when she stepped out of the car, she went around to the passenger side and helped Callie out.

They walked across the new driveway together.

'Hi, Jenna. Wow, the place is looking fabulous. You certainly have a magic touch,' Callie said.

'Thank you. I'm really happy with what we've achieved this week especially. How are you, Callie? You've grown even bigger since last week when you called in.'

'I know! How much bigger can I get? Jenna, this is my sister-in-law, Sophie. Braden insisted she drove us in this morning. We've dropped the boys off to school, and caught up with some friends in town.'

Sophie waved her hand. 'Welcome to town, Jenna. I can't believe what you've done. This place is going to be a showpiece. Once you get your signs out the front, you'll be pretty busy.'

'Thank you. We've had so much support and help, it's been overwhelming. Even as far as Charleville, plus the lady from the Morven Information Centre called me yesterday asking for brochures. The Charleville Information Centre gave her my contact details.'

'And don't forget the north. Send some to Tambo and Blackall as well,' Sophie said.

'And Barcaldine,' Callie chipped in.

'And if you need more help when you open, give me a call,' Sophie added. 'I'd be happy to volunteer a couple of days a week when you open. I'll give you my mobile number. I'll be driving the boys to school once Callie has the bub.'

'For a couple of weeks,' Callie protested.

'We'll see.' Sophie grinned.

Jenna thought Sophie seemed lovely. How kind to offer to volunteer. 'I might take you up on that offer.'

'Please do.'

'Between my husband and my sister-in-law, my life is organised for me!' Callie shook her head. 'Anyway, we just called in to drop this off.' Callie reached into her bag and passed a folded piece of paper to Jenna. 'It's an invitation to the get-together next Sunday at the park. It's going to be a big day.'

'We'll be there. Callie, while I think of it, I've been putting Mr MacGilvray's stuff into a box. I've found quite a few of his things. Do you think he'd mind if I visited him?'

'I'm sure Reg would love it. He's moved into the home, but it's probably best to visit him at the pub. You can always find him sitting at the table outside the side door.'

'Will he be at the get-together?'

'I hadn't thought of that, but I'll make sure he is. I'll see you there.'

'You won't be in hospital by then, will you?'

Callie laughed. 'Don't you start! The whole family have a bet going that when I go to the obstetrician next week, he's going to send me to the hospital in Charleville. I'm not going to miss the welcome picnic. I've instructed the baby to stay there until after next Sunday.'

Jenna put her hands up and chuckled. 'I won't take sides. You just stay healthy and have that baby soon!'

'Okay, we'll see you Sunday.'

'Yes. Nice to meet you, Sophie, and thank you for your offer. Alana and I are off to Charleville soon to collect some furniture. Kirk's cleared a spot under the side veranda to put some tables.'

'I was pleased to see you hired Kirk. He's a dynamo,' Callie said.

'He's fabulous.'

'And very easy on the eye.' Sophie chuckled.

'Alana noticed that the minute he arrived here looking for

work.'

'How long do you think it will be before you open?' Sophie asked as Jenna walked across to the car with them.

'The plan is for another three weeks, but we won't advertise until we're certain we can do it.'

'Did you get the flyers done?' Callie asked.

'We're picking them up today.'

'Sounds great. See you soon.'

Jenna smiled as she watched Sophie help Callie into the high car. The more time she spent here, the happier she was.

'Alana,' she called. 'Are you ready to go to Charleville?'

Chapter 14

Warrego River Campground -Sunday

Jenna and Alana walked from the car park behind the pub to the picnic site by the river just before midday on Sunday. As they crossed the road, Kirk's blue ute came around the corner and he parked about fifty metres up the road.

'I'll see you in a while, Jen. I'll just go and say hello to Kirk.'

Alana had been a tremendous help, and she seemed as happy as Jenna was. Kirk was a lovely guy and he seemed smitten with Alana too. Jenna just hoped it didn't go pear-shaped before the opening. She couldn't afford to lose either of them.

As she watched, Kirk climbed out of his ute and held his hand out to Alana with a big smile.

So far, things were looking rosy.

A big marquee was set up under the trees near the river, with three smaller tents beside it. Happy squeals came from a jumping castle in the middle of the flat park. A man led a child around on a small pony, and Jenna noticed a queue of children behind the roped-off area. At the far end of the grassy park, three caravans filled the space under the hill. The smell of barbequing meat and onions drifted across and Jenna's stomach rumbled.

'Jenna!'

She turned as her name was called. Sophie was walking across the grass towards her.

'Hi, Sophie. Looks like you've got a good crowd here already.'

'We have, but mostly locals so far. There are a few new

arrivals over near the drinks tent, and they're getting to know each other. Come with me, and I'll introduce you. But first the local brigade.'

A group of women manned a table in next to the barbeque. Rows of buttered bread and sauce bottles filled the table. A tall good-looking man wearing an apron manned the grill.

'Hi everyone,' Sophie called out. 'This is Jenna, the already famous Jenna of *Margie's Cottage Café*. Jenna, you won't remember all the names, but this is Amelia and Laura, and Dr Harry is the one in the sexy apron.'

The man flipping steaks on the barbeque smiled. 'Welcome, Jenna.'

She smiled shyly.

'And this is Kimberley. She's deputy at the primary school.'

'Hi, Jenna. Are you going to do coffee deliveries? I have a captive clientele for you at the school.'

Jenna shook her head. 'I hadn't even thought of that.'

'Worth considering.'

'I'll give it some thought.'

Sophie put her arm through Jenna's and they walked across to the drinks tent. A couple were chatting at the front and they both turned with a smile.

'This is Fallon and Jon. Guys, meet Jenna.'

'Hi, Jenna. This is my mum, Ruth,' Fallon said nodding to the older woman holding a baby. Another woman behind the counter turned around and waved. 'Welcome to town, I'm Bec, and the guy setting up the microphone is Matt.'

'I'm overwhelmed,' Jenna said. 'Please forgive me if I call you the wrong name.'

'I told you we should have had name tags, Sophie.'

Jenna turned as she recognised Callie's voice.

'Hi, Callie. That's one name I do know.'

A tall man with a rugged face had his arm around Callie.

'Jenna, this is my husband, Braden, and the three terrors over there looking at the cake stall are Rory, Nigel, and Petie.'

'Good to meet you, Jenna,' Braden said. 'Callie, we gave up waiting for the horse ride. Petie can go later. I'll grab your chair out of the car. Where do you want me to put it?'

'Can you get both chairs please, love? Reg agreed to come across as long as he could sit near the beer tent, so put them over there.'

'Will do, and then I'll go over and prise him from his table at the pub.'

Jenna noticed the way Callie and Braden's eyes connected and a message passed between them.

'I'll take Petie with me, okay?' Braden said.

'That would be good. I'll organise drinks and cake for the boys. Jenna, everything has been donated so don't try to pay for anything.'

'Come with me, Jenna. I'll take you over to the new group and you can learn some more names,' Sophie said.

Jenna smiled at the people she'd met. 'Great to meet you all. I'd love to chat later.' She followed Sophie across the grass.

Sophie lowered her voice. 'Callie's a bit on edge because the last time we were all together, there was an accident and Petie ended up in hospital in Brisbane for a few weeks. He's fine now, thanks to Matt who saved him, but Braden and Callie are very protective.'

'Understandably,' Jenna commented.

'It happened at our wedding, but all's well now. Come and meet my husband, Kent, and then we'll go over to the new group. I'm going to go and rustle up some name tags!'

Jenna spent the next hour chatting to the other new arrivals in town. Alana joined them, and Kirk went over to the beer tent to help out.

Everyone seemed really nice, and there were a lot of comments about how good it was to see new businesses coming to town. Three of the other new arrivals had started innovative agricultural projects, and there were two new nurses at the hospital, as well as a new casual teacher at the school.

Jenna excused herself and walked across the grass to the beer tent. She'd noticed that Reg had arrived and was sitting in one of the chairs that Braden had set up. There was no sign of Callie and Jenna frowned.

'Hello, Mr MacGilvray,' she said when she reached him. He looked up at her and his eyes widened.

'It's Reg. No one calls me that. Mr MacGilvray was my father. God rest his soul.'

'Is Callie all right?' she asked looking around.

'She's gone to the ladies' room,' he said gruffly looking away from her.

'May I sit with you for a while? I'd like to talk to you.'

He shrugged, but Jenna sat in the empty chair. 'I'll go when Callie comes back.'

Someone had placed a table in front of the two chairs, and a pot of tea and a bowl of sugar sat next to a plate of different types of cake slices.

'Do you want a cup of tea if you're going to chat?' Reg asked placing his cup on the table.

'That would be good, thank you. I'll go and find a cup.'

'No, stay there' He jumped to his feet, very sprightly for a man his age. 'I'll get one for you.'

'Thank you.'

Reg disappeared into the crowd and Jenna looked at the cup on the table, her eyes narrowing. She reached over and picked it up. The cup was burgundy on the outside with a gold handle; the inside was stained almost black. There was no saucer.

She frowned; she was sure there was a set in that same colour with gold handles in Gran's timber box; she'd have a look when she was at the cottage tomorrow. That was another job to add to her list now that the kitchen was almost finished. Wash up all the fine china and put it in the new cupboards.

And hand wash, not put them in the dishwasher. Gran would turn in her grave.

Jenna spotted Reg coming back, and she put the cup back on the table, but he obviously had good eyesight.

'Why were you looking at my cup?' He put a plain white teacup in front of her and sat down. 'I don't clean the inside because it makes the tea taste better.'

'Oh, I was just looking at it because I think I have some with the same pattern in the cottage.'

'Probably some modern copy,' he said picking the teapot up. 'Did you want milk because I'll have to go and get some if you want white tea.'

'No, black is fine, thank you.'

He poured her tea, refilled his own cup and picked it up. 'Mine is an *original* cup.'

'Mine are too,' she said.

He stared at her. 'Where did you get them from? I didn't think girls these days liked old-fashioned things.'

'They were my gran's. She came from Augathella. That's one of the reasons I moved here.'

Reg stared at her. 'What was her name?'

'Margaret.'

'Margaret who?'

'Margaret Hope.'

'And she's your grandmother, you said?' His voice seemed forced.

'Yes.'

'I think I remember a Margaret Hope. What can you tell

me about her? Where is she now?'

'Gran passed away three years ago.' Jenna blinked tears away; it still hurt.

Reg made a strange sound. 'Was she happy?'

'She was. Did you really know her before she moved away?'

'I think so. My old memory's not real good these days,' he said. 'Tell me a bit about her.'

'She moved to Brisbane when she was nineteen and she did dressmaking. She loved all the vintage stuff, the old clothes, the fine china, and I inherited the same interests. I miss her so much. She was my best friend.'

'What about your grandfather?' he asked slowly. 'Is he still around?'

'I never had one. Gran was a single mum. She only ever had my mum.'

'I think you look like her.'

'My mum always said that. So, you do remember her?'

'Aye, lass. I do. Where is your mother?' His voice was shaky, and Jenna wondered if he was sick.

She looked over at him, and he was watching her intently. 'Mum and Dad live in a caravan, and they are travelling around Australia. Why do you want to know?'

'I just wondered if your mother ever came back here to visit. I might have met her.'

'I don't think so. But they will come and visit when I open the tea shop.'

'How old is your mother?'

What a strange question from a stranger.

Reg's eyes were wide and his hands were shaking.

'Are you okay?' she asked, concerned.

'How old is your mother?' he insisted.

'Mum's fifty-four next month. She was born in 1969 on the day Neil Armstrong walked on the moon.'

Reg jumped up and picked up his cup. 'Nice talking to you, girl. I'll see you around.'

Jenna shook her head as he disappeared into the crowd.

What a strange man.

Chapter 15

Jenna sat at the table for about ten minutes after Reg left, and then she looked around with a frown; Callie was a long time coming back from the ladies' room. Maybe she'd got talking to somebody on the way back.

Jenna stood and walked around looking through the crowd; there must be over two hundred people here. She went in the beer tent and the barbeque tent and then looked over to where the children were lined up waiting for a horse ride. She also glanced over at the playground.

There was no one at the unmanned cake stall as all the cakes were gone. The group of new people that had been over towards the river had joined in with the main crowd, and most people were sitting at tables along the grassed flat.

Braden was holding a small boy's hand as they waited for a ride on the Shetland pony, she guessed it was Petie. There was no sign of Callie. Jenna didn't want to worry anyone, so she decided to go and have a look in the restroom near the road before she asked if anyone knew where Callie was.

The building was about a hundred metres from the picnic ground and she walked over looking around the park. She walked around to the front of the concrete building; it smelled of disinfectant and was spotlessly clean.

As she entered the dark interior, Jenna called out, 'Callie, are you in here?'

The answer came first in the form of a ragged groan, and she ran inside. The door to one of the cubicles was closed.

'Callie, are you in there?' she yelled out.

'Yes, Jenna, it's me. Thank God you're here. I need help. I'm stuck.' Callie's voice broke. 'The baby's coming. I need help. Can you get the door unlocked? I'm on the floor with my back against it.'

Jenna pulled her phone out of her pocket. 'I've got my phone here. I'll call an ambulance and then I'll run over to Braden.' She thought quickly; she couldn't leave Callie here by herself. She sounded terrified.

'No, better still, I'll call an ambulance, and then I'll call Alana to get her to tell Brayden.'

'Oh, thank you. I feel so much better now. I knew someone would come in here eventually, but it's been ages, and the concrete is so cold on my bottom, and my waters have broken, and I'm sitting in a pool of water. *Argghh!* Another contraction's coming!'

Callie's deep groan made goosebumps rise on Jenna's skin. Someone had to hear her across the field.

Her groaning ended and Callie was quiet for a moment then she panted out, 'Jenna, the contractions are only a couple of minutes apart and awfully strong. I'm terrified the baby's going to be born here in the bloody public toilet in Augathella.'

'It won't be, Callie, Trust me. Keep talking to me while I make a call.'

Jenna dialled triple zero, and once she'd chosen ambulance from the selection, the operator picked up straight away.

'I'm at Augathella, and there's a pregnant woman in labour in the public toilet at Riverside Park,' Jenna said quickly.

'Is there any sign of the baby coming yet?' the operator asked.

'Yes.' Callie groaned from behind the door. 'Yes, I think the birth is imminent.'

'I need you to answer some questions for me, and then we'll get some help on the way. First what's your name, and what is the exact address of where you are.'

Once the details were given, the operator spoke again. 'Okay, this is what I need you to do, Jenna.'

Jenna replied urgently. 'I can't do anything; Callie's locked in a cubicle. I'm going to get help. Please send an ambulance.'

'Callie, they're sending an ambulance now. It's okay. I'm on the phone.' Jenna disconnected from the operator, then called Alana's number. 'Answer, Alana, please answer.' The phone rang out, and then Jenna remembered that she had Sophie's number; she had given it to her the other day in case she decided she would need her help. She searched for it on her contacts and when she pressed call it picked up straight away.

'Hello?' Sophie answered.

'Thank God, Sophie. It's me, Jenna!'

'Jenna, where are you?'

'I'm over in the restroom with Callie. The one across the park. She's gone into labour.'

'Oh my God,' Sophie said. 'I'm on my way.'

'I've called an ambulance. Can you bring Braden?'

'Yes, and I'll get Dr Harry and Laura too. She's a midwife. We've got lots of help here. Stay there, Jenna. We'll be there in about two minutes.'

Callie groaned again, and this time it rose to a scream. Jenna felt absolutely useless with the closed door between them. She got down on her knees and looked underneath the door that hung a few centimetres above the concrete. She reached her hand through and felt around, touching Callie's back.

'I'm here, Callie, and help is on the way. Can you just hang on for another minute or two?'

Callie started panting. 'Oh my God, Jenna, I don't know if I can. This is nothing like the classes that Braden and I went to. This is what it's supposed to feel like at the end of labour, not at the beginning. I don't know what to do. I can't have our baby here.'

'Hang in there, Callie. Help is coming. Dr Harry will be here in a minute and Laura.

She could hear voices and she jumped to her feet stood and hurried to the door. 'We're in here!'

Braden's face was set and pale as he rushed to the door. The man who had been wearing the apron at the barbeque was behind him.

'Thank goodness,' Jenna said. 'The door's locked from the inside. Callie's on the floor and she can't reach the lock.'

'We'll sort it. Thanks, Jenna,' Braden said as he ran past her. 'We're here, love. It's going to be okay.'

Relief flooded through Jenna. Callie was in good hands now. Her hands started shaking as reaction set in.

The doctor went inside after Braden and they were followed in by the pretty woman with the long braid. Laura, the midwife.

'Callie, look up,' Braden said. 'I'm going to climb over the top of the stall from this side. Then we can open the door.'

'Thank goodness the door opens outwards,' Dr Harry said.

There was little sound as Sophie and Jenna moved outside.

'I'll wait here with you, Sophie' Jenna said. 'I feel totally useless.'

'Don't be silly. You called for help,' Sophie reassured her. 'I'd better go back and check on Petie.' Her forehead wrinkled in a frown. 'But I don't want to leave here.'

Jenna shook her head. 'Look, you stay here. I can go and watch Petie. Is Petie the little boy who was queued up with Braden for the horse ride?'

'Yes, he's with Amelia now. Do you remember meeting her?'

'Yes, I do. She was the one that had the dog with her, Chilli. She introduced me to him when I went back to the tent after I met the other new people.'

'Yes, that's Amelia. Can you just make sure Petie's okay and stays in the tent? We are very, very careful with him since the accident.'

'I will. Should I tell anyone what's going on? They'll wonder when they see the ambulance arrive.'

'I'm sure Callie won't mind. Just don't worry the three boys.'

'I'll be careful what I say if they ask.'

Jenna took off across the field and was soon at the beer tent. She looked around for Petie; he was sitting at the back of the tent playing with Chilli, the dog. She sat down beside Amelia and told her what was going on.

'Oh no, it's sort of good news and bad,' Amelia said. I know Callie wanted to get the birth over and done with but not here at the park. At least Harry and Laura are here today.'

'They're with her now. And Braden and Sophie. Sophie was worried about Petie.'

'Yes, I'll never forget that afternoon at their wedding. We'll make sure he doesn't get into any trouble. Actually, you sit here with Ben and Petie and I'll go and get Rory and Nigel. Are you going to tell them what's happening?'

'No, not just yet.'

Amelia stood. 'Oh, I don't think you've met Ben, have you?'

'No, I didn't. Hello, Ben.' Jenna sent him a brief smile.

'You'll be getting to know Ben soon,' Amelia said. 'He's a local building inspector.'

Jenna nodded. 'I'm almost ready for you, Ben.' She squeezed her hands together. Callie had been in such distress; it really worried her. She was supposed to go to Charleville and have the baby because she was so big.

'It's okay, Jenna. Don't worry. Callie's in the best hands. We're very lucky to have Doc and Laura in town.'

Chapter 16

Reg put his head into his hands and groaned. He sat at the table that filled the small window alcove in his new room. He'd unpacked his precious box and his cup and clock took pride of place in the centre of the table. His thoughts were in turmoil about what Jenna had said.

He hadn't been wrong.

His reaction when he'd spotted her on the veranda of his house the other day had been right. She was the image of his Meggie, and she had to be her granddaughter.

The big question was, was she also *his* granddaughter? Her mother had been born in July 1969. The dates lined up perfectly. Meggie had spent the night at his house four times in late October and November 1968. He remembered well; because the first time had been for his birthday on the twenty-eighth of October that year; she'd cooked him a roast dinner. They'd sat outside and looked at the stars and then she had stayed the night. The first night she had slept in his bed was imprinted in his memory. Meggie's birthday was in November and she'd stayed that night, plus two more nights that month after the Saturday night dance. She wasn't seeing anyone else. He knew that.

It had been the end of November when he'd driven the truck to Darwin for Horrie Andersen and when he came home just before Christmas, Meggie was gone.

All that was there waiting for him was the letter she'd left him.

And now Meggie was truly gone. She'd been gone three years and he hadn't even known.

Reg looked down with surprise as a wet drop landed on

the table in front of him. He reached up and touched his eyes; tears were streaming down his cheeks.

His Meggie was dead. He'd never seen her again.

And now I never will.

Had she known she was pregnant when she left? How the heck was he going to find out, or was he just being a silly old man? Should he just let it go?

He'd gone his whole life without knowing that he had a daughter and a granddaughter; why should he change now?

What a waste he had made of his life. He had done nothing memorable; shorn a few thousand sheep, driven a truck and fallen in love with his beautiful Meggie. Somehow, she'd decided that she didn't want to be with him.

He'd spent the rest of his life sitting at the pub hoping Meggie would come looking for him.

Reg opened his wallet and carefully pulled out the letter and read it for probably the five thousandth time in his life. Even when he'd first read it all those years ago, he'd had no idea what it really meant. He knew that she loved him; she'd told him so many times. And she wouldn't have slept with him if she hadn't, would she?

Meggie had known that he loved her much more than he'd ever loved the bush. He would have followed her to the ends of the earth. He would have lived in a hippie commune if that's what she'd wanted.

Maybe he should talk to Callie and get a woman's point of view about the letter and what her words actually meant. Was he not reading enough into them? Had he always missed the meaning behind the words? Was there a hidden message he'd missed?

He should have gone to Brisbane and looked for Meggie as soon as he'd got back. But he'd had no idea where to go, and she had specifically told him not to follow her.

He'd drunk himself into oblivion for the first three

months. Another tear rolled down his cheek, and Reg was disgusted in himself; always had been, always would be. He was an absolute waste of space.

He wanted to go to sleep tonight and not wake up. At least it would free up the room for some other sad bugger.

Chapter 17

Callie sat up in the bed of the maternity ward at their local hospital. Harry had decreed that they didn't have time to either wait for the ambulance or take her to Charleville. By the time Braden had climbed over and opened the door, Sophie had brought their four-wheel drive onto the park. Kent had come across to help lift Callie into the back seat.

She had been in the delivery room within minutes, and Harry and Laura had been at their professional best.

Braden stood next to the bed looking down at her with tears in his eyes.

'Are you okay, love?' she asked.

He reached down and kissed her. 'Am I okay? I should be asking you that!'

'I'm wonderful. A bit shell-shocked, and amazed that it was all over in less than an hour.'

'You are amazing.'

'Can we call her Meg?' Callie whispered as she looked at the crib at the end of the bed.

'I think that's perfect for her.' Braden reached down and held Callie's hand as though he was never going to let go. His grin was wide as she stared up at him.

'And what about "Muesli"?' he asked looking at the other crib to the side.

'I'll give you "Muesli"! she said laughing.

'What about Munro? Meg and Munro Cartwright?' Braden's lips moved against her forehead.

'I like both,' she said. 'Oh my God, Bray, how am I going to look after two babies? I haven't had any time to get my head around one, let alone twins, and we need so much stuff.

Double everything I've bought.'

'We'll sort it. I think you're going to have lots of helpers.'

'I think I'll need them. How could I have not known it was twins?'

'The obstetrician and the ultrasounds didn't even pick it up, so how could you? Harry explained it to me when Laura was weighing them. They were so close together that the smallest baby, in this case, our little Meg, his behind her brother.'

'And as simple as that we now have five children.'

Braden chuckled. 'I'd better go and buy some more cattle to pay the bills. I don't think you'll be going back to work at the school for a while.'

Harry and Laura came to the door, smiles on both faces.

'How are you feeling, Callie?' Laura asked. 'I have a very happy Auntie Sophie and Uncle Kent out here, and three very excited little boys. Are you up to a visit?'

'I am. And can I have a cup of tea? I missed out at the picnic.'

'I'll make it myself,' Dr Harry said, and he disappeared into the hall.

Callie's heart filled with love as Sophie and Kent, and Rory, Nigel, and Petie came into the room. 'Come and meet your new brother . . . and sister, boys,' she said. 'And Auntie Sophie and Uncle Kent, you now have a new nephew *and* niece.'

The three boys hurried over to the two cribs and Sophie stared at Callie and Braden, her eyes wide with shock.

'Twins? You had twins?'

'We did,' Braden said proudly. 'Your turn next, Soph.'

Chapter 18

Three days later

Jenna had called at the pub three afternoons in a row when she came to town to visit the hardware store. She brought the set of cups that were the same as Reg's with her but wanted to compare them to make sure. She'd taken a photo and done a reverse image search on Google. The set was a Shelley piece called Pink Roses. Inside each of her cups was a bouquet of pink roses and she was going to ask Reg if she could clean his and see if it was the same pattern.

But he hadn't been there. She'd asked Sean at the bistro if he knew where he was, but he shrugged.

'We wondered too, but we figure he has all the company he wants at the home now. But we do miss the old bugger,' Sean said.

'I hope he's not sick,' she said. 'I might go there and see if I can visit him tomorrow.'

The next afternoon, Jenna changed out of her work clothes and scrubbed the paint off her hands. As well as seeing Reg, she'd call in to see Callie at the hospital. Even though it was winter, the day was warm, and she put on her favourite dress. Like the set of Shelley cups, it was patterned with pink roses on a cream background. She left her hair loose and headed to town.

The first stop was to see Callie and the twins. Callie was pleased to see her, but Jenna kept her visit brief as there seemed to be a stream of visitors going in and out. Callie had even made the *Western Times newspaper* with her surprise twins and their birth at the picnic.

'Thanks for coming, Jenna,' Callie said as she made to

leave. 'And thank you again for getting me help so quickly.'

'My pleasure. I'm off to visit Reg now. I have a bit of a mystery to solve.'

'A mystery?' Callie asked.

Jenna quickly explained how she had a set of five of her late grandmother's cups, and she suspected that Reg might have the missing sixth.

Callie's eyes widened. 'What was your grandmother's name?'

'Margaret, but she always went by Margie or Meggie.'

'Margaret Hope?' Callie said softly.

Jenna nodded. 'How did you know that? Did Reg tell you I asked him about her?'

'No, but I think you'd better go and talk to him. Go gently with him, Jenna. But I think this might make him very happy,' Callie said enigmatically.

##

Jenna was thoughtful as she walked to the back of the hospital grounds where the aged care facility was situated. Like Reg's box, she carried her precious cups in a small timber box. She pushed open the door and walked across to the desk. Three elderly people were watching television in a large recreation room, but there was no sign of Reg.

'Hello.' The woman at the desk smiled at her. 'How can I help you?'

'I was hoping to visit Mr Reg MacGilvray.'

'Oh, I'm so pleased. He's been really sad since he came to us last week. Are you a relative?'

'I . . . I think I might be,' Jenna said slowly. 'I need to talk to him.'

'He's in his room. I've just taken him a cup of tea in that stained old cup he insists on using. Would you like to have one with him?'

'I would, but could I ask a huge favour? Would you

make it in this cup?' She opened the box and passed a china teacup to the carer.

'Of course. I'll bring it down. He's in room six at the end of the hall. Just go down and tap on his door and open it. He might be dozing.'

Jenna carried the box under her arm and walked down the hall. The strangest feeling filled her chest and her hands felt light as she took in deep breaths, not knowing what to say to him.

Jenna tapped gently on the door, and a gruff voice called, 'Come in.'

She turned the knob and pushed open the door, balancing the box in her other hand. Reg was sitting at a table by the window looking out onto a pretty rose garden. 'Hello . . . Mr MacGilvray.'

'Reg, please.'

She walked over slowly and put the box on the table and looked down at him. His face was unshaven, and his eyes were shadowed, and even though it was two in the afternoon, he was wearing blue-striped pyjamas.

Before she could speak again, there was a tap on the door and the carer came in with Jenna's cup of tea.

When she placed the cup on the table, Reg's eyes widened. The woman looked at each of them, and sensing the emotion in the room, she left and closed the door quietly behind her.

Jenna sat down and picked up her teacup. She took a sip. Her voice shook as she looked at him, and saw the tears forming in his eyes. Eyes that she now recognised as being very much like her mother's.

She cleared her throat, which felt thick and heavy. 'Instead of calling you Reg, I think I would like to call you Grandfather. You knew as soon as you saw me that day, didn't you?'

Tears rolled down his unshaven cheeks as he held her eyes. 'Aye, I did, lass. I did. You are the image of your grandmother.'

She nodded and her tears spilled over. 'I know.'

'My Meggie.' Reg reached into the pocket of his pyjama shirt and pulled out a clean handkerchief. As he leaned over and wiped Jenna's tears away, his touch was gentle.

An Augathella Baby

ANNIE SEATON

Augathella Short and Sweets: 2

Chapter 1

Sophie – Lara Waters

Sophie glanced across at Kent as she climbed out of bed. She inched out slowly, not wanting to wake him, even though her husband had said last night he'd have to have an early start today. He and Jon Ingram were off mustering at six-thirty.

It was still dark, but the moon shining through their large bedroom window highlighted Kent's face. Sophie stood beside the bed and looked down at him. Sound asleep and breathing evenly, his features appeared totally relaxed. He looked like the sixteen-year-old boy she'd fallen in love with, not the rugged cattleman of these days.

Despite his deep slumber, Sophie knew as soon as the alarm went off at five-thirty, Kent would spring out of bed full of energy and enthusiasm about the day ahead, no matter what he had planned. She adored this man; his constant positivity and happiness had made such a difference to her life.

Sophie's only regret was that they'd split up before they were engaged and she'd spent—no, she'd wasted—three years with Jock Evans, three years which she'd blocked from her memory.

Those years of emotional—and some physical—bullying by Jock, during the months after the accident that had killed Braden's wife, Julia, had been hard. Sophie had taken in her brother's three sons to mother because Braden's grief had consumed him. The regret that she had left Kent before all that had happened was always with her, but she knew she had grown into a stronger person from the choices she'd made. When Kent had accompanied Braden to Innot Springs last year to rescue her from a difficult situation, Sophie had come to her senses.

Thank God, Kent had never stopped loving her, and she knew that he had always been the man for her. She had fallen for Jock's sister's malicious lies when she should have known to trust Kent.

Their wedding had been a joyous affair until the accident that had threatened her nephew Petie's life. He had recovered and they had set off on their delayed honeymoon in Fiji. In the months since then, their married life at Lara Waters station had been happy and fulfilling.

Sophie let out a soft sigh; only one thing made her a little less happy at times. Kent desperately wanted a baby. He was already talking about when they had boys like Braden's three—actually four boys and a girl now with the arrival of little Meg and Munro a couple of months ago. He was looking forward to their kids being old enough to get out on the motorbikes and four-wheelers. Sophie had managed to brush off his comments or just simply smile.

The truth was, she wasn't ready, and her big worry was that she never would be. It was not a conversation she wanted to have with Kent in the first year of their marriage, but it had given her some sleepless nights as he talked more and more about their future family.

Turning to the door, Sophie picked up her satin bathrobe and slipped it on. She'd had every intention of getting up early—five a.m. was perhaps a little bit early—but making the biscuits and being ready to deliver them to Jenna for her grand opening had meant getting out of bed before dawn.

Sophie yawned, quietly closed the bedroom door and padded barefoot to the kitchen. She and Kent had gotten hooked by a comedy series about soccer in England last night, and they'd binge-watched a whole season after dinner. Of course, it was midnight before they went to bed, on the one night they should have gone to bed early. She had the baking to do, and then helping Jenna with what she was sure would be a very busy day at the official opening of the Vintage Tea Shop on the highway. Kent was behind on the mustering. Luke Elliott, one of the managers from Dwyer Holdings, was flying up from Narrabri today to see if the cattle were ready.

As well as the huge workload managing the stock on their property entailed, Kent also managed a thousand head of cattle on the property adjacent to Lara Waters. The property was owned by the Narrabri company and was currently between managers. Kent and Luke had become good mates over the past months. Sophie enjoyed Luke's company too, and instead of staying in the staff dongas on his last couple of visits, they had hosted Luke in their home.

She filled the kettle and switched it on; a cup of coffee would get her moving. Another yawn overtook Sophie as she stood at the kitchen window looking out as the first rosy pink glow tinged the eastern horizon, gradually creeping across the dark of the night.

It looked like the weather promised to deliver a good day for Jenna's opening. The sky was clear, and the last stars of the night quickly faded as the sky lightened. She turned her head to the side as the lowing of a distressed beast drifted in through the open kitchen window. She'd have to tell Kent about that as soon as he appeared.

After a quick coffee, her tiredness and yawns gone, Sophie set to work and half an hour later when she heard the alarm go off in their bedroom, four trays of jam drops were cooking in the oven. Kent appeared in the doorway as she lifted two of the trays out of the combustion stove.

'Yum. Jam drops for breakfast.'

She glanced across at him and shook her head as he

reached out for one. 'Nope. If you want jam drops, you have to come to the opening.'

'Spoilsport.' Kent reached for Sophie instead and pulled her into his arms. He smelled clean and fresh, and his hair was damp from the shower. 'Good morning, my darling. It was lonely waking up in an empty bed.'

Sophie looped her arms around his neck, and her fingers brushed the damp curls on Kent's neck as she looked up at him. 'You need a haircut. And the bed wasn't empty. You were in it.'

'But I didn't have a wife to cuddle.'

'I have to make dozens of biscuits. I promised Jenna. She's panicking that she hasn't got enough food for the opening this afternoon.' She reached up and pressed a kiss on his lips. 'Any chance at all of you getting there before it's over? Everyone's going to be there. Please, sweetie?'

'As much as I'd love to, Soph, I'm going to be too busy. It's the only day Jon could give me. I guess Fallon will be disappointed too.'

'She will. It can't be helped. I know Luke's coming through today.' Sophie hid her disappointment. 'That reminds me, I could hear a beast out there before. It sounds like it's in trouble.'

'Okay, a quick cup of tea and I'd better get out there. You know if we keep having these late nights and separate mornings, we're never going to get those babies made.' He pulled her back against him, and Sophie closed her eyes as Kent kissed her thoroughly.

The oven timer dinged, and Sophie pulled away. She smiled as Kent poured hot water on top of half a dozen Weet-Bix. By the time he'd finished his cereal, Sophie had two trays of Anzacs baking and was mixing up a batch of Melting Moments. Quickly drinking his tea, Kent carried his plate and cup to the sink before looping his arms around her waist again. 'Have a lovely day, sweetie. I'm sorry I can't be there, but I promise if there's any way that I can get into town before three, I will. Okay?' He bent down, and his lips were warm against her neck. 'I'm sorry I can't come. You have a good time,' he said. 'Bring me home something nice to eat.'

Sophie softened, and she cupped his cheek with her hand. 'What would you like me to bring home?'

'Does Jenna have any vanilla slices?' he asked.

Sophie chuckled. 'Jenna makes the best vanilla slices ever. Not with SAOs but with real puff pastry. I've got to stop sampling all her cakes. My jeans are getting tight.'

'You still look beautiful to me.' He dropped another kiss on her cheek and her mood thawed a little. 'I must come into town as soon as I get these cattle sorted and sample all these cakes. And catch up with Reg. I haven't talked to him for ages. Oh, and while I think of it, Ben and Amelia are going to come over for a barbie one night next week. Ben and I have been invited to play at the Tambo pub the night of the show. We want to practise some new songs.'

'That would be nice. You just make a date with Ben, whatever suits them.' She raised her eyebrows. 'Then again, Ben and Amelia will probably be at the opening today. I can talk to them.'

'Don't put the guilts on me, love. I'd love to come, you know that.'

'I wasn't. I was just making an observation.' She hid her annoyance. 'How about I help you with the cattle tomorrow?'

'Great. I have to go over and help Braden before the end of the week. Do you want to come with me?'

'That'd be good. Callie said she's right for a couple of days this week, but any opportunity to see Meg and Munro is one I'll take. Plus, I can help you and Braden with the cattle,' she added as an afterthought.

Kent's lips were warm as he kissed her goodbye. 'Drive

safe, sweetie.' He picked up the tucker box he'd packed last night before they went to bed and turned to the door. Sophie crossed to the sink where the trays of biscuits were cooling. 'Hang on, I'll put some jam drops in your tucker box.' Kent was still smiling as he looked back at her when he walked out the back door.

Chapter 2

Kent - Lara Waters

Kent jumped on his motorbike and rode the kilometre to the front gate. He was on time but Jon wasn't there yet. He climbed off the bike and put it behind the large timber mailbox, securing it with the padlock and chain he carried. Times had changed so much since he was a kid. They'd never had to secure anything back in those days. Now you had to lock up the house when you went to town and make sure there were no keys left in the station vehicles.

He unlocked the mailbox in case one of his neighbours had left something there, but it was empty. Now that the postal service had cut back rural deliveries to outlying stations—Lara Waters wasn't far enough out of town to qualify for delivery by air—he or Sophie made sure they were in town at least a couple of times a week to pick up the mail. Now that Sophie was helping Jenna at the new shop on the highway near Augathella, he didn't have to go to town so often.

Kent grabbed his tucker box off the back of the bike, climbed up on the fence rail, and sat waiting for Jon to arrive. He could see the plume of dust from Jon's vehicle approaching, but he was still a couple of kilometres away. He was worried about Sophie; if he didn't know better, a man would think his wife was avoiding him, but he shook himself and reminded himself of the loving kiss Sophie had given him as he'd left.

But one thing he hadn't missed was the way she was avoiding talking about having kids. Whenever he mentioned it, she either just smiled or changed the subject. It didn't mean anything; maybe if he was honest and told her he had some worries, they could talk about it, but so far, the opportunity hadn't arisen. They were both settling into married life and had a lot to adjust to. Sophie was busy; she was helping Jenna at the tea rooms plus baking at home; she was also going across to Kilcoy Station two or three times a week to help Callie out with the twins, as well as going to town to pick the boys up from school twice a week.

Sometimes he wondered if she was keeping busy so she wasn't at home with him, but again, he knew that it was just Sophie being Sophie. She was a good person, and she pitched in and helped wherever help was needed. And to be honest, he'd been so late home over the past few weeks, she would have been home by herself anyway. He always had to push away the thought that they'd broken up once. And that made him all the more determined to be honest and tell her what he was worried about. Communication and talking things out together was the key.

Having to work today sent guilt spiralling sky-high. If Luke hadn't been flying in, Kent would have taken the afternoon off and made sure he was at the opening. Jenna's Vintage Tea Room on the highway was the talk of the town, or rather the talk of the district. And Sophie was really enjoying helping out.

He had to learn to stop worrying and to trust; sharing his worries with her would lighten the load. He was so immersed in his thoughts he didn't even hear Jon pull up until he called out to him.

'You coming, mate?'

Kent jumped off the fence and climbed in. 'Gidday, mate. Thanks for collecting me.' He slammed the door of the work ute shut and Jon took off again.

'Sorry, I was a bit late. Ryan had a bad night. Teething,

we think.'

'Bit young for that, isn't he? Not that I know anything about babies.' Kent reached over and put his tucker box behind the seat.

Jon yawned and nodded. 'According to Ruth, five months is normal. But honestly, mate, I can take the crying, the poor little mite; it's the nappies that are the worst. It's worse than calf scours.' Jon looked over and caught Kent's grin. He chuckled. 'I know. Whoever thought we'd be having this sort of conversation? Wait until it's your turn. I'll be the expert by then.'

'You will,' Kent said.

'Okay, so what's the plan once we get out to the back paddock?'

'The boys should have that mob in by the time we get out there. I want to check them over and make sure the cattle that we've brought in are in prime condition for Luke to assess.'

'They were looking good when I flew over there last week.'

'Yeah, I hope he's happy. Managing the cattle for Dwyer's is certainly worth it financially. Once you get your property set up, I'd suggest approaching them. They're great to work with.'

'I will. Times have changed, haven't they, mate?'

'They have. The days of family properties are long gone. Big business has come to the bush.' Kent shook his head.

'Since the drought ended, I reckon the country'll end up with more corporate stations than family concerns.'

'You're right, and they have the money at hand to improve everything up front.'

'But are they doing that? I'm yet to be convinced. I saw it when I was up in the Territory.' Jon changed back a gear as they reached the gate in the fence that marked the boundary of Kent's land. 'There's a lot of lip service paid to things like sustainability and reconciliation, and the employment of women but . . .'

'But?' Kent prompted.

'I might be biased, but in the past, pastoral companies typically had staff with solid hands-on experience from the ringers right up to management, even at the board level. These days, the experience just isn't there. Unless they've got a good manager, some of these holdings are going to go bust very quickly. They chase short-term profits. Anyway, I'll get off my high horse.'

'It is a worry. I know exactly what you mean. We're losing so much out here in the bush.'

'Not only the skills on the land either. As the older generation passes away, we're losing so many of the stories. The larrikinism, the bush ethos, and the old ways.'

'Yeah, old fellas like Reg. So many stories,' Kent said. 'I'm looking forward to you meeting Luke today,' Kent said. 'He's a good bloke and he knows his stuff. He came from a large family spread, went to uni and then got his helicopter licence. Dwyer's are really lucky to have him.'

'Look forward to it. What time are you expecting him? I'd like to get home as early as I can this afternoon.'

'Ryan?' Kent asked.

Jon looked sheepish as he pulled the ute over near the cattle yards 'Um, not really. Would you believe the opening of the Vintage Tea Room? Fallon said she won't go unless I do too.'

'I'm in the bad books with Sophie because I'm working too,' Kent said.

Chapter 3

Sophie

By nine o'clock, Sophie had six dozen jam drops, three dozen Anzac biscuits, and two dozen Melting Moments cooling on the kitchen bench. She went into their bedroom, wondering what would be suitable to wear today. She'd offered to help out in the kitchen, but she still needed to look the "vintage" part. Jenna had already worked herself up into a right state when Sophie left yesterday, and Sophie didn't want to give her anything else to worry about. So dress the part, she would.

'What if we haven't got enough food? What if nobody comes to the opening?' Jenna said.

Sophie laughed. 'Well, I think you're going to hit that magic middle spot. You won't run out of food, and you'll have enough people to eat it. The whole town's talking about the opening, you know. Actually, the whole region. Plus look how much food you've got. We've got four Victoria sponges ready to be filled, and the biscuit jars are full.'

Jenna had nodded. 'I'm going to make some more tonight, plus a tray of vanilla slices. I'll fill the sponges in the morning so they're not soggy. We've also got eight different slices, and Jenny Riley has offered to make me two dozen plain scones and a dozen pumpkin scones. Oh, and Mrs Rees sent in three jars of lemon whisky marmalade for the scones.' Jenna had put a hand over her mouth. 'Oh, no. Maybe we've got *too* much food. Being a Saturday, everyone might be busy.'

Sophie smiled as she calmed Jenna. 'How long have you

been in town?' Sophie asked.

'For three and a half months.'

'And you've made a huge hit in the community,' Sophie said. 'Everyone loves you. Not only will you have all the tourists going up and down the highway calling in, but I think half the town is going to be out here every day for their morning cuppa.'

'It has been good this week. It was a good practice week. But I don't know.' Jenna chewed on her lip. 'I don't think that volume will be sustainable, you know. I think our main clientele will be the tourists. It's just a novelty for the townsfolk to come out and see what's happening.'

'No.' Sophie shook her head. 'You've injected enthusiasm into the community, and when Jenny Riley was here yesterday, she said because of the extra tourists that are stopping out here and with all the brochures you've been handing out, already more caravans are stopping overnight in town. I think that we'll see a lot more people doing that. And Jenny is talking about opening her gift shop again. She closed it up before I went away about four years ago, but she still owns the premises. Her Calico Cottage was a hit before COVID, but hopefully, if she opens it again, that will be another business for tourists to visit.'

'That would be great.' Jenna looked more hopeful.

'Jenna, I think you are responsible for getting Augathella well and truly back on the tourist map.'

Jenna smiled. 'Really? As long as the gala opening goes well tomorrow, I'm happy.'

'And your mum's still going be here for it?' Sophie asked.

'Yes, that's why I made it two o'clock and afternoon tea instead of morning tea. Not only will all the Saturday sports be over, but it will give Mum and Dad time to get here. They're staying at the pink pub at Dulacca tonight, and they said they will be here by noon, so it'll just give them time to get the van set up, have a shower, and get dolled up.'

Dolled up, Sophie thought now as she stood in front of her wardrobe looking at the clothes hanging in front of her.

Nothing in her wardrobe suited the vintage line. There weren't many dresses there; most of the hangers held jeans and T-shirts. There was a bridesmaid dress she'd worn when she was a bridesmaid for one of her school friends, and she still had her white dress from the Debutante Ball when she was eighteen. It should still fit, but it wasn't the right style.

Sophie frowned and reached to the back of the wardrobe, where there was a green velvet skirt she'd bought years ago for a fancy dress party. She pulled it out and slipped it over her hips. It almost fitted, but thanks to Jenna's cooking, it was snug over her tummy. She needed a loose top over the waist. A T-shirt wouldn't do.

Kent's mother, Rhonda, had left quite a few of her clothes here when they moved to Brisbane, and Sophie remembered a cream top that she had worn every time Jenny Riley had one of her spring garden parties. She walked down the long hallway to the master bedroom that was still Kent's parents' room.

Since Kent's dad had been sick, they didn't get home to Lara Waters very often. They'd moved to Brisbane before the wedding so that his dad was close to the specialist.

Sophie was sure Kent's mum wouldn't mind her borrowing a blouse. As she opened the wardrobe, she wrinkled her nose as the cloying smell of camphor drifted out.

Her eyes scanned the rows of blouses, and finally, they settled on the cream cotton blouse that she was looking for. Pulling out the padded hanger that her mother-in-law had all her clothes on, Sophie walked to the mirror and held the cream top up in front of her. It was a loose waist-length style with a scooped, gathered neck and puffed sleeves.

It would be perfect. She sniffed it carefully; the camphor aroma wasn't too bad. She could air it for an hour or so, and a splash of perfume would cover the smell of mothballs.

She carried the blouse back to their bedroom at the other end of the house and hung it up on the shower rail in the ensuite. She turned the hot water on in the bath to let the room steam up to freshen the shirt and hopefully take out the few wrinkles.

Sophie hurried back to the kitchen, took the final batch of biscuits out of the oven, and put them on the benchtop with the others. Before she went back to the bathroom to turn the water off, a quick call to her mother-in-law was in order.

Chapter 4

Jenna's Vintage Tea Room

Matilda Highway tourist route

Jenna Wilson smiled as she stood beside the antique Welsh dresser that she had found for her newly-opened business, the Vintage Tea Room, and watched her grandfather deep in conversation with an older man in the car park outside.

Since they'd opened last Saturday, Reg—her *newly-discovered* grandfather had asked that Jenna call him Reg—had asked for a lift out to the tearoom from town with Jenna and Alana each morning so that he could sit outside and wait for the customers to arrive.

Jenna had had no idea that the property she'd bought—for a very reasonable price—was owned by the grandfather she'd never met.

The grandfather she didn't even know she had, let alone one who lived in the town she had decided to move to. Today, her mother was arriving to meet Reg, her father, for the first time. Jenna swallowed the lump that had been in her throat ever since she'd got up at four a.m. It was going to be a very emotional day. The meeting of her mother and Mum's father, and the official opening of her new business. It was sure going to be a day to remember.

Reg gestured to the house—the house looked nothing like it had when Reg lived there—and Jenna knew that he'd be telling their first customer how he'd used to live here, and what a wonderful job his granddaughter had done, converting it into a tearoom on the highway.

Customer! Gosh, had she turned the urn on when she arrived? Alana had stayed at Kirk's place last night—that romance was hotting up quickly—and Jenna was out of their usual routine setting up by herself. It was going to be a long and busy day, so she'd told Alana not to come until ten.

Last week had been hectic and had surpassed Jenna's expectations. She was going to have to look for more staff . . . and quickly. She couldn't rely on Sophie's goodwill forever, even though she'd appreciated her help so much as the newly opened business had been flooded with customers every day.

Boy, had those customers arrived! They had only been open about fifteen minutes on their first trading day when six caravans had pulled up and a dozen people had spilled out of the cars, looking delighted they could get a cup of tea.

Reg had been there that day and had thoroughly enjoyed talking to the travellers.

'Good to meet some new people, love,' he said. 'It was pretty much always the same ones who used to come into the pub. We did get a few tourists there, but it was the good old regulars who used to keep me busy talking.'

Jenna had hidden a grin at that. Now that the emotion of discovering her grandfather had passed, they were settling into a comfortable relationship, and she was quickly learning that "Old Reg", as the town referred to him, sure enjoyed a yarn.

The phone conversation she'd had with Mum when she discovered that Reg was her long-lost grandfather and her mother's unknown father had been a difficult one.

Mum and Dad had been in Exmouth, Western Australia, and had immediately hightailed it across the country to Augathella.

Heading back to the east, their journey had been interrupted by floods along the road from Broome to Kununurra. They had stayed in touch by phone as the journey progressed, but Mum had refused point-blank to speak to Reg.

'The first time I speak to him, I want it to be face-to-face,' her mother's voice was teary. 'Don't tell him you've told me, will you, love? I want to see his face.'

Jenna questioned the wisdom of that. 'I'm surprised he hasn't asked, Mum, but I haven't mentioned you at all yet. He just asked once where you were, and he hasn't mentioned you since.' Jenna understood her grandfather's hesitation; it was hard enough for him to get used to having a granddaughter in town, let alone thinking about the daughter he hadn't known he had. 'But he does know you're on the way. For one thing, we don't want him to get a shock, and it will also give him time to prepare if he knows you're coming.'

'Okay, darling. I'll leave it up to you.'

'It will all be fine, trust me,' Jenna had promised. Now two weeks later, her parents had got through the flood water and last night had spent the night four hundred kilometres away, ready to arrive in time for the official opening.

Jenna hurried inside while Reg was still talking to their first customers for the day, and was pleased to see she *had* turned the urn on, as well as the coffee machine. She set a tray with cups and an assortment of biscuits and cupcakes, hoping that the early arrivals weren't expecting a breakfast menu.

Chapter 5

Sophie

Sophie dialled the Brisbane number and waited for Kent's mum, Rhonda, to pick up. She wouldn't feel right just taking her clothes and wearing them without checking first.

The phone picked up quickly, and Rhonda's happy voice greeted her. 'Hello, is that
Sophie or Kent?'

'Hi, Mum, it's me, Sophie. Kent's gone out to work already.' Rhonda had insisted that Sophie call them Mum and Dad as soon as they got married. As she and Braden had lost both their parents a few years ago, it was bittersweet.

'I thought he might be. It's so lovely to hear from you, love. How are you both?'

'We are good. How's . . . um'—even though Mr Mason insisted she call him Dad, it was hard to do that—'how are you both?'

There was a long silence for a moment until her mother-in-law spoke.

'Dad hasn't had a good week, but he's a bit better this morning. So, yes, we're fine. We're looking after each other. We were hoping that you and Kent would come down to Brisbane and visit because I don't think we're going to be able to get back home for a while.' Her voice was slow, and Sophie read between the lines. Kent's dad was obviously not well.

'Yes, Kent and I were only talking about that the other day. We'll come down for a weekend soon.'

'How soon would that be, Sophie? As soon as the

mustering is finished?'

'It's almost done, I think they'll be finished in the next couple of days.'

'Dad's keen to hear about this new setup with Ronnie Stuart's property.'

'I'll talk to Kent and we'll get down very soon. I promise.'

'Thanks, Sophie. You're a good girl. It's so good to have Jacinta and Ryder close by now when I need a break, but I—we—miss you and Kent too. Now I've been rabbiting on too much, it's early for you to be ringing, can I help you with anything?'

'Actually, yes.' Sophie glanced at the clock and crossed to her chest of drawers. She tucked the phone between her ear and shoulder as she pulled out her underwear to take into the bathroom. 'I think I told you about Jenna? The new arrival in town. The one who bought Old Reg's house on the highway.'

'You did. She's opened a tearoom for the tourists you said. How's it going?'

'Well, it's been open for a week, and the town has been supportive. It's certainly filled a need locally. The tourists have been stopping in their dozens too. I was talking yesterday to Rory, the builder, and Jenna's going to have to extend the car park to accommodate all the caravans that have been stopping already.'

'That's fabulous news. One day, I'll get out there and see it.' Rhonda's voice was soft.

'That would be lovely,' Sophie said. 'But what I'm ringing about, I've got to dress up for the grand opening this afternoon, sort of vintage style, and you know what my wardrobe's like. I found an old green velvet skirt that I had, but I didn't have a shirt. So, I hope you don't mind. I went down and had a look in your wardrobe because I remembered that cream top with the puffed sleeves you used to wear to the garden parties that Jenny Riley had when I was in high school. I found it in your wardrobe.'

'Yes, that's not a problem at all, sweetheart. Not only wear it but keep it. I doubt whether I'll be wearing puffed sleeves these days and low necklines with my wrinkled chook neck.'

'Don't be silly, Mum, you're still gorgeous.'

'And you're a gorgeous daughter-in-law to say that. I have to go. I can hear Dad calling. Say hello to Kent. Give him my love, and a big kiss and hug from his mum, and I hope the opening goes really well today. Send me a photo when you're dressed up.'

'I will.'

It was only when Sophie got in the shower that she remembered she hadn't told her mother-in-law about Reg being Jenna's grandfather.

Chapter 6

Jenna's Vintage Tea Room

Matilda Highway tourist route

The first week of the Vintage Tea Room operating at Road Mailbox 182 on the Matilda Highway, five kilometres from the town of Augathella, had been amazing. Jenna had been overwhelmed by the response of both locals and tourists. What she had entered in her business plan to earn in a month, the tea shop had taken in the first two days, and that had meant a quick rethink of food orders, baking, seating and numerous other organisational things.

Word had spread quickly, and locals had come from Tambo in the north and Charleville in the south for a stickybeak and a cup of tea.

Reg had shaken his head after three days. 'It's good for you, love—' he'd said to Jenna, '—but when it's all said and done, it's only a cuppa tea.'

'Everyone who's stopped by has said how wonderful it was that there was somewhere on the highway to stop for a break that wasn't a petrol roadhouse.' Jenna nodded, enjoying the warm feeling that filled her when her grandfather called her "love". 'I was pleased to see that many of the caravans turned into town after they had a cup of tea here too. I think what we've done already with our local knick-knacks and brochures has fired an interest in the local area.'

Jenna had worried about taking business away from the establishments in town, but the owners of the small coffee shop up from the butcher's and the small cafe down from the pub had both called in through the week and offered her their best wishes.

'There's plenty of room for all of us,' the owner of the coffee shop had said. 'We've already seen more tourists in town this week,' the café owner had assured her.

Augathella was a lovely town with a supportive community, and Jenna was getting to know many of the locals. She'd been invited out to dinner at the pub to join a group of local young people, and the Cartwrights had invited her out to dinner at their station last week. Their new twins were the cutest babies and had actually made Jenna feel clucky for the first time ever.

When she'd mentioned that to Callie, Callie had smiled. 'You never know what will happen out here. If anyone had told me a year or so ago that I'd be married, and have three stepsons and now baby twins, I would have told them they had rocks in their heads. And now look at me.' The way Callie had looked at the babies in the double pram with such love had just about melted Jenna's heart.

Callie had told her about the on-air incident that had led to her fleeing Brisbane and had filled her in on who was related to who in the district.

Jenna was gradually picking up the family connections, which families were related, and who ran what businesses in town. But the best thing she'd encountered was the support and enthusiasm that everyone had shown for her new business. Half the day—when her feet weren't aching—Jenna felt as though she was walking on air.

Alana—her friend who'd come west with her from the Gold Coast to help set up the business—hadn't been as social as Jenna. She hadn't taken up many of the invitations because she and her new boyfriend, Kirk, were getting pretty hot and heavy.

Jenna smiled again; it was all she seemed to be doing lately. She hadn't been this happy for such a long time, and on top of that, the joy of finding her grandfather—well, words simply couldn't describe the happiness that had brought. She was just impatient for Mum to arrive and discover the same happiness.

But there was work to be done to prepare for the day. Hopefully, Sophie would be here soon to help her get her head around what needed to be done. Alana would be here soon too, but her head was in the clouds in the throes of love, and it was hard enough for her to get the tea and coffee orders right at the moment.

Chapter 7

Sophie

Sophie turned onto the Matilda Highway and crunched the gears as she changed back when a road train approached from the north. She waited, wondering whether to turn or wait.

Common sense prevailed and she eased off onto the side of the highway and closed her eyes as she waited for the huge vehicle to approach. Disappointment had impacted her mood as she'd driven in but she wasn't going to let it affect her safety. She waited until the road train had passed her car, and wrinkled her nose at the smell; even though she should be well used to the smell of cattle—it had always bothered her— but today, more than usual. She swallowed as nausea threatened.

It was so cruel to see the beasts all crammed into the two levels of the road train.

Braden always laughed at her, but Kent had tried to reason with her. 'You're a country girl, Soph. That's what we do. We raise cattle for market.'

She sighed. 'I know, it's just a soft part of me. Poor things. We look after them, feed them and fatten them and then. . .'

Even though Kent had hugged her and promised to try to come to the opening this afternoon, she'd detected the impatience in his voice when he'd thought she was trying to put the guilts on him; Sophie was sure Kent believed she didn't care about the property enough.

It was unusual for her new husband to be like that, but

she was a bit cross too. She'd been so looking forward to the opening and she would have loved Kent to be here with her. It had been such a busy time getting ready as she'd worked with Jenna and Alana. They'd worked hard and the Vintage Tea Room looked absolutely divine. Jenna had sourced so much memorabilia, and the outfits she and Alana had bought at a vintage store in Brisbane before they'd headed west were fabulous.

And Kent wasn't going to see any of it. Her temper simmered and she tried to get over it, but the niggling annoyance remained.

Maybe it was hormonal. Or maybe it was her age—she was heading for her mid-twenties. Maybe it was seeing Callie with the new babies, but something deep inside told Sophie that she wasn't ready to be a mother yet. What she worried about most was if she'd ever be ready to be a mother.

Chapter 8

Sophie

The road train passed and Sophie's eyes widened as she approached the turnoff to Augathella and looked at the newly renovated house sitting on the crest of the hill. Not in a million years would you ever guess that the Vintage Tea Room business was the dilapidated house that Old Reg had lived in until a few months ago. Every time Sophie saw the house, she still couldn't believe the difference the builders had made.

They'd left most of the original rustic timber, replacing the rotten boards and Kirk, the handyman who had taken up with Alana, Jenna's friend, had done an amazing job of sanding it back and touching up the new planks to match the existing weathered timber. Rory, a builder from Charleville had done the structural work, replacing the veranda floors and the windows. He was the one who'd found the vintage front door with the stained-glass panels on a demolition site.

The roof had been fixed and painted a brilliant red that contrasted with the deep blue outback sky. Kirk had built a new set of front steps, and now as Sophie parked away from the house to leave room for the customers' cars and caravans, her bad mood finally lifted and she smiled as she climbed out of her car. Reg was in the car park, cigarette in hand, but dressed to the nines and showing an early customer where to park his van.

Sophie threw a cheery good morning in his direction before she hurried around the side of the house and put two of the baskets with her baking on the bottom step. She hurried back to the car and took out the other two. She stopped to have a quick chat with Reg on her way past.

'Morning, Reg, sorry I couldn't stop before. I've got to get this baking inside to Jenna.'

'You're a good girl, Sophie, helping my Jenna out.'

'Anything we can do to help; she's doing a great job. Last week was incredible, wasn't it?'

'Sure was,' Reg said. 'More people called in here than I've seen at the pub in the last ten years.'

'You must be very proud.'

'Proud's not the only word. I'm blessed. Never thought I'd have a granddaughter in my old age.'

'And a daughter,' Sophie said quietly. 'I believe she's arriving today. Is that why you're all dressed up, Reg? Braden said you'd been shopping.'

Reg was wearing a new pair of trousers, a white shirt, and a nice jacket, not quite a suit, but he was more dressed up than his usual navy blue work clothes.

'Not every day a man meets his daughter,' he said, his voice husky.

'Are you nervous?' Sophie asked.

He cleared his throat. 'If I tell the truth, I am. Very nervous. I mean, who'd want to meet an old reprobate like me and find out he's your father? I feel sorry for the girl.'

'Reg, you're a good man. Don't be silly. And you know we all love you, and I'm sure your daughter will too.'

He grunted and lifted the cigarette to his lips.

'One thing I'd suggest,' Sophie said. 'Maybe it's time to put the cigarette out. Not a good look for the customers.'

'Just nerves, love, just my nerves.' He stubbed out the cigarette, dropped the stub in the garden and used his boot to cover it up. 'When I'm ready for another smoke, I'll go around the back near the dunny.'

Sophie chuckled. 'Okay, I'll get these biscuits upstairs.

Get some courage up, Reg. Be prepared.'

'I am, lass. I am.'

Sophie walked up the back steps, carrying the first load of jam drops. She'd come back for the others after these were upstairs.

Jenna was in the kitchen when she opened the back door; the tables were covered with plates of cupcakes and biscuits.

'Morning, Jenna.' Sophie smiled when she spotted the tray of vanilla slices ready to go into the fridge. One of those would have Kirk's name on it shortly. Jenna was leaning over the oven, and her cheeks were flushed. She stepped back and wiped her hand over the perspiration trickling down her cheek.

'Okay, Miss Vintage Tea Room—' Sophie said with a grin— 'get yourself away from that oven and get out there and greet your first customers of the day. I'll take over whatever you're watching.'

'Morning, Sophie. Thank you, but I need to watch these biscuits. I burnt the first batch.'

'Do you really need to bake more biscuits?' Sophie gestured to the table. 'I've got four baskets for you.'

'Oh, you are a pet! Thank you. I just want it to be perfect. I can barely think straight because Mum just rang. They left Charleville an hour ago.'

'So, they'll be here soon,' Sophie said.

'Yes. I told Reg. He's waiting for them out the front, and I worry about them meeting him without me out there with him.'

'He is in the car park, and he's nervous too. He could do with you beside him. I think you should be there when they arrive. It's not every day that Reg meets his daughter for the first time.'

'I know, Sophie.' Tears welled in Jenna's eyes. 'Whoever would have known that me finding this house on the Internet, and then buying it, would lead to me finding my grandfather and Mum's dad!'

'It was meant to be, Jenna.'

'It's so unexpected and so special. Mum is beside herself. She could barely keep her voice steady on the phone. Reg is excited too, and I see he's got new clothes.'

'Yeah, Braden had to go to Charleville a couple of days ago, and he took Reg down with him.'

'You don't think he's a bit over the top?' Jenna asked.

'I think he looks pretty swish, and if that's what he chose, let's tell him how good he looks.'

'He does actually. I think he's put a bit of weight on too. Do you, Sophie?'

'I do. We all have with your cakes!'

'He's not living on beer anymore,' Jenna said. 'He has so many cups of tea when he spends a day here. And he does love his cake.' Her smile was affectionate. 'Although he is keen to get back to town to the pub for half an hour on his way home to have his one beer for the day.'

'He seems really happy. I've never seen Reg so animated. He's always been up for a chat and interested in what's going on, but he's got a new spark in him.'

Jenna turned around and Sophie reached over and brushed a dab of flour from her cheek before she enfolded her friend in a quick hug. 'Congratulations on the opening of your tea rooms, Jenna. You've done a wonderful job. You should be very proud.'

'I couldn't have done it without your help, Sophie.'

'My pleasure. Now, I'll stay in here in the kitchen once I get the last biscuits up here. You tell me what needs to be done and then go out and wait with Reg. Go to the bathroom, and put some cool water on your face. I'll look after the customers.'

'How's my hair?' Jenna asked as she reached up and

patted the 1940s style that she had rolled her hair into that morning.

'You look gorgeous, but put a bit more of that red lippy on. Did you know the mayor's coming?'

'I know. Unbelievable! Listen, those biscuits have to come out in three minutes and then leave them two minutes before you take them off the tray. Put them on that cooling rack on the sink there.'

'Anything else, boss?' Sophie grinned.

'No. The tables are ready, and the coffee machine's on. Alana will be here soon, plus the four girls from the high school who are going to waitress for us this afternoon. Can you show them what to do when they get here? Amelia said she'd help too, if we wanted. Oh my God, Sophie, I am so nervous I feel sick.'

'I can show them. It will all be fine. Now go, or your parents will arrive before you're out there.'

Sophie smiled as Jenna hurried towards the bathroom. It was a wonderful day for her friend. She walked out of the kitchen to the tea room and crossed to the window; the first customers were halfway up the steps.

She looked out; there was no sign of Reg. A motorhome drove in and parked close to the gate. A door slammed, and a woman jumped out and hurried up the steps. Sophie knew straight away who it was as soon as she stepped onto the veranda. She quickly seated the first customers who were waiting at the counter.

'I'll be back to take your order in a moment.'

'No rush, love. Take your time.'

Sophie raced into the kitchen, took the biscuits from the oven, and then hurried back to the tea room. The new arrival was standing in the doorway looking around.

'Good morning,' Sophie said. 'I'm guessing you must be Jenna's mum. You could be her twin sister.'

The woman raised a shaking hand to her face. 'Yes, I'm Jenna's mum. I hope she doesn't mind us getting here too early. I wanted to get here as soon as we could.'

There was no sign of Jenna, but Reg walked up the steps and stood on the veranda.

Jenna's mum gasped and left Sophie and hurried to the door. Sophie picked up the order pad and crossed to the table near the door where the couple were waiting to order.

'Have you decided what you would like?' she asked, keeping one eye on the couple on the veranda. As the two of them stood there, she looked down at the motorhome in the car park; Jenna's dad was also giving them privacy as father and daughter met for the first time.

As she took the order, she missed Jenna's exit from the bathroom, but a soft cry had her looking up. Jenna stood at the door, tears rolling down her cheeks.

No words had been spoken, but on the veranda, Reg held his arms out, and Jenna's mum stepped into them. She was crying, and a tear rolled down Reg's cheek as he looked over at Jenna. He patted his daughter's back awkwardly.

Jenna waited a moment and then went out to the veranda. The three of them were in tears as they hugged.

Sophie had always considered herself quite hard-boiled. She'd never been one for emotion, and the months living with Jock Evans had beaten out any softness that she ever had. Having the boys had helped her soften her attitude a little. She had enjoyed the nighttime cuddles with Rory, Nigel, and Petie when Braden hadn't been able to deal with them after Julia's death. Being with Kent had opened her up even more, and her emotions had softened, but she still rarely cried.

Sophie sniffed as she went back into the kitchen, reached into her pocket for a tissue and dabbed at her eyes. She filled the plates with the food order and then went back out to the counter to make the pot of tea on the order. Once she'd put the pot, the cups, and a jug of milk on the table, she smiled at the couple.

'Enjoy,' she said softly before she walked slowly to the front door and looked outside. Two caravans and a motorhome had parked in the car park, and three more couples were heading towards the house. Alana and Kirk were walking towards the back door.

Jenna and her mum were standing next to Reg. He was still dabbing at his eyes with his white handkerchief. Jenna was chattering away, and her mother was looking at Reg as if she couldn't believe what she was seeing. As Sophie watched, Reg reached out and took his daughter's hand and raised it to his lips.

Tears welled in Sophie's eyes again. God, what was wrong with her?

She leaned around the door and caught Jenna's eye. 'Jenna, there's some more customers coming up. Alana and Kirk have just arrived too.'

'We'll go back downstairs,' Jenna's mum said. 'Reg can meet your dad.'

Jenna nodded. 'Before you go down, Mum, this is Sophie. I couldn't have got everything done without her and Alana. Sophie, this is my mum, Margaret.'

The woman, who was a dead ringer for Jenna, turned around and held out her hand to Sophie, taking one of her hands in both of hers. Her skin was soft and a faint sweet fragrance drifted over to Sophie. 'I've heard lots about you, Sophie. Thank you so much for helping Jenna.' She gave a small smile and glanced across at Reg as the customers reached the top of the stairs. 'I hope we didn't throw a spanner in the works, but I couldn't stand to get here any later, so we drove right through the night and stopped for a sleep about three o'clock this morning.'

'Well, Mum,' Jenna said. 'I think you and Dad will be in

dire need of a cup of tea. I need to give Dad a hug too. Take Reg downstairs to meet him and then I'll set up a table for you all.'

Reg's chest puffed out with pride as he crooked his arm for his daughter to put her hand through. Jenna and Sophie looked at each other and smiled as they went down the steps.

'A pretty special day for Reg and your mum,' Sophie said.

'He was pretty nervous,' Jenna said. 'He said he was just about to go around the back for another cigarette when they pulled up.'

Sophie nodded. 'It's certainly been an emotional start to the day, hasn't it? Anyway, I've got customers to look after. You go down and see your dad.'

Jenna wiped her eyes. 'It's certainly been an emotional start. It's not every day that your mum meets her dad, her daughter opens her new business, plus she gets to meet half the district where her father grew up, and where her mother and father met all those years ago. I need to pull myself together. We have a big day ahead.'

'We do. I'll get to work,' Sophie said.

Chapter 9

Sophie

Sophie was in the kitchen when Alana and Kirk came in the back door. 'Hi, Alana. Hi Kirk. It's a great day for the opening, isn't it?'

'Sure is,' Kirk said. 'I've come along to help, so give me a job, Sophie.'

'Hi Sophie, you look absolutely gorgeous.' Alana's gaze went from the top of Sophie's hair to her toes. 'Even your shoes are vintage.'

Sophie smiled. She'd found the black lace-up ballet shoes in the bottom of her shoe box. She'd forgotten she had them from the ballet stage she went through in her early teens.

'Not only do they look vintage, but they are super comfortable,' she replied.

'So,' Alana said. 'We didn't like to interrupt Jenna and her mum downstairs. It looks like the meeting has gone well; they're all smiling and chatting.'

'I think we're going be pretty busy. I've noticed a few vans pull up in the last couple of minutes. Kirk, seeing it's such a lovely day, you could get some more of the tables and chairs out of the shed and put them around.'

'Right, I'm on it,' he said and headed out the back door.

'He is such a great guy, isn't he?' Alana said dreamily, smoothing her hand down her floral dress; it had a sweetheart neckline and was cinched in at the waist.

'You look lovely too, Alana. Love your dress.'

'Thank you. I hope we weren't too late getting here, but Jenna insisted that we come in late because Kirk and I worked pretty late last night.'

'No, it's fine. We're all organised. I've got a mix of biscuits already on plates'—Sophie gestured to the benchtop— 'and I've done quite a few mixed plates, because last week, it seemed that's what the customers preferred—a mixture of sandwiches, a selection of cakes, and biscuits.'

'Yes, they did, and didn't we go through some food!' Alana reached for one of the aprons hanging on the back of the door. 'Oh look, Ben and Amelia just pulled up. They're early. I'll finish off here; you have a bit of a break. I think you've been here for a while by the look of things.'

Sophie tucked up a strand of hair that had fallen from the French roll that she'd done her hair. 'Amelia's offered to help out today too.'

Alana shook her head. 'I can't get over how you all pitch in and help. Very different to where we came from.'

Sophie was waiting at the top of the steps when Ben and Amelia reached the veranda. Amelia reached over and hugged her, and Ben kissed her cheek.

'Hey, how's it going, Soph?' he said.

'We're pretty organised. Are you here for a cuppa?'

Amelia shook her head. 'No, I'm here to help. Ben's got to go out to a property and do a job, and I figured I might as well be here for the morning instead of sitting at home.'

'Oh, that would be great. Jenna's got some girls coming out from the high school, but an extra pair of eyes to supervise would be good. It's going to be a pretty special day because there are so many people coming from far and wide. If we stuff up, it's going to get back, and it'll affect the business.'

'We're not going to stuff up,' Amelia said after Ben had left. 'It's going to be perfect.'

'Come into the kitchen, and I'll show you where everything goes,' Sophie said. Amelia followed her in and after a quick chat with Alana, she listened as Sophie told her what had to be done.

'Not a problem, I'll start cutting up the slices for you,' she said.

Sophie headed for the door. 'I'll go and man the coffee machine. 'Oh, Amelia, while I think of it, Kent was talking about inviting you to our place during the week.'

'Yes, Ben mentioned it this morning. Apparently, they're going up to the Tambo show next week. Are you going too? I've never been to the Tambo show.'

Sophie chuckled. 'I haven't been for a few years, but yes, I'll go. I love hearing them sing. We can travel up together.'

'That sounds good. I'll run it by Ben.'

Sophie thought about the coming week. 'How about we make it Thursday night? Does that suit you?'

'It's okay with me, and I'm sure it will be with Ben. He's keen to practise with Kent. He's actually written some new songs.'

'He's very talented,' Sophie said.

'Thursday night sounds good. Don't go to too much trouble. I'll bring the salads or make a dessert. What would you prefer?'

Sophie laughed. 'I think after being here all last week, I couldn't face a dessert. Let's just have some salads with the steak.'

'That sounds good to me. Besides, I'm watching what I eat,' Amelia said, looking down.

'Don't be silly, Amelia. You don't need to lose weight.'

Alana had gone out to the laundry and Amelia lowered her voice.

'Can you keep a secret, Sophie? I'm busting to tell you.'

'I can?' Sophie glanced down the short hall and could hear the tap running in the laundry.

'More than okay. We were going to tell you guys when we came out for the barbecue, but I can't keep it to myself any longer. We're having a baby.' Amelia's face lit up in a huge smile.

Sophie froze and then forced a smile onto her face. How rude of her not to be happy for Amelia, and to be selfish and think that would make Kent want to push her even harder.

She reached over and hugged Amelia. 'That's fantastic news.'

'It sort of is,' Amelia said. 'Entirely unplanned. I mean, we got engaged at your wedding, but we weren't going to rush into organising our wedding, and then we were planning on having kids in a year or two. I wanted to wait until Mum and Dad and all my brothers could come down for the wedding, but that could be ten years away.' She rolled her eyes. 'But it happened. I was pregnant and had no idea. I'm almost halfway.'

'Wow, you can't even tell,' Sophie said.

'I've been watching what I eat, but I've started to pop out now.'

A strange feeling—almost a tinge of envy— shimmied through Sophie as Amelia turned sideways and pressed her loose dress flat against her front. There was definitely a baby bump there.

'Anyway, we wanted to talk to you when we come out on Thursday.' Amelia kept talking as Sophie tried to process what she was feeling. 'We're going to have a small wedding and we'd love to get your ideas on where to have it and how to do it. I've got no idea, and even though Ben's on the Shire, and he knows where everything happens, he hasn't got a clue about wedding venues. We both want to get married in the next month or two so that we can have the wedding done and dusted and focus on the baby and getting our house ready.'

Sophie's eyes widened.

'That's our other news. We've bought a house at the end of Ben's mum's street. It's on an acre and has the most beautiful rose garden. And it backs onto the paddock, so I won't feel like I'm in town.'

'Wow, you're certainly full of news this morning. Ssh, here comes Alana.'

'So how are things with you, Sophie?' Amelia crossed to the drawer and took out a wide-bladed knife to cut the slices as Alana came back in. 'You actually look a bit tired, are you okay?'

Sophie nodded and smiled. 'I'm fine. We had a late one last night. We were watching that funny soccer show on Netflix that Ben told Kent to watch.'

'Ben and I watched that series last week. It's really good, isn't it? Are you sure that's all? You seem a little bit subdued.'

'No, I'm fine,' Sophie said forcing her smile to widen. She wasn't going to share what she was worried about; if she was going to share her worry, she'd talk to her sister-in-law, but then she bit her lip. That wasn't fair; Callie had her hands full with their family.

'Well, that's good to hear,' Amelia said. 'I'll look forward to having more of a chat on Thursday night.'

Sophie moved across to the window at the front of the tea room. 'I think we're going to be busy. Oh, my goodness, how many people are in that group?'

Alana joined her at the window and counted quickly. 'Would you believe twenty-four? I hope Kirk's got those tables ready to go. I'll just grab some tablecloths and run down and cover them.'

'I'll get out and start taking orders until you come back up, then make the drinks. If Jenna thinks she should come up, can you tell her that we're fine up here? We'll call out if we need her. And look, another car just pulled up. I think it's the girls from the high school.'

'Amelia, we'll put you in charge of the girls,' Alana said.

'Tell them what to do, while I go and get the outside tables organised.'

'Okay, you and I will take the orders to start with, and then I'll make the tea and coffee,' Sophie said. 'The tables up here are numbered so the girls can take the food out.'

Alana nodded. 'I'll number the ones on the lawn too.'

'Sounds good to me.'

Alana picked up the numbers from beside the phone on the kitchen bench and headed out the back door.

'Amelia, when you've done with the slices, can you man the cash register?' Sophie asked. 'Do you know how to use that Square thing?'

'Yes, I do. I was using it at Jenny's the other day.'

'Jenny's?' Sophie asked as she headed for the tea room to greet the customers who were coming up the steps.

'She's actually starting to set up the gift shop.'

'That's fantastic. Augathella won't know what's hit it soon!'

Chapter 10

Kent

'Well, that was a great start,' Kent said.

'Yeah, not having to repair any of the fences was great. Luke must've organised for the contractors to come in and do it since the last time I was over here,' Jon replied.

'So, we're ahead of schedule.' Kent grinned. 'We might even get to the tea room after all.'

'We probably should go home and get changed first,' Jon said.

'If you have a café like that in the country, you have to accept the customers who have to work too,' Kent replied.

'Yeah, but not on the opening day when the mayor's there.'

'True,' Kent said. 'But we won't be there until after all the official stuff is over, so we can have a bit of a wash over at the bore before we head off.'

'I'll give Fallon a call later and tell her I'll meet her there. What time do you reckon?' Jon asked. 'And it depends on Ryan too.'

Kent frowned and screwed up his face. 'All depends on what time Luke arrives.'

'It's only just gone eleven-thirty. He should be here soon,' Jon said.

'Yep, and then he might come into town with us. I think he was planning on staying the night.'

'And then maybe we can go to the pub for a beer after the cup of tea thing,' Jon added.

'Sounds like you've got my social calendar planned for the rest of the day.' Kent chuckled.

'Blame Fallon, she's been such an organising influence on me, especially since Ryan arrived. If you're not organised with a baby, nothing gets done.'

'Half your luck, mate.'

'What's up?' Jon looked at Kent curiously. 'Sounds like you've got something on your mind.'

Kent ran his hand through his hair. 'I shouldn't say anything, but it's good to talk to a bloke. I probably should talk to Sophie about it, but we've been on eggshells a bit around each other some of the time lately.'

'Doesn't sound good.'

'Don't get me wrong. We're fine. Everything is great. Marriage is fantastic. We're settling in well together. Life's good. It's just that the few times that I've mentioned kids, she seems to clam up.'

'Early days, mate. You've only been married a few months. You're probably imagining it. You know what they say. Men are from Mars, and women are from somewhere else, or something like that. I find it hard to read Fallon a lot of the time. I just listen, and I know when not to say anything and when to just smile.'

'You're probably right, Jon. Don't say anything to Fallon, will you?'

'Not a word, mate. Secret men's business. And if you ever do need to have a chat, feel free. Not that I can set myself up as a marriage expert. Who would've ever thought a couple of years ago we'd all be settled into marriage now? Callie showed up and then Braden remarried and his three boys are doing so well. The twins arrived and Callie's settled right in. Fallon flew in, and look what happened there. And Sophie came home and you pair got yourselves sorted and hitched.'

'Yeah, just ignore me. I'm making something out of nothing,' Kent said. 'But you're right. Life's good, hey?'

'Sure is.' Jon pointed to the east. 'Here comes Luke in the chopper now.'

Two hours later, Luke had checked out the cattle, done a headcount as best he could, and announced that he was more than happy with their condition and that they were ready for the market.

Kent breathed a sigh of relief. 'That's great, mate. We can get the truck going, load 'em up, and not have to worry about letting them out in the paddocks again and then doing another muster.'

'I know,' Luke said. 'Time's precious.'

Kent leaned back and looked up at Luke, who towered over him at over six and a half feet. He shook his head. 'I wonder how you fit in that tiny little helicopter.'

Once introduced, Jon and Luke had hit it off straight away; it turned out they had a lot of acquaintances in common up in the Territory.

'I didn't know you'd worked up there in helicopters as well,' Kent commented.

Luke laughed. 'I reckon every helicopter pilot that I've met has done some time up in the Territory.'

'Can't argue. I've never even been up there,' Kent said.

'Yeah, but you've got your family spread here, and now you're married. Plus, you've got all our stuff to look after. I can't see you getting there for a while.'

'I don't even know if I want to,' Kent said. 'It's pretty good here.'

'Right, I'll take the chopper over to your place, and I'll meet you there, will I, Kent?' Luke asked.

'How about flying into town? Land at the aerodrome in town, and we'll pick you up. There's a bit of a shindig out on the highway, and we're both calling in to keep our partners happy. You can either come with us or we can meet up at the pub afterwards. It's up to you, Luke, what do you reckon?'

'What's happening at this shindig?' Luke grinned.

'There's a new girl come to town, and she bought an old house on the highway. Belonged to Old Reg, a local identity, but you wouldn't have met him. Turns out that Jenna's his granddaughter, and she's had a whole stack of building work done at the house over the past couple of months. She's opened what she calls a "vintage" tea room on the highway. It's doing really well.'

'Anyway,' Jon interrupted. 'To cut a long story short, today is the grand opening. The mayor's come up from Charleville and there are a lot of people coming from all over the district.'

'Sophie got up at some ungodly hour this morning and baked thousands of biscuits,' Kent added.

'Sounds good to me,' Luke said. 'Might be a bit early for a beer, so a cup of tea and a homemade biscuit or two would hit the spot.'

'We've had lunch. We took a break for smoko about an hour ago. Have you eaten?' Kent asked.

'I had a bacon and egg roll at Thargomindah,' Luke said. 'I had to fuel up there on the way over.'

Jon nodded. 'You sure get around, mate.'

'Yeah, we've got properties in Narrabri, Cunnamulla, and west of Charleville. And one just over the border into the Territory and another one just past Cameron Corner. Keeps me busy getting out and looking at them,' Luke said, 'but here is my favourite stop. I know that you look after the beasts really well out here, Kent. Sure makes my job a lot easier.'

'Thanks, mate,' Kent said.

'Okay, how long will it take you guys to get into town?'

'I'll probably be about half an hour,' Kent said.

'Rightio, pick me up at the aerodrome. On the way in I might have a bit of a fly over a couple of places I've got my eye on. The company's looking for more land out this way. Do you know of any properties that are coming up out here?'

Kent looked at Jon. Jon raised his eyebrows and nodded slightly.

'If you head southwest from here—' Jon said, '— about five ks as the crow flies, you'll see a place with a brand-new green Colourbond roof. Have a look around the eastern side of that. That's my new place. If you're seriously looking for some more land, I'm happy to take on some stock for you. I've worked as a manager at a lot of stations both here and in the Territory so I can provide references.'

'I'll suss it out on my way over,' Luke said. 'Thanks, mate.' He held out his hand to Jon and shook it. 'Good to meet you, anyway. See you in town. See ya, Kent.'

A couple of moments later, the whop whop of the chopper filled the air, and red dust swirled around them as Luke took off and headed southwest.

'Thanks for priming me on that, Kent. I probably wouldn't have said anything if you hadn't mentioned it,' Jon said. 'Luke seems like a good bloke.'

'He is. You ready to head?' Kent asked.

'Yep. Do you mind driving? As soon as we get into service, I'll give Fallon a call and see if she's got to the tea rooms yet. I'll let her know we'll be there soon. Around three o'clock, do you think?'

'Three sounds good to me,' Kent said as he climbed into the driver's side.

Chapter 11

Sophie

Five hours later, Sophie kept one hand in the washing-up water and reached over to wipe her left hand with the hand towel on the side of the countertop. It had been an incredibly busy day. The attendance at the gala opening had exceeded any of their expectations, and there weren't going to be any jam drops left over to freeze for the week ahead. They'd been through so many of the cups and saucers it was quicker to hand wash, dry, and put them back out on the benchtop for Alana to take back out than to run the dishwasher, even on the thirty-minute cycle.

Perspiration trickled down the side of Sophie's face, and she used her shoulder to wipe it away.

'Sophie, I need you out the front,' Jenna's voice came from behind her, and Sophie turned, wiping both hands on the towel this time.

'Not a problem. What would you like me to do?'

'If you don't mind, I'm going to take a quick break. Mum and Dad are about to go into town and park up their van. Is that okay? Then I'll come back up and you can have a *long* break. You haven't stopped all day.'

'Of course, it's okay. Alana is handling the orders, and Amelia is plating up the food as the orders come in. She's just gone downstairs to have a short break. The four girls have been fabulous.'

'We're down to the last Victoria sponge,' Jenna said,

looking in the fridge.

'Go on, scat. Hang on, take your apron off and put some lippy on before you go. You've got to look the part.'

'Was the official bit okay?' Jenna asked hesitantly. The two o'clock official opening had gone well. The shire mayor had given Jenna and the business a huge rap.

'It was great. I think the mayor sees your business as the turning of the tide for this northern part of the region.'

'I can't believe it, just after a week of trading. Do you think the numbers will be sustainable?'

Sophie nodded. 'Jen, I've lived in this district all my life, except for a couple of years away recently, and this is the best idea I've ever seen. I've seen businesses come and go. I've seen people move here and leave just as quickly, but over the last couple of years, since the drought ended, a lot of new younger people have arrived in the district. There's a lot of innovation happening with organic farming, the new date palm place, and we're getting a real unique flavour here.'

'It's been the best day.' Jenna was positively beaming.

'It has, now I'll look after the front of house. I think there are quite a few starting to leave. It's nowhere near as busy now. What time do you want to close?'

'I guess we'll just play it by ear and see how long everyone wants to stay.'

Sophie smoothed back her hair and checked her apron. It was still clean enough to go out to the front of the house. Alana had just reached the serving bench as Sophie followed Jenna out.

'Okay, Alana, I'm on it now.' Sophie picked up the order pad and pencil and hurried down the steps. The tables downstairs were still full, even though upstairs had emptied out. It was such a lovely afternoon, everyone wanted to sit in the sun. It was such a shame Kent hadn't got here; he would have had lots of locals to talk to. She reached the table at the side of the steps, and her smile widened as she saw her brother and sister-in-law sitting there.

'Hey, guys, I didn't think you were able to come. How's our little bubs?'

Braden and Callie were sitting at the table with a pram between them. Braden's proud expression as he looked down at his twins almost brought another tear to Sophie's eye.

'Perfect children,' he said proudly. 'Not a peep out of them since we got them out of the car.'

'Where are the boys?' Sophie asked.

'We dropped them into town to Ruth. She didn't want to come out here today. She came out last week and gave Jenna her nod of approval,' Callie said. 'I think the boys would have been bored here once they ate their cake. Running around the tables on a sugar high with all that good china wouldn't have been a good idea. They were playing in Ruth's garden when we left.' Callie grinned. 'Now look at this quiet pair. They've had a feed and they're sleeping quietly.'

Sophie leaned over the pram and gazed down at her new nephew and niece. It was still hard to believe that Callie had had twins. It had been totally unexpected. Sophie would never forget that afternoon.

'Black tea for you, Braden?' she asked. 'And a skinny cap, Cal?'

'Yes, please. Where's Kent?' Braden looked around.

'Couldn't make it. Luke was flying in today to check the beasts over at the Stuart place.' Sophie pushed away the ever-present disappointment as she headed back upstairs with the order. Despite her comfortable shoes her feet and lower back were starting to ache. She stretched and rubbed her back as she walked up the stairs.

Chapter 12

Sophie

Finally, only a few stragglers were left. Amelia had stayed in the kitchen and helped them wash up the last of the dishes before loading up the dishwasher. Braden and Callie had come up to say a quick goodbye.

'We're thinking about going to the pub for tea, Sophie,' Braden said. 'Give Kent a call to come into town.'

'Pass. I think I need an early night,' Sophie said, rubbing the nagging ache in her lower back again. 'He'll be tired too.'

'Sophie!' Braden shook his head sadly. 'Make the most of it before you have kids.'

Sophie pulled a face at her brother. 'Maybe I'd like to spend some time with Kent. We're newlyweds, remember!'

Amelia was putting the last half of the leftover sponge in the cool room that Kirk had installed at the end of the short hall behind the laundry.

Jenna walked into the kitchen as Sophie pulled out the tray from the refrigerator that held the milk and the slices.

There were three vanilla slices left—now she had an order for two—so she took the three out, put the third one on a plate, covered it with cling wrap, and put it at the back of the top shelf.

'I'll pay you for that one, Jenna.' she said. 'That's Kent's afternoon tea, or more likely tonight's dessert.'

'You will not pay me for it at all. Don't be silly.' A knowing smile tilted Jenna's lips. 'I won't be charging for his cup of tea either.' She walked over to Sophie and undid the colourful apron that was covering her cream shirt and green skirt. 'I don't think I told you this morning how fantastic you look. I was so worked up about Mum and Dad arriving.'

'Thank you,' Sophie said. 'So do you. It's been a great day.'

'And about to get even better. Hang that apron up and go stand on the front step,' Jenna said.

Sophie wrinkled her nose with curiosity. 'What do you mean? Stand on the front steps for what?'

'It's way past time you had a break. Anyway, I think it's time you sat outside at one of the tables, got a feel for the place as a customer, and had a cup of tea.'

'I don't really need one,' Sophie said, wondering what Jenna's sneaky smile meant.

'Sophie,' Jenna said. 'Outside. Now.'

'Yes, boss.'

The official opening had gone well, and the crowd was finally starting to thin. There were quite a few empty tables in the front tea room and on the veranda. The two smaller rooms were empty now and Amelia was wiping down the tables. As Sophie walked through the house, there were still several local people looking happy and chatting with friends. The last caravan had pulled out when she had been on the veranda taking the last order. She stood on the veranda looking at the tables below, and her heart jumped as she saw Jon's ute pull into the car park.

'Kent! Jon!' she called, as her husband climbed out of the driver's side. Kent looked up and grinned as she waved to him madly. 'Oh, what a sweetie. He made it.'

She watched as the back door of the twin cab ute opened and Luke climbed out. Sophie ran lightly down the steps and across to the three men. Kent held his arms out, but she stood back with her hands up. 'Cream shirt. How dirty are you?' she said, gesturing to Kent's mother's blouse.

'It's only red dust,' Kent said. He wasn't too dirty but he

leaned over and kissed her without touching her.

'I'm clean, Sophie. Not like this pair,' Luke said.

'Hello, Luke, it's good to see you,' she said as he bent down to kiss her cheek.

'Good to see you too, Sophie. You're looking very "fifties".'

'Jenna asked us to dress up vintage. It's gone so well she's going to buy some clothes especially for the staff next time she is at a retro shop.'

'Jenna?' Luke queried.

'Yes, these are Jenna's vintage tea rooms. She's been in town for about three months. You probably haven't met her yet. I don't think you were here the last time we all met at the pub for dinner.'

'I hear there's a plan tonight. But how about a cuppa now?'

'Of course. I'm pleased to see you all here. Come and sit down and put your orders in. And, Kent, guess what I saved you?'

'One of Jenna's delicious vanilla slices, hopefully.'

'Sure is, and it even has passionfruit icing for you. Jenny Riley's passionfruit.'

Kent reached out and took Sophie's hand. 'I knew there was a reason I married you.'

'Careful, there's only one piece left. I can still give it to someone else,' she replied as Kent grinned at her.

'I'll just go and try to call Fallon again,' Jon said. 'I'll be back in a moment.'

As Sophie led Kent and Luke across to a vacant table at the edge of the lawn, she took notice of how pretty the place looked this afternoon. The winter sun was low in the sky as the afternoon closed in and gave a beautiful golden sheen to the house and garden. The landscapers had done a great job; yellow roses trailed over a trellis, and a bed of colourful winter annuals bordered the fence along each side of the gate.

Jenny Riley—the local with the green fingers—had come out and given them advice and gifted some rose bushes and shrubs to Jenna. Jenna had been overwhelmed.

'You guys sit here,' Sophie said, gesturing to the vacant table.

Kent was looking over at Reg where he was still sitting with his daughter and son-in-law.

'Looks like it's all gone well,' Kent said. 'Reg is beaming.'

'They've been sitting there talking since about ten o'clock this morning,' Sophie said. 'Jenna hasn't stopped smiling since her mum and dad arrived, and when she looks at Reg, she's as proud as punch. I've lost count of the cups of tea they've had. They came out a while ago to take the van into town, and they still haven't left.'

Luke looked over at the table. 'What's she proud about?'

'All this.' Sophie gestured around. 'A lot has happened in town since you were last here, Luke. Jenna arrived and started the tea rooms. Turned out that Reg from the pub is her grandfather, and today her mum met her father for the first time. Reg didn't even know he had a daughter and a granddaughter until a couple of weeks ago.'

'Readymade family,' Luke said. 'Sounds like something out of *Neighbours*.'

Sophie rolled her eyes. 'Don't tell me you watch that. Is it still on?'

'My mum used to watch it when I was a kid.' Luke grinned.

'So did I,' Sophie took the order pad from the pocket of her apron. 'I was addicted. Now what would you like for your afternoon tea?'

Kent chuckled. '*Smoko* for us.'

Sophie shook her head with a chuckle. 'No, Kent, show a

bit of class. When you visit us here at the Vintage Tea Room, you have *afternoon tea.* We've brought some style to town.'

'Very well, my love. I will have a cup of strong black tea for my afternoon tea, please.'

'Luke?'

'I'll have a cup of tea too, thank you, Sophie. Can I give you a hand to carry it?'

'I'm good, but thank you,' Sophie said. 'Any preference in the food line, Luke? There's a little bit of everything left. Scones, biscuits, fruit cake, cream sponge—'

Luke looked hopeful. 'Vanilla slice?'

'Sorry, Kent gets the last one. I've been saving it for him, but I can cut it in half.'

'No, you can't.' Kent wagged his finger at her. 'That's got my name on it, that vanilla slice.'

'How about marshmallow slice?' Sophie said. 'That's one of Jenna's specialties.'

'I'll let you choose,' Luke said.

'Okay, I'll bring an assorted plate out.' She looked up as Jon walked across to them. 'Did you get on to Fallon, Jon? I thought she and Ruth would be here today.'

'She's on her way now. She was waiting for Ryan to wake up. She won't be long. Ruth's minding Braden and Callie's boys, so she won't be coming. She was out in the yard playing cowboys and Indians with them.' Jon shook his head. 'That woman has so much energy.'

'Tea or coffee for you, Jon?'

'I'll have a large flat white, thanks, Sophie.'

Kent grabbed her hand as she went to walk away. 'You look lovely, Soph. I do love the cream shirt. Is it new?'

'It's your Mum's. I called her to see if it was okay to wear it.' Sophie hesitated, and then decided not to say anything about his dad yet; it wasn't the place and there'd be time enough for that tonight. 'I promised we'd go and see them soon,' she said.

Kent knew her well enough to read between the lines, and he squeezed her hand. 'Yes, sooner than later,' he said quietly.

'Love you,' she whispered. Sophie reached up and kissed his cheek before she hurried back to the kitchen.

Amelia had finished clearing the tables in the two rooms and was back in the kitchen.

'Probably one of the last orders for the day,' Sophie said. 'Two pots of tea and a large flat white. And a plate of assorted cakes and biscuits and of course Kent's vanilla slice.' She reached for her apron and put it back on. It was a miracle the cream shirt had stayed clean. 'Jenna, come out and meet Luke. He's a regular visitor in town. He drops by in his helicopter—or that is, his company's helicopter—to suss out the cattle. He's got a really interesting job.'

'I will. Amelia, will you please make Sophie a coffee too? You take that apron back off and go and sit with them, and I'll bring it out when it's ready,' Jenna said.

'Thank you, I'll leave the apron on, I think. I don't want to spill anything on my shirt.' Sophie smoothed her hair back and quickly put some lipstick on. She ran lightly down the steps and sat beside Kent. The three men were talking cattle and she sat watching them. Kent looked tired, but the shadows under his eyes were nowhere near as dark as Jon's.

Jon looked over at her and smiled, sensing her eyes on him.

'A late night?' she asked.

'Teething,' Jon said with a nod.

Sophie wondered how Fallon coped so well with the change in her life. She'd gone from being a helicopter pilot working with the mustering to being a full-time mum. But she seemed really happy and never looked tired.

Maybe having her mum, Ruth, close by made the

difference. That was one thing she and Kent wouldn't have if they ever had children. Sophie and Braden's parents had passed away about ten years ago. Kent's parents were in the city, sadly dealing with his dad's Alzheimer's disease.

Sophie thought about how she would cope with broken nights of feeds and teething. Having a tiny human being dependent on her.

She wouldn't.

The panic began to build in her chest again. She was going to have to talk to Kent about how she felt; she needed to be honest.

Pulling her thoughts away from her worry, she looked over at Luke. His eyes had widened and he was staring at the house. Sophie turned to see what he was looking at.

Jenna stood at the top of the stairs, holding a loaded tray as she scanned the garden. She smiled as she spotted them sitting at the table on the lawn.

Luke jumped to his feet. 'I'll help Jenna.'

'Do you know Jenna, Luke?' Sophie asked, curious as to why he'd stared at her so intently.

'What? Sorry, Sophie, what was that you said?'

'I asked if you already knew Jenna?'

'No, I've never seen her before, but wow, what a beautiful woman. She looks as though she's stepped straight from a movie.'

'Not *Neighbours*, Luke?' Kent said jokingly as he caught Sophie's eye and smiled.

She raised her eyebrows.

Kent leaned over as Luke hurried over to the steps to help Jenna. They watched as she smiled her thanks at him as he took the tray from her. 'Invite Jenna to dinner at the pub to finish off the day? She's sure got Luke's interest,' Kent said.

'Maybe,' Sophie said. 'All depends on what Jenna's planned with her mum and dad and Reg. Although I think they're pretty tired; they'll probably go back to the van. They might come in and have dinner later.'

'And Reg'll go to the pub for his one beer and then back to the facility for his dinner.'

'Dinner? He won't need it,' Sophie said with a smile as she looked over at Reg. 'He's still eating cake! Okay, can you give Braden a quick call and tell him we'll come? He mentioned going for dinner when they were leaving before and I said I was a bit tired, so he'll need to book a bigger table. And Jon and Fallon, and probably Luke and Jenna. And we'll ask Amelia and Ben too.' She put her hand to her mouth and covered a yawn.

Kent moved his chair closer and put his arm around her shoulders. 'You okay, Soph?'

'It's been a big day after an early start, but I'm fine now that I've had a sit-down. It'll be good to see everyone there.' She smiled. 'And Luke and Jenna can get to know each other, plus I won't have to cook dinner.'

Chapter 13

Sophie

Dinner at the Augathella pub that night was a joyful affair. The celebration for the opening of the Vintage Tea Room moved to the pub, and many people came over to Jenna and congratulated her. Sophie was pleased to see that Luke had snagged the chair next to Jenna. Every time she'd looked over, they were deep in conversation, and Jenna's cheeks held a rosy flush.

Sophie had found her second wind and thoroughly enjoyed the evening. Kent raised his eyebrows when she took turns holding little Meggie and Munro while Callie and Braden enjoyed their dinner.

She closed her eyes as Meg snuggled into her, savouring that delightful, sweet baby scent. At least she knew she could hand Meg back to Callie.

'Do you want a nurse, Kent?' Sophie asked.

'Too right I do. Pass my little niece over here.'

Sophie handed Meg over to Kent and then turned to Braden, taking Munro from him.

'It's fabulous having babysitters in the family,' her brother said. 'Now, I can enjoy my dinner and use both hands.'

Sophie smiled as Braden leaned over to Callie and kissed her cheek. Braden's happiness was complete. Ruth and her husband had joined them at the pub for dinner, and Rory, Nigel and Petie sat opposite Sophie and Kent. Her nephews were growing quickly, and Rory's conversation with Kent about the cattle agistment made her realise there was another cattleman in the making.

Nigel? She wasn't so sure about her middle nephew, but time would tell.

And little Petie. Her youngest nephew held a special place in her heart.

Sophie watched Kent as he turned from Rory and looked down at Meggie in his arms. Yes, seeing him hold the tiny baby made her feel happy. It suited him perfectly, and as he gazed down at the baby with her long eyelashes framing her cheeks, and her sweet little rosebud mouth pursed in a cute bow, Sophie knew in her heart that they would have children one day. She had to gain her confidence; it would be cruel to deprive Kent of the chance to be a dad.

For some reason, there had been a shift in her thinking this weekend, but she still held doubt.

As they headed out to the car park after Sean called last drinks, Jenna caught up with Sophie. 'You've worked your butt off, Sophie, and I'm going to pay you for today. If you won't give me your bank details, I'll just give you cash,' Jenna said.

'No,' Sophie replied. 'That's an argument you're not going to win. It was my pleasure to be able to help, and having us volunteer gives you such a good start to your business.'

'Well, I owe you,' Jenna said.

Sophie shook her head. 'It's the country way, Jenna. It's the way we do things out here.'

Jenna hugged her. 'Thank you. You're a good friend.'

'And that's exactly right,' Sophie said. 'It's friendship. You came to town, you didn't know anybody, and I was more than happy to help. Now I'm sure you'll be hiring some more staff, and I'll get back to my normal routine. I can come Wednesday and help you. I normally go over and help Callie on Wednesday, Thursday, and Friday, but she and Braden have an appointment in Charleville at the hospital for Petie this Wednesday.'

Jenna's eyes widened. 'Little Petie, is he okay?'

'Oh yes, he's fine now. He was involved in an accident at our wedding a few months ago, and they just give him a bit of a checkup every three or four months now. He's fine.'

'He's a little cutie. Wouldn't you love to have one just like him?'

Sophie sighed, and her head spun a little. 'One day, not just yet. What about you? Do you want to have kids?'

'One day,' Jenna said. 'I've got the business to look after, a grandfather to get to know a bit better, and on top of that, I haven't met anyone I want to share my life with. Not yet, anyway.' She looked around. 'You do look like you're half-asleep on your feet though. Where's Kent?'

'He's inside talking to Luke. He's staying at the pub because his helicopter is at the aerodrome just out of town, and he's got an early start to Longreach tomorrow.' Sophie looked at Jenna and smiled. 'You and Luke seem to have hit it off tonight.' Even in the dim light of the car park, Sophie noticed Jenna's cheeks turn pink.

'Yeah, he's a nice guy, but there are a lot of nice guys like that. Guys caught up in their careers, not ready to settle down. But you were right, he does have an interesting job. I was the same on the Gold Coast with my job at the agency. Too focused to get involved with anyone. I just had the occasional dates. As we travelled across to here, we stopped at several pubs for the night and met several guys who were very friendly and wanted to get to know us better.' She grinned. 'But Alana and I were women on a mission.'

'Yes, and your mission certainly has been accomplished so far. I'll see you Wednesday,' Sophie said. 'I hope the week continues to be busy.'

'See you then.' Jenna reached out and hugged Sophie. 'I truly, truly appreciate the help that you've given me today.'

Kent and Luke came out of the pub and walked over to them.

'Thanks for a great night, all of you. I'm heading home now.' Jenna lifted her hand and started to walk away.

'Wait up, Jenna, I'll walk you home,' Luke said. 'I'll see you next time, Kent. Bye, Soph.' He reached over and kissed her cheek. 'It was great to catch up.'

'See ya, mate,' Kent said, shaking Luke's hand 'And thank you for talking to Jon. He's excited to join up.'

Sophie turned as Kent opened the door of her car for her. As they drove out of the car park she smiled. Jenna and Luke were still standing under the lamppost, deep in conversation.

'Now that would be a nice romance,' she said. Kent glanced across at her and smiled. 'You know, love, I thought exactly the same thing. Two really nice people without partners.'

Sophie laughed. 'But two really nice people who live a long way apart.'

Chapter 14

Jenna

Jenna and Luke were still standing under the lamppost, deep in conversation.

Jenna looked up at Luke, but his face was in shadow, his back to the light. 'It was great to meet you tonight, Luke. I'm sure we'll see you again. Your job sounds so interesting. You must get to meet a lot of people and visit a lot of pubs.'

'Would you believe not really?' he replied. 'I'm usually on the go. It's like this in Augathella, but that's few and far between.

Jenna tipped her head to the side. 'What about at home?'

'Home is when I catch up on all the auditing and paperwork from the trips that I do. I'm not a lot of fun, you know. I'm a bit of a workaholic. But from what I saw today and you told me tonight, I sense I'm talking to someone who understands being focused. I'm really impressed with the business you've set up out here. It's been a quiet little town the eighteen months or so I've been coming out, and it certainly was buzzing this afternoon. Did you enjoy yourself?'

'I did,' she said. 'And for lots of reasons. Did you see me talking to the older guy before we came to the pub when you guys were sitting out in the garden? He left with my mum and dad; they were in the motorhome.'

'Yes, I saw him climb up at the front of the motorhome. He sat in the middle, and I had a bit of a smile to myself. He was sitting there, looking as proud as punch as they drove out. Sophie told me he was your grandfather.'

'He is. It's a long story, but a good one. We've only just

found him, so today was pretty special.'

'And on the day of your business opening.'

'Yes, I was on a high when the mayor gave me a huge rap, but that didn't compare to the joy of watching my mum and her dad meeting each other for the first time.' She was surprised when her eyes welled with tears, and she blinked them away. 'A very special day,' she said quietly.

'Hey, don't cry,' Luke reached out and wiped away the tear that was hovering on one of her eyelids.

'Happy tears,' she said. A pleasant shiver ran down her back at Luke's gentle touch. They stood together for a moment before she spoke again. 'Anyway, I better get going home.'

'I'll walk you there.'

'It's okay. We just live two streets away.'

He shook his head. 'Not at night by yourself.'

'This is Augathella, Luke. It's very safe.'

'Nevertheless, a gentleman never lets a lady walk home by herself. Do you live alone?' he asked.

'I actually share an apartment, a two-bedroom apartment with my offsider, Alana, but since we've been in town, she's found herself a man, and she spends most of the time at Kirk's place, so I'm alone most of the night.'

'Okay, well, I'll definitely walk you home.' He crooked his elbow as she stepped out of the car park, and Jenna threaded her hand through. Luke was tall and strong, and she really liked him. His bare arm was warm against her fingers, and she moved a little closer. They'd had a great chat through the night, mainly about what he did and what an exciting life he led.

It wasn't far to her place. They walked straight from the pub, and she stopped outside the gate of the unit block. 'This is home.'

'It's been good getting to know you, Jenna. I had a great

time at your tea room, and I really enjoyed spending time with you at dinner.' He raised his eyebrows. 'Maybe next time I come to town, we could have dinner together.'

She smiled. 'I'll look forward to that.' She reached over and put her hand on his forearm. 'Now, you fly safely, won't you? I'll be listening for the helicopter when you leave tomorrow morning.'

'Don't worry about that. I will.'

Jenna was surprised when Luke reached down, and his lips brushed her cheek.

'Sweet dreams, Jenna,' he said, before turning away and walking back up the street.

She watched until he reached the corner and smiled when he waved before he disappeared. Jenna was surprised to feel her hand shaking as she reached into her bag and took out her key and opened the door. What a nice guy Luke Elliott was.

Chapter 15

Sophie

As it turned out, having a couple of days at home turned out to be a blessing. Sophie and Kent both woke up in the early hours of Monday morning. Sophie's stomach was gurgling, and she just made it to the bathroom in time before she was sick. All she could taste was the chips she'd had last night at the bistro.

She was washing her hands in the ensuite when she heard Kent call out.

'Damn, me too.' He went racing down the hall to the other bathroom. Hearing him being sick didn't help Sophie's queasy stomach at all.

They were both miserable when they went back to bed and spent the rest of the night up and down to the bathrooms. Sophie had recovered by the time the sun was up, but Kent was too ill to go out to work on the station. He spent most of the morning in bed or in the bathroom.

Sophie's stomach had settled but she still felt deathly tired so she had a very easy morning. She made herself some dry toast and a cup of tea and managed to keep that down. Then, after she checked on Kent and found him sound asleep, she went into the study to catch up on some of the paperwork for the property. She looked after the accounts and was way behind because she'd been so busy with Jenna as well as helping Callie with the twins. She hadn't had much time at the computer over the last couple of weeks.

Focusing on the accounts, the numbers, and organising the bills took her attention away from her still tender tummy, and the morning passed quickly. She looked in on Kent a couple of times, and he was still sound asleep each time she peered around their door. It had been at least two or three hours since she'd last heard him go to the bathroom. She filed receipts in their filing cabinet, shut down the computer, and wandered out to the kitchen.

Sophie was still in her PJs and wondered whether she should go and have a shower before she made herself some lunch. She was actually hungry and feeling a lot better. Standing at the kitchen window, she thought back to last night as she stared out at the garden. She'd neglected that too, and with spring coming there were seedlings to put in. Rhonda had always had the garden planted out by now, and Sophie was determined to do the same.

Her stomach gave a little gurgle and she thought about what they both ate, and she wondered what had made both of them ill.

They'd both had a different meal and hers had tasted fine. The only thing that had been the same was the hot chips; she had eaten some of the chips from his meal while she'd waited for her salad to come out. Kent had a steak with pepper sauce, and he had commented the sauce had been very creamy. Sophie had a chicken salad, and it had tasted fine, but it was too much of a coincidence that they had both got sick at the same time.

She had Jenna's phone number in her contacts, so she walked out to the back porch in the late morning sun, pulled out her phone and pressed speed dial. Jenna picked up very quickly.

'Hi, Sophie, what's happening? Don't tell me you want to come in and work because I'm not going to let you.'

Sophie chuckled.

'No, I just wanted to check you're okay.'

'I'm fine, why?'

'Kent and I ate something at the pub last night, and we've

both been crook all night. I just wanted to check you're okay, seeing you're by yourself.'

'I'm fine. I'm out at the tearoom now, just sorting out and seeing how much is left in the freezer and how much baking I need to do to reopen tomorrow. I'm even thinking about opening up this afternoon. There's a bit of traffic going past, and I can handle it by myself.'

'Don't overdo it, Jenna.'

'I won't. You take care of yourselves.'

'We will. I've got to go. Kent's just surfaced.'

'Okay, I'll see you later in the week. Bye.'

Sophie looked at Kent as he shambled into the kitchen. He was still in his blue checked PJs, and his hair was tousled. His face was deathly white, and there were dark shadows under his eyes.

'Holy hell, I hope I don't ever feel like that again,' he said. 'I don't think I'll eat pepper sauce again.'

'Come and sit, and I'll make you a cup of tea. Could you handle a hot drink?'

'Just a black one, thanks. How are you?'

'I'm fine. I got up at about seven, and I haven't been sick since then. I think I'm over whatever it was.'

'It'll have to be that pepper sauce. I can still taste it,' he said. 'You didn't have any of that, did you?'

'No, I had the chicken salad,' Sophie said. 'I'll have to have a talk to Sean and just check that the cleanliness in the pub kitchen is up to scratch. He had a couple of new kitchen hands in there yesterday, but it looked okay.'

'As long as he hasn't poisoned the whole town.'

'I've called Jenna. She's okay.'

'Crumbs, Luke had the steak too, I think. I didn't notice what sauce he had. I can't give him a call. He'd be long gone by now, but then again, if he's crook, he wouldn't have left. I might call the pub after my cuppa and see if he got away on time.'

Kent managed to finish his cup of tea, and then he yawned. 'I think I'll lie down for a while, and then I'll have a shower. Do you want to come and lie down with me for a while?'

'I was just thinking about having a shower too. But I'll come and have a bit of a snooze with you.'

Sophie settled next to Kent on top of the bed and he put his arms around her. She only intended to have a short lie down, but soon he was breathing rhythmically, and her eyes fluttered closed and she was soon asleep.

Sophie opened her eyes slowly, surprised to see the shadows on the bedroom wall.

'Wake up, sleepyhead.' Kent stood beside the bed and she was pleased to see he had a nice healthy pink in his cheeks.

'Well, you look a bit better,' she said.

'I feel a lot better. How are you?'

'I feel on top of the world. I slept so well I can't believe it. I never sleep in the daytime.'

'How about we go and have a shower?' he said with a grin. 'Together?'

'How about we do,' she said, with a smile.

Chapter 16

Sophie

Monday

Sophie couldn't stop thinking about what Kent's reaction would be tomorrow night when Amelia and Ben came for dinner and announced their news.

'You pretend you don't know,' Amelia had asked her on the weekend. 'Ben will probably be cross if he found out that I told you, but I really wanted to share.'

'I know nothing,' Sophie had said. 'And I will act suitably surprised and delighted when you tell us on Thursday night.' She knew that Kent would be very happy for them too. As long as it didn't cause tension between them.

She pegged his work shirts on the line and headed inside, even though she'd had a lot of sleep yesterday, she'd woken up tired again this morning. At least she hadn't been upset in the stomach like she had been yesterday morning. Kent had made a full recovery and managed to eat a normal dinner last night, but she was still not feeling terribly hungry. She'd managed Weet-Bix this morning, but it hadn't sat comfortably in the stomach.

The phone rang just as Sophie was about to go out to water her vegetable garden.

'Hi, Callie, how are you? Feels like ages since we've had a good chat. We didn't get to talk to each other much at Jenna's opening or the pub, did we?'

'No, and we left early. I looked for you to say goodbye, but you were talking to Fallon and Jon. We left pretty quickly because the twins both woke together as usual,' Callie said.

'Have you all been okay?' Sophie asked. 'We were both a bit sick after dinner on Saturday night.'

'Sort of. I've kept Nigel home from school today. He's got a bit of a queasy tummy.'

'Maybe it's a bug we've had? Poor Sean, his ears must be burning.'

'Could be. Braden was a bit sick the other night, and then Nigel threw up last night, so I've kept him home from school today. I think the kids picked something up at school. Maybe.'

'Oh well, we wouldn't have caught that because we haven't seen you guys long enough to catch anything.'

'I don't know about that. They're pretty good at sharing germs. Anyway, Nigel's okay, he's out playing on his bike now, so I think he was just pleased to have a day off. Are you and Kent okay now?'

'Yeah, we're fine. Kent's gone back out to work today, and I'm just pottering around.'

'You're not working out with Jen. I thought you were going to work with her today.'

'No, she insisted on me taking most of the week off. I'm just helping her out so it's pretty flexible. It's just a friendship thing.'

'You're a good girl, Sophie, and I'm going to impose on your goodness. Is there any chance of you coming over and sitting with Nigel for me for a while? I've had an unexpected call into town, but don't panic, I won't leave the twins with you. I'll take them with me, but I just don't want to take Nigel into town in case he gets carsick on the way. I have to go to the bank at eleven o'clock and sign some papers with Braden.'

'You don't need to tell me what you're doing,' Sophie said. 'It's your business, Cal. I'm more than happy to come and sit with Nigel. It'll be nice to have some one-on-one time with him.'

'I know you and Nigel have got a special relationship. I think he might have been a bit of a favourite when you had them over those months you cared for them.'

'He's a little rogue, but I love them all.'

'I know you do. He is a good boy.' Callie chuckled. 'Most of the time.'

'Okay, what time is it now?' Sophie asked.

'Just after nine,' Callie said.

'What time do you want me there?'

'Whenever it suits you. I will probably need to leave here about ten-thirty. Braden took the boys to school in the work ute, and I'm going to drive in the Land Cruiser.'

'Yep, not a problem. I'll be there in half an hour.'

'Thanks, Soph. You're a champion. I'll get the twins feeding now.'

Sophie went inside, put the washing basket in the laundry and took her jeans off the ironing board. It was a little bit too cool to wear her shorts out to the farm because no doubt Nigel would have her outside playing. She pulled her jeans on and struggled to get the button done up. She'd sampled too many cakes at Jenna's over the last couple of weeks; the jeans were quite snug around her waist.

'Sensible eating from today. No more snacking on jam drops and Anzacs when I'm helping out,' she said to herself.

It didn't take long to drive across from Lara Waters to Kilcoy Station. Callie was standing on the front veranda, watching Nigel ride his bike up and down the path to the gate.

'Aunty Sophie!' he squealed as he threw the bike onto the grass and came racing over, his arms open wide.

'Hey, there how's my boy?' Sophie scooped him up and planted with kisses all over his cheek. 'Can I have a kiss back?'

'That's for girls,' Nigel said.

'It's for big boys too,' Sophie held him close and he stayed there. 'So, give your aunty a kiss.'

'Yucky,' said Nigel, squirming in her arms. 'Go away. Mum said you came to mind me. Did she tell you I threw up in the night? It was all orange and yellow.'

Sophie put a hand on her stomach. 'That's enough, Nigel. I don't need to know the details. Hi, Callie.' As her nephew ran back to his bike, she reached over and gave her sister-in-law a hug. 'You look fantastic. How are those twins this morning?'

'They've actually been good so far today. Megan slept six hours last night, and Munro did four and a half. Mind you, they both woke up at different times, so Braden and I didn't get as much sleep as we'd hoped for.'

'Where are they?'

'They went to sleep, so I've put them in the car already.'

Sophie looked at the car parked near the gate, the two doors on the Land Cruiser were open and Callie had her bag next to it ready to leave. 'Okay, you go into town, and I'll look after this young man.'

'I'll only be a couple of hours, so we can have a good chat when I get home. Is there anything you need in town?'

'Oh, if you're anywhere near the IGA, maybe a couple of litres of milk and a large box of Weet-Bix. Kent goes through it like it's going out of fashion.'

Callie laughed. 'That's easy. Nothing else you can think of? Chocolate biscuits?'

Sophie put her hand on her stomach. 'No, I'm putting on weight from eating too much at the tearoom!'

Callie looked at her curiously. 'You're not eating for two, are you?'

Sophie froze. 'No, Callie.' She blinked, surprised to feel tears welling up in her eyes. 'God, what's wrong with me?'

'What's wrong, Soph?'

'Everybody keeps asking me when we're going to have a baby.'

'I'm sorry,' Callie said. 'I shouldn't have said anything.'

'No, it's okay. It's just me being super-sensitive.'

'You're not ready yet, you've only been married a little while. And you've got plenty of time.'

Sophie ran a hand through her hair, reached up, and tightened her ponytail. 'I don't know if I'm ever going to be ready. That's my problem.'

Callie looked at her for a long moment before she spoke. 'You're the only one who can make that decision, and it's a decision that you and Kent will have to make yourselves. But if you want my tuppence worth, and please don't be offended, and *please* don't think I'm putting pressure on, but I know that you would be an absolutely amazing mum.'

Sophie shrugged. 'Maybe. I don't know. I feel like I haven't got the maternal gene. I mean, I know Kent really wants kids, and it would be nice if we had some boys to help him on the property. I know how much Braden loves having your three with him, but it's a lot to think about Cal. I have to get pregnant, go through nine months of being pregnant, then give birth and then the hard part starts. I would be responsible for looking after a newborn baby. I see what you're going through with the twins. I don't know if I can cope with that. I honestly don't know if I could handle it.'

'Petie wasn't very old when you had him for those eighteen months,' Callie said. 'And from all accounts, you coped with that just fine. I hope it's not that experience with the boys that's made you doubt yourself.'

'Maybe it threw me in too quickly, and it's different when they're not yours. I love being their Auntie Sophie, but . . .'

Callie hesitated. 'It sounds like I'm trying to tell you what to do, but I'm not. All I can do is tell you of my experience. I didn't know if I wanted children, but when I fell pregnant with the twins, it made an absolute quantum shift inside me. All of a sudden, I wasn't Callie Black, I wasn't Callie Cartwright. I was Braden's wife, but I was also a person who was carrying a new life inside her. Please don't think I'm trying to tell *you* how to feel. I just want to tell you how I felt. I didn't want . . . I didn't know consciously if I wanted children. I worried about it too, and I thought that three boys would be enough. But when I fell pregnant, I felt different. I felt like a totally different person. I still do. Don't get me wrong. I'm still Callie. I'm still the same Callie I was, but it's created a new dimension for me. I've given birth to my children. I love the three boys as much as I love the twins, but the twins are little humans that I carried and gave birth to.'

Sophie smiled gently, never dreaming that she would have a conversation like this with Callie.

'That's a lovely way to describe it, Callie.'

'We'll keep talking when I get home. I don't want to pressure you, and I don't want you to feel like I am. But I want you to talk to me whenever you need to, and please talk to Kent about how you feel. Don't feel as though you've got to go along and agree with everyone's expectations. It's your lives. You let him know how you feel, and you guys can sort it out together. Will you promise me that?'

Sophie hugged Callie. 'You get to town, girl, and yes, I promise. As usual, you're full of sage advice. Love you, Cal.'

Callie's smile was gentle. 'You be a good boy for Aunty Soph, Rory.' She walked across to the car and checked on the twins in the back before she climbed up to the driver's seat. 'Won't be long. See you soon.'

Chapter 17

Kent

Kent called in at Kilcoy Station on his way back from the agistment property. He hadn't had a good catch-up with Braden, and he wanted to ask him a few things about the black Angus cattle.

He was surprised to see Sophie's car parked next to Callie's Land Cruiser at the house, but he pulled into the shed where Braden's ute was parked.

'Hey, Braden, how's it going?' Kent said as he walked across the shed to where Braden had his head under the bonnet of his ute.

'Good to see you, mate. What are you up to?'

'I was just coming back from the Stuart property, and I wanted to run a couple of things by you about the drench I've been using.'

'Not a problem. Did you see Sophie's car at the house?' Braden lifted his head.

'I did.'

'Yeah, she and Callie have been chatting out on the veranda ever since I got home at three o'clock with the boys. We'll go and have a cuppa with them in a minute. I'm trying to replace the blasted fan belt.'

'Okay, stand back,' Kent said. 'Give me the tools.' Braden might be an excellent cattleman, but if there was one thing he couldn't do, it was motor vehicle repairs. Mechanical skill came naturally to Kent; he took the spanner from Braden and got to work as Braden stood back and watched.

'I wish I had your skill,' he said.

Kent nodded. 'Not hard, mate.'

Braden stared at him intently for a minute and Kent glanced over at him.

'Tell me if I'm out of line, Kent. Is everything okay with you and Sophie?'

Kent froze, looking up at his brother-in-law. 'Why do you ask?'

'I don't know, she just seems a little bit subdued.'

'We've both been sick. Did she tell you that?'

'Yeah, but you had it worse by the sound of things. Cal said that you and Sophie both had different meals.'

'Yeah, Sean poisoned me at the pub on Sunday night with the pepper sauce, I reckon. But we're okay now.' Kent turned back to the motor.

Braden looked at him long and hard. 'We're talking about my sister here, mate,' he said.

'And my *wife*.' Kent's voice was tight.

'I'm sorry,' Braden said. 'I may be overstepping the mark, but I've always worried about my little sister.'

'Okay, can we have a man-to-man?'

Braden stared at him. 'I knew there was something wrong. What is it?'

'There's nothing wrong,' Kent said. 'It's just that . . . I don't know . . . every time I talk about having kids, I know Sophie, she freezes and she won't engage in a conversation about it.'

'Maybe she's not ready. I mean, she spent eighteen months looking after my three.'

'I know.'

'She did a damn good job too,' Braden said.

'She's probably not ready.' Kent put the spanner down and wiped his hands on the rag on the side of the ute. 'I mean, we've got plenty of time. She's only twenty-five. I don't want to be one of those parents who are in their forties, and if we have boys, they won't be able to help me on the property, or if we have girls, I won't be sexist.'

'Have you talked to her about it? I'll never forget what she said to me when she brought the boys home.'

'What did she say?'

'She said "I can't do it anymore. I spent my twenty-first birthday changing Petie's nappies." I've never forgotten it. I put a huge load on my little sister when I was weak.'

'It wasn't a weakness, mate. It was a terrible tragedy.'

'It was. But now you've got me worried about Sophie.'

'I think I'm making it worse because I can't talk to her. I've got a bit of an issue,' Kent said. 'That's why I'm keen to see if we can have kids straight up.'

Braden frowned. 'What do you mean, a bit of an issue?'

'Well, do you remember that rodeo when Sophie was up in the stands with that jerk? I lost focus and came off that cranky bull.'

'Yeah, I heard about it. I wasn't there. I know you got taken to the hospital.'

'Yeah, well, I got kicked in the nuts pretty hard. I didn't give it a thought before, but now, when we've been married six months and we're not using anything, and Sophie's not pregnant, I'm starting to worry that maybe it did some damage.'

'Well, mate,' Braden said. 'There's one way to find out, see the doc. But the first thing you have to do is talk to Sophie about this.'

'Yeah, I know. I was just hoping that I wouldn't have to share my worry and she'd be pregnant by now. You know, if she was pregnant, I'd know that everything was okay in that department.'

'Talk to her, and if Sophie isn't ready when you talk to her about it, you need to go and get yourself checked out.'

'Thanks, good advice, mate.' Kent reached up and closed the bonnet. 'Ready for that cuppa?'

'Yeah, but I could go a beer, not a cup of tea,' Braden said.

They were laughing as they walked up to the veranda together, and Kent was determined that he would talk to Sophie tonight. He followed Braden out to the veranda where his beautiful wife was waiting for him with a wide smile on her face.

His heart did a funny flip as the love he felt for Sophie filled him as it always did.

Chapter 18

Jenna

Friday

'Will you have a look at that?' Alana said with a giggle as Jenna placed the last tray of sponge cake slices into the fridge.

The end of the week had slowed down a bit, and the traffic and customers at the tea rooms had been manageable. She and Alana had been running it by themselves all week. Jenna had arranged for Ellie and Aimee, two of the girls from the high school to come in on Saturday, and Laura and Elisabeth, the other two on Sunday.

'Have a look at this.' Jenna turned and walked over to stand with Alana near the kitchen window.

'You see all sorts of folks, don't you?' Alana said, shaking her head.

Jenna stood on her toes to peek over Alana's head as she leaned over and rested her elbows on the empty countertop.

A huge flash caravan with all the fancy gizmos on top, and a big four-wheel drive was parked at the edge of the car park closest to the house, leaving no room for other cars to turn around.

'He's a hefty bloke. Check out his plumber's crack. Not a pretty sight.' Alana giggled.

'His what?' Jenna looked out. There was a fairly substantial man bent over at the wheel, and his jeans had slipped down at the back.

'Haven't you heard that before?'

'No' Jenna smiled. 'I can see what you mean, but why is it called a plumber's crack?'

Alana shrugged. 'I don't know. I'll Google it.' She pulled out her phone and her words were interspersed with laughter 'Here's your lesson for the day, Jenna. A plumber's crack is from the stereotypical image of a plumber being a heavyset man bent down beneath a sink with a tool belt around the waist. The position and belt tend to pull down the back of the pants, and if those pants are too tight, they can accidentally reveal the "crack" of the upper buttocks. And that dear Jenna is where the term came from.'

Jenna laughed. "I am so pleased I have you to educate me, Alana. I must have led a very sheltered life!'

Alana giggled. 'Oh look, they're coming up now. Should I tell him to pull up his jeans? If we get any of the grey nomies coming in, the older ladies will be quite scandalised.'

Jenna laughed. 'I don't think they'll be scandalised; they'll probably just turn away. Oh my God, Alana, look at the lady with him.'

A young woman of a similar size to the overweight man walked around the back of the van and bent over next to him. From the tops of her thighs down to her knees, the backs of her legs were covered with tattooed writing.

'I wonder what her tattoos say,' Alana said. 'Will I read them when she comes up? Her shorts are very short.'

'No, I think reading her legs would be a bit obvious,' Jenna said.

'Well, why would you get sentences tattooed on the backs of your legs if you didn't want people to read it?'

Two more couples followed the woman under discussion up the steps. 'Come on, back to work. You take the orders, I'll get the food and make the drinks,' Jenna said.

Alana grinned at her and walked out. Jenna missed her in the apartment. Alana had now moved in permanently with

Kirk in his house down past the primary school.

'I know it's a bit quick,' she'd said when she told Jenna she was moving in with Kirk two days ago. 'I knew as soon as I met him, he was the one.'

'As long as you're happy,' Jenna said.

'I couldn't be happier, even thinking that I'll probably end up settling here in Augathella. Kirk is quite settled here.'

A few minutes later, Alana came back in with the orders for three flat whites, two cappuccinos, and a pot of tea. 'Two plates of assorted cakes please.'

'Coming right up,' Jenna said as she worked on the coffee machine.

She set the trays neatly and placed one of the roses that Jenny Riley brought in for her every afternoon, on each tray.

Alana came in and took the trays with a smile. She spoke quietly. 'Mr and Mrs. Tattoo took a while to decide, but they would like two large lattes, please, made on skim milk with only half a shot. And that's *my* please, not theirs. They are rude people. They wanted vegemite toast, but I said we only have what's on the board. He wasn't happy.'

'I'll check the freezer,' Jenna said. 'I think there's a loaf of wholemeal bread in there. But tell them we can do jam but not vegemite.'

A couple of minutes later, she put the two lattes on a tray ready for Alana to take out. Jenna frowned as the sound of raised voices reached her from the tearoom.

Alana was quickly back in and shook her head as she picked up the tray. 'No, he said he doesn't want any of that wholemeal stuff. He wants white bread.'

Jenna shook her head. 'We haven't got any until lunchtime when the delivery comes, not that it really matters as toast isn't on the menu. Would you like me to go out and tell him?'

'No, it's all right. I can handle that,' Alana said. 'There's a few more coming in. Mrs Clark is on the way in for her regular decaf if you want to start making it.'

A few more arrivals kept Alana and Jenna busy for the next half hour or so.

Jenna had finished the last order and gone back into the kitchen when Jenny Riley arrived with the roses.

'Hi, Jenny,' Jenna said. 'You're early today.'

'Yes, I'm on my way to Charleville, so I picked these for you yesterday afternoon and put them in the fridge. I'm going down to do some paperwork for my new shop.'

'Oh, that's fabulous. You're going ahead with it,' Jenna said.

'I am,' she said. 'Listen. I've had an idea. I'm only opening it a couple of days a week because I've got a school-based apprentice working in my garden with me, doing some horticulture. They've done everything they can at my place because it's established already. How would you feel about it if they came out here with me and I worked with them for a couple of weeks to get your gardens ready for spring?'

'Really?' Jenna said. 'That would be fantastic. They're already looking good thanks to your work, but if you could do some more, that would be awesome.'

'You can get your own roses going out here, and then you can pick your decorations for your trays,' Jenny said.

'That sounds wonderful. Would you like a cup of coffee before you head out to Charleville?'

'Just a quick one.'

Jenna put the roses in the cool room and then walked out to the front with Jenny where the coffee machine was near the cash register. Alana was standing over in the corner with her hands on her hips, talking to the man at the register.

'Take a seat, Jenny. I'll come back and make your coffee,' Jenna said. She walked over to the counter, and the man glared at her.

'Are you the owner of this place?' he demanded.

'I am. Is there a problem?'

'Is there a problem?' he yelled, and heads turned. 'First off, you didn't have any white toast, and second, my coffee was stone cold.'

Jenna bit her lip, tempted to say that it would be cold because it was half an hour since she'd made it.

'Not a problem, sir. I'll make you a fresh one.'

The customer is always right, she told herself.

'Don't bother,' he said, nudging his wife beside him. She put her hands on her substantial hips.

'We don't want another one because my coffee tasted off.'

Jenna couldn't help looking down. The woman's legs were lily-white, and she wore the shortest pair of shorts that Jenna had ever seen. 'Very well. If you don't want more, that will be nine dollars and fifty cents.'

'Well then, if you insist on us paying for that shit you call coffee, make us another one.' The man clomped back to the table muttering under his breath, but his tirade was interrupted by a calm voice.

'I think you should apologise for your language, sir.'

Jenna's head flew up as several others in the tearoom nodded and voiced their agreement with the new arrival.

The plumber man had sat down again and Luke was standing beside his table. Her heart beat a little faster as he walked across to the counter.

'You handled that very well, Jenna, but I'm here to back you up if you need it.'

'It's okay. If he comes back and refuses to pay a second time I'll just ask them to leave. It's not worth the argument.'

The man stood, hitched up his jeans and scowled. 'Come on, we're leaving,' he said to his wife.

Luke and Jenna watched them leave, and then she turned

to Luke. 'Good morning, Luke, you're a surprise visitor.'

'I was hoping I could talk to you about dinner at the pub tonight.'

'You'll never get a table at the pub on a Friday night,' Jenna said. 'It's always busy.'

His grin was wide. 'I called in there on my way past and booked a table, hoping that you'd say yes.'

Jenna's heart soared and she smiled. 'That sounds lovely. Are you out working today?'

'No, I'm not.'

She frowned. 'So, you just called into Augathella on your way past?'

'No, I came especially to ask you out to dinner.'

'In the helicopter?'

'No, that wouldn't be the right thing to do. I had a rostered day off today, so I drove up to see you.'

'You drove up? How long did that take?'

'It's not far. I like being in the car for a change.'

'How far?'

'About four hundred kilometres. I stopped overnight at the Nindigully Pub.'

Disbelief flooded through Jenna. 'You drove that far just to see me?'

'I did. And now that I see you, I know it was worth every minute.'

Heat ran into her cheeks, and Alana winked at her from behind Luke.

'We don't close here until three. What are you going to do all day? Drive out to see Kent?'

'I thought you might have some odd jobs here I could fill in the day with. I believe you've got volunteers working with you. I'm happy to be one too.'

'All day? Really? On your day off?'

'Not a problem at all.' Luke rolled up his sleeves. 'Give

me a job.'

'A job?' Jenna put her head to the side and her cheeks warmed as he held her gaze.

'Yes, I figured if we couldn't spend the day together—which I knew we couldn't when I headed up here—I could still spend it in your company.'

Pleasure filled her as she smiled back at him. 'Thank you, Luke. It's good to have you here. And as well as appreciating your help, I'll enjoy your company too.'

Chapter 19

Kent

Kent helped with wiping up and loading the dishwasher before going for a shower. When he came through to the bathroom, Sophie was already in bed with only the bedside light on.

'It was a nice night, wasn't it, Sophie?'

'Yes, it was. Amelia and Ben are a lovely couple.'

'I'm looking forward to the Tambo show. I'm pleased that you and Amelia are coming with us.'

'And Ben's written three new songs.'

'I liked the sound of the one that he sang.'

'Yes.' The unspoken issue between them was Amelia's pregnancy. Ben and Amelia told them as soon as they arrived, which created tension between Kent and Sophie all night.

Sophie had pretended to be suitably surprised, and Kent had smiled widely as he shook Ben's hand and hugged Amelia. 'Great news, guys.'

Now, they lay side-by-side in the dark, and Kent sensed that they were both lost in their thoughts.

'I hope the barbeque sausages weren't off,' Sophie said. 'I feel a bit queasy again. How about you?'

'No, I'm okay,' Kent replied.

More silence followed. Sophie closed her eyes, and a tear squeezed out from beneath her closed lids. She had seen the look on Kent's face when Amelia and Ben had announced their pregnancy, and it had broken her heart. Maybe she was going to have to reconsider. Perhaps they needed to try harder, even though she wasn't ready and they weren't using any birth control. But so far, nothing had happened.

Sophie was about to open her mouth to talk to Kent about her feelings and her love for him when he spoke first.

'Sophie?' He rolled over and put his arms around her, holding her close. 'I need to talk to you,' he said.

She stiffened in his arms. 'What's wrong?

'Calm down, relax, it's nothing bad.'

'It's about Ben and Amelia having a baby, isn't it?' she asked, her voice trembling.

'Sort of. We haven't been talking as much about things, have we, darling?'

'No, we haven't,' Sophie admitted. 'And it's because we're both worried about things, I think. Kent, I know you want to have a baby, and I sense that you aren't sure if I'm ready.'

'I've wondered. You haven't talked much about it.'

'I'm coming around to the idea,' Sophie replied. 'When I held little Megan and Munro at the pub last Sunday night, something shifted inside me. I'll be honest; I don't know what kind of mother I'll be. I don't know if I can do it or if I'll be any good at it.'

'Sophie, you'll make a great mother,' Kent reassured her. 'You're such a loving person. But if you're not ready, we'll wait. Even if it's two years, five years, or ten years, we're both young enough. We don't have to rush. But I do want to tell you what's worrying me. If we choose not to try for a baby now, I need to go to the doctor.'

Sophie rolled over, turned on the bedside light, and propped herself up on one elbow, looking down at her husband. 'What do you mean you need to go to the doctor?'

'Well, we're not using any contraception, and we've been married for nearly six months, and nothing has happened yet. That doesn't mean there's nothing wrong,' Kent admitted. 'I occasionally experience a bit of discomfort down there, so I worry that maybe there is a problem.'

Sophie sat up and folded her arms. 'That's it, Kent Mason. You are going to see the doctor tomorrow. Not to determine if you can have children, but just to make sure that everything is okay. Remember that campaign young Jerry Munsie from school started when his older brother got testicular cancer? You, of all people, should be aware of that. He was even in your year.'

'I'm not worried about anything like that,' Kent said.

'Well, you should be,' Sophie replied. 'As soon as we wake up in the morning, we're going to make an appointment to see Dr. Harry together.'

Kent grinned and reached out, pulling Sophie down so her head was nestled on his shoulder. 'That's my Sophie,' he said. 'And listen, let's forget about babies for a while, okay? We can enjoy Maggie and Munro without any pressure.'

'No,' Sophie said, shaking her head. 'We will go and get you checked out, and then we'll just let nature take its course.'

'Wouldn't you like to let nature take its course now?' Kent asked, his lips warm against her neck.

Sophie nodded and put her arms around her husband's neck and lost herself in his kiss.

Chapter 20

Kent

Friday

Since Sophie had insisted on scheduling an appointment with Dr. Harry the next morning, Kent decided not to go out to the farm. They slept in, and around eight o'clock, he rolled over.

'There are plenty of tasks I can handle in the shed before Harry opens at nine. I'll get up, have a shower, and we can have breakfast together. Then I'll go and do some work in the shed.'

'No, you stay right there,' Sophie replied. 'I was just about to get up and have my shower.' He nodded and lay back on the pillow as Sophie headed for their ensuite.

The previous night, when Kent had unburdened himself to Sophie, had lightened his worry. Knowing how she felt had cleared the air between them. Afterwards, they held each other all night.

Kent smiled as Sophie emerged from the bathroom and walked over to her chest of drawers. Her strong, lithe figure, the result of her hard work around the property, was evident. Her calves were finely defined, and her figure was slim and toned. But when she turned around, Kent's eyes widened.

He stared at Sophie and then sat up. 'Sophie, where are you feeling those tummy pains?'

'It's not exactly pain, just discomfort down here,' she replied, turning the light on and standing there in her underwear and bra, pointing to her lower abdomen.

'I think you should see the doctor today too.'

'I'm feeling better now, Kent. I'm fine. I don't need to see the doctor, but I'm going there with you.'

'But your tummy is all sort of bloated.'

'No, it's not,' she said looking down.

'It looks normal from the front, but you look puffy above your panty line.' Kent pointed.

Sophie reached down and touched her tummy. 'You're right. Maybe I should go and see Dr Harry.'

Kent climbed out of bed and approached her, putting his arms around her. 'We'll be fine, sweetheart. We'll get ourselves checked out and healthy, and then maybe we'll head down to Brisbane to see Mum and Dad next weekend. What do you think?'

'I think that would be a great idea. It'd be wonderful to see Jacinta and Ryder again too. I was talking to her on the phone yesterday. She's got a job at a small primary school in the hinterland of the Sunshine Coast.'

'That's quite a commute for her, isn't it? It's not close to Mum and Dad's place.'

'It's halfway between, apparently, but she mentioned that they are seeing a lot of your dad.' She nodded. 'I think you're right. We should plan a visit soon.'

'We will,' Kent said. 'Anyway, my dear wife, get out there and fetch me some breakfast while I get showered.'

Sophie laughed and picked up the pillow and tossed it at him. 'You can make your own breakfast. I've already had mine.'

'You have not. You just got out of bed.' The pillow went sailing back towards Sophie. Her giggles made Kent smile.

***

'Hi, Sophie. Hi, Kent,' Laura, Dr Harry's partner and receptionist, greeted them. 'Haven't seen you guys for a while. How have you been?'

'Well,' Kent replied with a grin, 'I'd like to say we're doing great, but seeing we're here to see the doctor, that might not be the right response.'

Laura smiled. 'I didn't mean personally; you know what I mean. How have you both been? Is life treating you well?'

Kent put his arm around Sophie's shoulders. 'Life's been good, thanks, Laura. We've been keeping busy, settling into married life, and overall, we're happy.'

'That's all we can ask for,' Laura said. 'You both look well anyway.'

'That's good to hear.'

Laura continued, 'Harry is ready to see you. He came in early this morning. He'll be at the hospital at ten. Thanks for taking the early appointment.' She led them to Harry's office, knocking on the door and then holding it open for them to go in. 'Harry? Kent and Sophie Mason are here to see you.' Laura stepped back. 'Harry's ready to see you now.'

After they greeted Dr Harry, he said, 'The weather's been good, Kent. I bet that bit of rain we had a couple of nights ago was good for your property.'

'Yes,' Kent replied. 'The station is looking great. We've been keeping busy, though.'

'That's the life of a farmer, isn't it?' Dr. Harry remarked.

Sophie remained standing when Dr Harry gestured for them to sit down. 'I'll let you go first, Kent. I'll go out and talk to Laura while you talk to Dr Harry.'

'Thanks, love.' Kent looked grateful. Sophie stood up, but he was at the door before her and opened it. She reached up and touched his face. 'It's all going to be fine, sweetie. Don't worry.'

'So, Laura, what have you been up to?' Sophie asked after she'd taken a seat near the reception desk in the small surgery.

'Well, Harry and I've been away. We went back to New

Zealand and visited some of my family. It was very good to catch up, and make our peace.'

'You do look happy,' Sophie said.

'I am,' Laura said simply. 'I love living in Augathella.'

'And you love living with Harry, Laura?' Sophie asked.

'I do. I could live anywhere with Harry. I think that's the main attraction of Augathella.' Laura shook her head. 'Although I'm enjoying living here. Jenny Riley and I have struck up a friendship, and I'm helping her with her garden party; it's not long away.'

Sophie said, 'No, it's not. It's going to be great. I think it will be a big event this spring. Have you been out to Jenna's new tearoom?' she asked.

'No, we only got back to town a couple of days ago. I believe the opening was very good. I think everyone has been there and has been talking about it and what a wonderful job she's done. We did notice it as we drove in. Looks fantastic.'

'Fancy Old Reg's house looking like that, and how about him already having a granddaughter and a daughter,' Sophie said.

'It's lovely, isn't it?' They chatted for a while longer and then the door opened, and Kent came out.

'Your turn,' Kent said, then smiled and added. 'All good.' He was holding a piece of paper. 'I have to go down to the hospital and have a blood test. Do you want me to do that while you go in?'

'No, wait for me,' Sophie said. 'I won't be long. I might have to have some blood tests too.'

Laura had put her head down and was typing, ignoring them to give them some privacy.

'Okay, I'll wait.' He opened the door for Sophie, and she stepped inside.

'Come on in.' Harry gestured to the seat. 'So, Sophie, how are you really? I sensed when Kent spoke to me that there might have been a couple of issues there, and that's why this has come up. If you want to talk to me about it, you know everything is confidential.'

'Thank you, Harry. I guess one of the reasons I haven't gotten pregnant is because I've been making sure I've been out of bed early around the middle of the month. I sort of don't know if I'm ready to have a baby yet, even though I know Kent wants to have one very much,' she said. 'But you know what, when I heard a friend was pregnant last week, there was sort of a bit of a change in me, and I think I might be ready now. I had a few doubts, but once Kent and I talked it over, I'm feeling better, and I guess if it happens when it happens, I'll be able to cope.'

'And why did you think you couldn't cope? "Cope" is a strange word to use.' Dr Harry sat back and waited for her answer.

'I guess having Braden's boys for those eighteen months made me realise what a responsibility it is.'

'Yes, however, three children might be a bit different to a newborn baby.'

'I know. I've been seeing Callie and Braden with the twins and how easily Callie does it. I was helping a couple of days a week, just with the washing, the cleaning, and cooking and stuff like that, but she's fine now, and she's got five children.'

'I'm sure if it's meant to be, it will happen, and you'll cope. I know that sounds like a platitude,' Harry said. 'But I'm a great believer in letting nature follow its course.'

Sophie smiled. 'That was the phrase we used yesterday morning. And last night we had a good chat. And why I'm here now is because of some tummy problems I've been having. Kent commented this morning that I was bloated and made me come with him to see you. I'm feeling better now, though.'

'Okay, hop up onto the table, and I'm going to have a little bit of feel of your tummy. Just lift your shirt, and I'll loosen your trousers.'

Sophie lay there and looked at the ceiling as Harry's warm, soft fingers gently prodded her tummy. He started above her waist and moved along the base of her ribs. 'Any pain there?' he asked.

'No, all good.'

He moved across the lower quadrants of her stomach and pressed gently. 'Any pain there?'

Sophie shook her head. 'No, I feel fine. All good, and like I said, I was only a little bit queasy yesterday, and apart from that, I'm fine. It's just what I ate.'

'Okay, I'd just like you to go into the back room here.' Harry handed her a small cup 'I'd like you to give me a sample of your urine. Now tell me about your periods first. When was your last period?'

'A couple of weeks ago.'

'Regular?'

'As clockwork. They've always just been light, maybe a little bit lighter over the last few months, but I haven't worried.'

'Have you ever been on the pill?' he asked.

'Only when I was with my previous partner,' she said reservedly.

'And how long have you been off the pill now?'

'About a year and a half.'

Harry nodded. 'Okay, leave the sample in there on the bench when you finish and come back out.'

Sophie did what he asked, and when she finished, she washed her hands and left the sample jar on the bench. She was starting to wonder what Harry was looking for. She went back outside and sat back down in the chair next to his desk. 'Will I need to have some blood tests too?'

'Yes, we'll do the whole raft of tests just to check how your general health is, but there is another test I want to do, but I'll just run one quick test while you wait. I'll be back in a moment.'

Sophie resisted looking at the computer as she waited patiently for Dr. Harry to come back out. He was only gone about five minutes, and the door opened, and she looked up as he came in. He sat on the chair beside her and looked at her for a moment before he spoke. 'So, Sophie, sometimes a woman's body follows its path in different ways.'

Her eyes narrowed. 'What are you saying, Harry?'

'Well, I'll tell you first, and then you can decide whether you want Kent to come in.'

'Tell me what?'

'You're pregnant, Sophie.'

Sophie put a hand to her throat and stared at him. 'I'm pregnant?' she whispered.

'Yes, the urine test confirmed my suspicion. At a guess, I'd say you're at least four months pregnant.'

'What? Four months?' she said, her voice squeaking.

Harry smiled. 'Yes, four months now. Tell me, what's your immediate reaction to that? Is it shock, horror, or disappointment? I want to know how you're feeling.'

Sophie's heart was racing, and she pressed a hand to her chest as a smile broke over her face. 'I'm having Kent's baby.'

Harry chuckled. 'Well, I was assuming it's your husband's.'

Sophie laughed with Dr Harry. 'How am I feeling? I feel incredible. I can't believe it. Is that why I was sick?'

'I'd say so. With the different symptoms between you and Kent, I'd say he was the only one with food poisoning, and you said you've been queasy on and off ever since. And there's no doubt that your pregnancy test is positive. You're pregnant, Sophie.'

Her voice shook. 'Can you ask Kent to come in, please?'

'I can.' Harry patted her shoulder as he walked to the door and opened it. Kent came back in and frowned as Sophie sat straight on the chair and composed her features.

'Sophie?'

They all sat there quietly for a moment, and Kent looked from one to the other. 'What's wrong, sweetheart? What's the matter? You look a bit pale. Harry, what did you tell her?'

'I'll let you tell him, Sophie.'

'Well, Kent, I don't think we need to worry about what you were worried about anymore.'

Kent's face screwed up in confusion. 'What do you mean? What was I worried about?'

'About your family jewels?' That brought a half-smile to Kent's face but he still looked worried.

Sophie jumped up and reached over and put her arms around his neck. 'Yes, Kent, it's all good news. We're having a baby. I'm pregnant.'

For a moment, Kent's eyes widened as shock set in. 'You're pregnant? We're pregnant? We're having a baby?' he repeated.

'We surely are, and we haven't got a long pregnancy to worry about.' Sophie's smile widened. 'In fact, I think I'm probably due the same time as Amelia. Whoops,' she said.

'It's okay,' Harry said. 'I know Amelia is pregnant, don't worry, it's not a secret.'

Kent stood and put his arms around Sophie and rested his cheek against hers. 'How do you feel about it, babe?'

'I feel really, really happy,' she said. 'It's... it's the right thing. The right time.'

'You really mean that?'

Sophie stepped back and looked up into her husband's eyes. 'I do.'

And she did.

Chapter 21

Three months later

Kent's sister, Jacinta and her partner, Ryder, drove Kent's parents to Augathella for the baby shower. The look on Kent's dad's face when he stepped out of the car at the homestead that he had lived in all his life had torn at Sophie's heartstrings. Mr Mason—she had always had trouble thinking of him as Dad— had been on the new trial for the drug, Donanemab. The drug had been able to slow the progression of his symptoms of Alzheimer's disease and to Rhonda and the family's great relief, his deterioration had stabilised.

As Sophie stood in their bedroom getting ready for the combined baby shower that Jenna was hosting at the Vintage Tea Room, she could hear the laughter from the shed, interspersed with the yells of three of her four nephews. Rory, Nigel, and Petie were feeling very grownup to be allowed in the shed with the men talking cattle. Munro, the fourth nephew and his twin sister, Meggie, were in the living room in their car carriers ready to travel to the baby shower with Callie.

Kent, Ryder, and Braden were listening to Mr Mason's stories of the property in past years.

'Sophie?' Callie's voice followed the soft knock on the door. 'Are you ready for me to do your hair?'

'Come in, Cal. I'm ready.'

The door opened and Callie stepped in, looking elegant in a pair of black trousers, a glittery gold top, and dangling black and gold earrings. Jenna had insisted that everyone dress up today. The women were helping Sophie get ready, not that she needed any help slipping on her floral maternity dress and jewellery, but she loved having the house full of family.

Sophie would never forget the moment when she and Kent had sat in his parents' kitchen in Brisbane and told them, and Jacinta and Ryder that Sophie was having their baby. Everyone had cried; even Kent and his dad had shed a tear. Jacinta had let out a huge whoop and danced Kent around the kitchen.

When they had come home, they had shared the news with Braden and Callie, but it was Amelia who had been one of the happiest to hear the news because as it ensued, she and Sophie were both due on the same day.

They fully intended to keep Dr Harry and Laura, the midwife, busy. The multipurpose health service had been fighting to keep the maternity section open, and both Sophie and Amelia were on a committee working towards that solution and so far, it appeared they would be able to have their babies locally.

'You look gorgeous, Sophie,' Callie said as she approached wielding the hairbrush.

'Thank you, Cal. As gorgeous as is possible with a huge stomach and swollen ankles!'

'You keep an eye on that, won't you?'

'Kent is checking on me all the time, and Dr Harry isn't too concerned, but he's got me on weekly visits now, just so he can keep an eye on it.'

Sophie sat at the dressing table and closed her eyes as Callie put her hair up into the same sort of French roll she had worn for the gala opening of the Vintage Tea Rooms. She hadn't even known she was pregnant that day, but her aching back and legs had shown her that she should have picked the symptoms. She would know next time.

And Sophie was sure there would be a next time. Hopefully, several.

The past three months had been full of joy, celebrating their pregnancy and their happiness, celebrating the improvement in Kent's father's condition. Watching little Meggie and Munro grow into babies that were taking notice and alert had been exciting, knowing that that was ahead for her and Kent.

'You know who I think is the most excited about you having a baby, Sophie?' Callie said.

Sophie looked up into the mirror and smiled at her sister-in-law. 'I know exactly who you're going to say. It's Petie, isn't it?'

'It is, he loves the twins, but when we told him that Aunty Soph was having a little baby he was beside himself. I think you'll have a readymade babysitter over the next few years.'

'Bless him,' Sophie said.

Footsteps pounded up the front steps. 'Are you girls ready yet?' Braden called from the front door.

There was a convoy taking them to the baby shower. The cars were full of laughter and chat as they drove into Augathella. Callie had Rhonda and the twins in their Land Cruiser, and Ryder was driving Jacinta and Sophie. When he turned off the highway behind Callie, Jacinta's eyes widened. 'Oh, my goodness, Sophie. That can't be Reg's old place.'

Sophie nodded and smiled. 'It is. Wait until you meet Jenna. She is so lovely.'

As Ryder parked the car and Sophie waited for him to come around to the back seat and help her down, Sophie admired the Vintage Tea Room.

Reg's derelict house had once been a faded building of rotten timber, surrounded by dead brown grass and old car bodies.

Now in the final month of spring, the grounds looked superb. Jenny Riley had been hard at work preparing for the

Spring Garden party which was going to be held at the tearoom next week. The gardens were already in bloom with masses of colour. Somehow with Jenny's green thumb, she managed to get plants unaccustomed to the climate of the west not only adapting but thriving.

Sophie caught her breath as Ryder helped her out and she looked at the house. Whoever had helped Jenna get the tea room ready for this afternoon's function had excelled themselves. Bunches of pink, blue, and yellow balloons hung off the front of the building and coloured ribbon wound around the railings of the front steps.

Amelia and Jenna appeared on the veranda, closely followed by Alana.

'Come on, Mrs Mason,' Amelia called down. 'It's time to party.'

Sophie grinned up at the newlywed Amelia. 'I'm on my way, Mrs Riley!'

An Augathella Spring

ANNIE SEATON

Augathella Short and Sweet: 3

Chapter 1

Emily

Emily Jansen parked her small station wagon outside the grocery store at the top of the main street in Augathella. She glanced across to the back seat and was rewarded with a beautiful smile from Ophelia, wide-eyed and happy in the baby seat.

Emily opened her door, climbed out, and went around to the passenger side to open the back door. 'You're awake, my sweet,' she said. 'You're such a good girl, not a peep out of you for the last two hundred kilometres. You've had a huge sleep. I'll bet you're hungry, darling.'

There was plenty of food in the camp fridge in the back of their station wagon, and she was thankful that Troy, her late husband, had set the fridge up in the car a couple of years ago. It had made her trip down from Townsville so much easier, being able to have fresh food for both her and Ophelia, and not having to stop frequently to buy food. However, she was getting quite low on supplies and did need to top up here, but first things first.

Emily unclipped the seat buckles and lifted out her little girl. Her skin was warm as Ophelia nestled into her neck. 'Mum-mum,' she said.

'Yes, darling, Mum-mum is here, and we just have to go and see a lady, and then we'll go over to that park and have some lunch.'

Emily had smiled when she'd seen the name of the park across the road—Meat Ant Park! She was certainly not in the tropics now and that suited her just fine.

The grocery store was surprisingly busy even though there were no other cars parked outside. Once inside, Emily soon realised that elderly people who lived in town must walk from their homes with carry bags.

Feeling guilty about going in just to ask a question, Emily went to the fridge near the counter and took out two litres of milk. There would be room for that in the camp fridge.

She walked across to the counter and stood behind the two elderly women waiting. An animated conversation was taking place.

'The new girl is doing an amazing job,' the shorter one said.

'No, Beryl, that's not the new girl I meant.'

'Yes, it is. That young one who bought old Reg's place out on the highway. Apparently, the café is going great guns and they say it's always busy.'

Emily had noticed the Vintage Tea Shop on the highway on her way in; there had been several caravans and quite a few cars parked there. If there was one thing she missed, it was her daily brewed coffee. It was a bit hard to do that with a camp fridge while staying in cabins and caravan parks. Stopping for a coffee had tempted her, but she knew she had things to do first.

'Yes, and do you know what she's decided to do?'

'No, Gladys, but I'm sure you do.'

The patient voice held irritation. 'Beryl, someone has to keep an eye on what's happening in town. You know, I couldn't believe it when old Reg went into the home. I never thought he would. He's been sitting outside that pub for a lot of years, you know.'

'Yes, that's all very well, but tell me what this news is you're busting to tell me.'

'Well, you know Jenny Riley's Spring Garden party that she has every year with the CWA?'

'Yes, I've already started baking for it.'

'Well, Beryl, this year that newcomer out at the tea shop has almost taken over. She's decided to put a big sign out the front saying "CWA fundraiser for the RFDS. Come into town and get your coffee and cake."'

Beryl nodded. 'That's good of her.'

'Yes, that may be, but don't you think she's a bit new in town to be getting involved in our town things? She's not a local yet. But the big thing, Beryl, is that Jenny Riley isn't calling it a spring garden party anymore.'

'She has to call it a garden party.'

'Absolutely. That's what it is, and that's what it's always been. Well, apparently, this Jenna girl reckons that if she makes it a little bit more modern, she's going to get all those caravans that have been coming into her tea shop.'

'So, what's it going be called?'

'It's going to be called the Spring Fair.'

Beryl shrugged. 'I suppose I can live with that.'

'I'll be saying my piece at the committee meeting, trust me! And for the life of me, I don't know why we have to have the meeting out at that girl's new tearoom! What's our town coming to! She'll be running for mayor before we know it.'

Emily hid a smile when she saw the other lady roll her eyes.

'That will be fifty-six dollars, Mrs. Tingle,' the cashier said. Gladys handed over her cash, and as the girl packed up her two bags of groceries, Gladys shook her head. 'Whoever thought I'd be paying twenty-five dollars for one bag of groceries. I don't know what the world is coming to. Do you, Beryl? With all this COVID stuff, somehow people are putting up all the prices of our groceries.'

Emily switched off as the conversation continued, and Beryl was served by the cashier. Finally, it was her turn, and she stepped forward and put the two litres of milk on the counter. The two older ladies, Gladys and Beryl, were still standing near the door, having a conversation about the state of the world. The cashier smiled at Emily and gestured her head towards them.

'Don't worry too much about them, dear. Gladys always has something to whinge about. Just the milk today, is it?'

'Yes, please.'

'Just passing through?' the woman asked.

'Well, I did want to ask you something. I noticed there's no real estate agent in town. In fact, I thought there'd be a little bit more of a shopping centre here.'

'Love, we've got very little here these days. Sign of the times. You could go up to the rural store behind Anderson's garage if you're looking to buy a house. They've got a few for the Charleville agents in their window.' Her eyes narrowed as she regarded Emily.

'No. I'm just perhaps looking for a local rental.'

'Good luck with that. Town's full at the moment; a lot of investors have bought up the real estate and are renting it out to the stockmen on the properties and the road workers working out on the highway upgrade. I sort of know what's available most of the time, but I really can't think of anything at the moment.'

Emily's heart sank. Her contract at the local primary school started after the spring holidays, and she really needed to be settled before then, plus she had to find somewhere for Ophelia to go during the day. As much as she hated the thought of leaving her with a stranger, Emily needed the work. When she'd seen the one-term part-time contract position at the local primary school advertised in the state education gazette, she'd somehow known this little town in southwestern Queensland was exactly what she needed.

Troy's money—*their* money—hadn't come through yet. Probate was taking a long time, and her solicitor said that while the manner of his death was being investigated, matters were even more complicated and the process slower.

Emily's throat closed, and she swallowed, refusing to dwell on those issues. Augathella was a new start, and she was going to do the best she could to move on. She *would* find somewhere to live in this town. The contract was only for ten weeks, and then she'd decide where she was going to go next.

'I heard the ladies talking about the tea shop out on the highway,' she asked quietly. 'Do they do coffee out there as well?'

'Do they do coffee? I'll say! Jenna makes the best coffee anywhere I've been in, love. Even though I'm working in this little town, I've had coffee in most places around Australia when Gary and I travelled around in our caravan. Jenna does a great job, and her cakes are amazing.'

'I might give it a try,' she said.

'You won't be sorry.'

Emily handed over the cash for the milk and walked outside.

The woman called Beryl stepped forward 'Hello, love. I couldn't help overhearing your conversation with Dawn in there. I know there's a room available in one of the three units down in Nelson Street. But you'll have to share.'

Gladys raised her eyebrows. 'Who with, Beryl?'

'Well, it's that young Alana who came to town with Jenna. She's moving on.'

'Oh, is she? That girl did most of the baking at the tea shop, I heard. Made the best cakes. If she's left it's doomed unless someone else can keep up to her standard. Where is she going?'

'Don't you worry about that now. And you're wrong. She didn't cook. Young Jenna does her own baking.'

Beryl turned back to Emily. 'I heard you say you were

thinking about going out there for a coffee. You ask for Jenna. I know she's got a spare room in her apartment, love.'

Emily nodded. As much as she hated half the town already knowing that she was looking for somewhere to live, it *would* make it easier if she had some inside information. 'Thank you very much, ladies. I'll do that.'

'What a beautiful little girl.' Gladys reached over and tickled Ophelia under her chin and was rewarded with a little chuckle. 'She's a sweet-looking little one, love.'

'Yes, she is, isn't she? Thank you, ladies. I appreciate your help.' Emily put her head down and walked to the car. Maybe moving to such a small town hadn't been such a good idea.

Chapter 2

Jenna

'I'm really, really sorry to leave you in the lurch, Jenna. I know I said I'd stay for a while when we moved here, but—'

Jenna put a hand up. 'Alana, It's fine. Rory's been given this great opportunity, and I don't mind at all. I've got more help here than I need, and the business has settled down now that the local interest has eased off a bit.'

'But it's still going alright, isn't it?' Alana asked.

'Between what I'm getting from the caravanners going past on their travels and the locals who are stopping in as they leave Augathella to go down to Charleville to work every morning, it's really good. Besides, I don't mind easing back a bit. We've worked hard setting up plus it gives me time to think about Jenny Riley's Spring Fair. Will you come back for that?'

'How long away is it?' Alana asked.

'Two weeks, but you don't have to. It's such a long way to travel from Moree back up to here.'

'No, it's not.'

Jenna chuckled. 'You're turning into a real bushie, Alana. Where's the woman who found it too hard to drive from Burleigh Heads to Surfers Paradise to work?'

'Yes, I know, but it's different out here. The roads are great to drive on, there's no traffic, and I really enjoy driving with Rory.'

'I think you just enjoy being with Rory.'

'I do, and listen, what's happening with you and Luke?'

Jenna shrugged. 'There is no me and Luke. I think we're just going to be friends. I like him a lot, but he hasn't been here for a couple of weeks.'

'But is there a spark? 'Alana looked hopeful.

'No, I don't think so. I've never had a spark so I really can't tell. Anyway, I know he's been busy up in the Northern Territory.'

'You'll know straight away when you meet someone and there's a spark, trust me.'

Jenna chuckled. 'We're just friends.'

'But you do fancy him, don't you, Jen?'

'Um, not in that way.' Jenna shrugged. 'He's a nice guy, but look, I'm busy with the business. I don't need to complicate my life with a partner. And like I said, no spark.' She folded her arms.

Alana regarded Jenna, a frown on her face. 'Seriously, just don't let the business take over your life like you did at the real estate office back on the coast. Look what happened there. Make some time for being happy and socialising.'

'I'm my own boss here. I'm the only one with expectations. I have never been as happy as I've been since we got here. The community is lovely, I've made lots of friends, and I'm loving my little business. I will miss you though, Alana. When do you leave?'

'In the morning. Is that okay with you?'

'Of course it is. You've stocked up the freezer to last me for ages, thank you. Sophie's happy to come in for a couple of days a week, and Ellie, one of the high school girls who worked for us at the opening is leaving school at the end of term this week. I've looked into getting a school-based traineeship for her. She wants to be a pastry chef. I know I haven't got the qualifications to supervise her, but she can do her work hours here and go to TAFE in Charleville.'

'Sounds like it's all working out pretty well.'

'Yes, Ellie is a lovely young girl, and she enjoys working here.'

Alana shook her head. 'It surprises me that the young ones in town stay local after they leave high school. I know we've seen the coast and we've had our years of going out on the town, but you'd think that after growing up here in this quiet little town, they'd want to spread their wings a bit.'

'Different strokes for different folks,' Jenna said. 'She's happy. Just wants to get her qualifications; she might move to the city then, who knows? Anyway, it's all getting organised. It's not definite yet.'

The tearoom was calm and quiet that morning, and that gave Jenna a good chance to get herself organised. She did a stocktake of the freezer, cool room and pantry and planned to close the doors around two-thirty when the lunch rush stopped. They were having a quick committee meeting for the Spring Fair and then she'd go into town after that to stock up on supplies and maybe do some baking at home tonight after she'd visited Reg.

'Here's another customer. Do you want me to look after them?' Alana said, looking out at the car park. She was rolling pastry for a last batch of the mushroom tarts that had been so popular with the tourists.

'No, it's fine, I'll go out. You keep cutting out those pastry circles. I hate doing them.' Jenna took off her apron and washed her hands.

A pretty woman with long blonde hair stood by the counter, holding a small toddler in her arms.

'Do I need to be seated or can I sit anywhere?' she asked quietly.

'No, you can choose a seat wherever you want, and then I'll come across and take your order. Would you like me to get a high chair?'

The woman smiled. 'Do you have one?'

'I sure do,' Jenna chuckled. 'Not that many of the grey nomads have babies with them, but we do get some Sunday tourists who come up from Charleville with little children.'

The woman nodded and smiled. 'That explains your little colouring corner over there; I wondered about it.'

'Take a seat, and I'll be back in a moment with the chair.' Jenna went to the storeroom beside the cool room that Rory and Kirk had set up for her and lifted out the small wooden highchair. She took it into the kitchen, gave the plastic tray a quick wipe down, and then carried it into the front tearoom. The woman had taken a seat by the window where she could see the garden. Jenna was proud of the beautiful blooms that had started to appear over the last couple of weeks. She and Jenny Riley had worked really hard on that garden, and it was looking beautiful. It amazed Jenna what grew out here: a riot of snapdragons, candytuft, and delphiniums edged the borders in front of the roses that were in heavy bud.

The only thing she was worried about with the lack of rain was that she didn't want to use too much of the tank water to keep the garden going. If it came to it, she'd order water in a truck because the garden made her tearooms that little bit extra special and caught the attention and comments of many grey nomads on their way past. Some of the women over the last couple of weeks had said that they'd stopped specifically to have a coffee because of the flowers. So, even if she had to pay for the water to keep the garden lovely, it would be worthwhile. Jenna made a mental note to follow that up this afternoon.

She carried the high chair across to the table, and the woman stood, lifting the little girl in.

'Hello, sweetie. What's your name?' Jenna asked.

'This is Ophelia,' the woman said.

'And how old is she?'

'She's eighteen months.'

Jenna sensed that the conversation was closed off, and the woman didn't particularly want to talk. Sometimes, some of the customers who called in wanted to talk for ages about the tearoom, the types of tea, and coffee, and the gifts. Who made them, and who helped her in the garden. Other times—and Jenna was very good at picking up when someone just wanted to place their order—there was no need for conversation. This pretty young mother was one of those. Jenna took her order with a smile and headed to the kitchen. She knew when to leave customers in peace.

***

When she took the coffee out, Jenna introduced herself, and her new customer smiled briefly.

'I'm Emily.'

Business became brisk. Jenna lost count of the caravans, pulling up one after the other for the next hour and a half. To her surprise, Emily stayed at the table the whole time. She refilled her coffee twice and had no problem when Emily asked if she minded if she brought Ophelia's food from the car and fed her at the table.

'Not at all, we're pretty easy-going here,' she said.

'It's just so good to have a highchair again,' Emily said with a little smile.

Jenna left Alana on the coffee machine and took the orders as it got even busier. She was aware of Emily watching her, and it was almost as though she was sizing her up.

Eventually, the rush receded. The vans pulled away, and it was time to start thinking about cleaning up and closing for the afternoon, but Emily still sat there. She was nursing the little girl, who had gone to sleep on her shoulder.

'Would you like another cup of coffee?' Jenna asked.

'No, I'm fine, thank you. Look, I hope you don't mind me sitting here.' Emily looked up and met Jenna's eyes.

Jenna looked back, unable to ignore the depth of sadness in Emily's eyes.

'I had an ulterior motive for coming here,' Emily said. 'I

209

went into town looking for real estate agents to see if there was somewhere I could stay in town.'

'There's a pub there with rooms, and they're quite nice,' Jenna said.

'No, I need somewhere to stay for the whole school term,' Emily said. 'I'm on contract at the local primary school for ten weeks until the Christmas holidays, and I need somewhere to stay. When I was in town at the IGA, at the grocery store, I met two ladies called Gladys and Beryl.'

Jenna smiled. 'And you managed to escape? It's a wonder you're still not in there with them, with them probing your entire life history.'

Emily's face closed, and Jenna realised she'd said something wrong. 'Anyway, what did they tell you?' she hurried on.

'They said that, and I'm assuming it's you, that the owner of the tearooms had a room that might be available to rent.'

Jenna looked at Emily, sizing her up. 'I do.'

'And is it available?' Emily continued. 'It's just the two of us, just Ophelia and me. Ophelia is the most well-behaved little darling.' Emily's eyes filled with tears, and a pang of sympathy hit Jenna squarely in the chest. She knew that Emily was sad, and the way she spoke and looked at her daughter reinforced that sadness, and she'd said she was alone.

'So, you're working at the primary school. A few of my friends are teachers there. I think you'll be happy there. It's a very nice little school, very social.'

'Yes, but my immediate problem is finding somewhere to live,' Emily gestured her head down towards the sleeping baby. 'And I need to find some daycare for Ophelia.' Her eyes welled with tears again. 'As much as I hate it, she will have to go to daycare while I work.'

Jenna's heart went out to her. 'Well, then you don't have

to worry about somewhere to stay because I certainly have a room. I can give you references and my solicitor's details if you want to speak to somebody to check I'm okay.' She smiled.

'No, it's fine.'

'I'm gone all day, so you'd have privacy and I'm often gone at night. I usually eat at the pub. The last thing I ever feel like doing when I get home from working here all day is cooking a meal in the kitchen, so I barely use the kitchen at home, although I am going home tonight to bake. My assistant, the one who made your great coffee, was sharing the house with me when we moved here from the Gold Coast. But Alana is leaving town with her new partner. So, Emily, you're welcome to stay with me until you get yourself settled. If that suits us both, that is.'

Jenna added that bit because she didn't want to leave herself open to someone moving in who wasn't going to work out.

'Oh, thank you, Jenna. You have no idea how relieved I am.'

'Would you like to come and have a look this afternoon? If it suits, you can move in today, if you like. Or are you staying somewhere else for the time being? Have you just driven up from Charleville for the day?'

'No, I drove south from Longreach today,' she said.

'You must be exhausted. No wonder the poor little one has gone to sleep.' Jenna couldn't help reaching out and touching the soft curls on the little girl's head. 'She's beautiful.'

'She is, she's my beautiful girl,' Emily said.

Chapter 3

Jenna

Jenna crouched in the garden at the bottom of the steps, and as she pulled on a particularly tough weed, the sound of an aircraft engine filled the air. She'd put the closed sign up and she was waiting for the committee members to arrive. Never one to waste a minute, she'd decided to weed the garden at the bottom of the stairs while she waited. Jumping up, she brushed her hands on her jeans and then looked up. Disappointment filled her as she realised it was a small plane flying over and not Luke's helicopter.

Jenny Riley had arrived early for their committee meeting and was working at the far end of the garden bed. She stood at the same time Jenna did.

'Time for a cuppa, love?' she asked, and then her gaze lifted to the sky. 'That'll be Amelia's brother.'

'Amelia's brother? I didn't know he was coming today.'

'Yes, he's got his own plane. She said he does some mustering up in the Northern Territory. We must make sure that he catches up with Fallon when he's here. Apparently, they knew each other in Darwin.'

Jemma nodded and pulled her gardening gloves off.

'You've been quiet this week. You okay, love?'

'Yeah, I'm good. Just a bit tired. Everything's settling well. The new girls are working out, and I finally managed to coax Sophie into not turning up here so much. It doesn't do her good being on her feet all the time.'

'She loves it though.'

'So do I.' She glanced up again. 'I've been half expecting

Luke to arrive this week. He hasn't been for a couple of weeks.'

'Have you heard from him?' Jenny asked.

'Not since the week before last.' Jenna shrugged. 'Mum told me to call him before they left yesterday.'

'Oh, that's why you're quiet; your Mum and Dad finally went.'

'Yeah, but they're only going up to Longreach and Winton to have a look around and then they're coming back for a couple more weeks. Mum said she wouldn't miss your garden party for the world.'

'Yes, the Spring Fair is getting close. We've got a lot to do in the next two weeks. We'll get everything allocated at the meeting today. ' She turned as three cars came into the car park. 'Here they are now.'

Jenna put her hands on her hips. 'I don't know what you're doing helping me weed my little garden when you should be working on yours.'

'It looks after itself,' Jenny said happily. 'I went out this morning and gave it a little light spray. The buds are beautiful. They don't need too much water; I don't want them falling off. It's just about perfect.'

'You make sure to tell me how I can come and help on the day or closer to the day. I can close up here.'

'You'll do no such thing,' Jenny said. 'You can't get a reputation for not sticking to business hours. People might drive here specially and find you closed.'

Jenna scrunched her face up. 'Yeah, I guess you're right, but I'll get the girls to work when you need me and I'll make sure everything is right. I'll spend the day and the evening before helping you get ready. And I'm going to bake for you too.'

'I think you've got enough baking of your own to do here, haven't you?'

'Yes, but it's not hard to make a double batch.'

Jenny smiled. 'It would be nice to have some of your sponge cakes. I've never met anyone that makes them just like you.'

'That's my pleasure. Come on, let's go and wait upstairs for this lot.'

'I'll put the kettle on.'

Jenna hurried up the steps and listened as the rumble of the plane faded. She wasn't sure what was going on with Luke. Mum had told her last night not to stress about it.

But Jenna was worried that maybe Luke was keener than she was.

She bit her lip as she went into the kitchen, got the large kettle and put it on the gas stove. She leaned against the countertop, waiting for the kettle to boil as she heard Jenny greet the committee girls and take them to the back tearoom.

Luke was an enigma. She liked him enough but was worried that he'd read too much into their relationship. He was always good to be with, and when they were together, he was totally considerate, but their relationship had never gone beyond a chaste kiss goodnight. Maybe she was reading more into it, maybe Luke just wanted to be friends too. When she'd said that to Mum last night, Mum shook her head, 'A friend who flies his helicopter hundreds of kilometres to come and visit you? He's certainly not coming for a cup of tea.'

'He has to come up here anyway for work, Mum, so he's just being kind. We're just friends.'

'But do you really *like* him, Jenna?'

'I do, he's a really good guy, but there's no point starting a romance because he lives so far away. Who knows, when he finishes with these properties, he might not have to come back here anymore.'

'Yes, and you're settled here, I think. I see what you mean. You certainly don't want to uproot all that if you did have a relationship and had to follow him to where he lives.'

'No chance of that.' Jenna had laughed. 'You're jumping the gun, Mum. We are *just* friends.'

She and Luke had exchanged mobile numbers, and after the first couple of weeks of coming up to visit her, Luke had started to ring her three times a week. They had lots of lovely long chats on the phone at night, and she began to look forward to seeing him again. After a while, she asked him when he was next coming up, and he said he couldn't commit to a date. Jenna realised that maybe that was the brush-off, but the strange thing was he kept ringing, so she didn't know what was going on. She wasn't in a hurry to figure it out, though. She had enough to keep herself occupied with the tearooms, and now that Mum had gone away for a week, she was keeping an eye on Reg too.

The kettle whistled, and she reached for the container of tea leaves. She filled the teapot that she knew Jenny liked. Maybe when Luke called next time, she'd ask him outright what was going on, and then she could stop worrying. Meanwhile, there was a Spring Fair to organise.

***

'Okay, ladies, I now declare the meeting officially open.' Jenny Riley sat at the head of the table in the smaller tearoom at Jenna's Vintage Tearooms.

Jenny had booked the room especially for the meeting because it meant Jenna could be there.

'Thanks for letting us have the room, Jenna.'

'My pleasure. I didn't want to miss out.' Jenna looked around the table and smiled. Sophie and Amelia, both very pregnant, sat together at the end of the table. Opposite them were Beryl and Gladys, and beside them were Fallon Ingram and Callie Cartwright. Laura, Dr Harry's partner, sat at the far end.

Jenny had formed a new committee for her revamped

Spring Fair and was keen to get some fresh ideas for the day.

'Thanks for coming, and thanks for your input so far,' she said. 'I'd just like to recap what everyone has said to me already because it's happened in bits and pieces, meeting some of you in the street, having phone conversations, and exchanging text messages. So, to confirm, we're right to go two weeks from this Saturday. The CWA is putting us under their organisation, so we'll be insured for the event, and as usual, all profit will go to the RFDS.'

There were nods and murmurs of assent around the table. Jenna relaxed; she'd been a little worried about Gladys Tingle. She'd heard that she could be a bit of a gossip and troublemaker. She paid attention as Jenny continued.

'This year, we're having a bit of a change. We've decided not to have any jumping castles or pony rides for the kids. Instead, we are thinking about getting a clown and having face painting.'

Callie raised her hand. 'I hope that's not because of what happened to Petie last year, is it, Jenny? I'd hate to think that we are depriving the kids of those fun things because of that. That was purely and simply an accident and was caused by the wind, not by any neglect or anything like that.'

'I know,' Jenny said, 'but that accident rattled us all. So, I took a look at our work, health, and safety guidelines. It's a Spring Fair, for selling plants, having cups of tea, and getting to meet up with some locals. We'll just have that one little thing for the kids.'

'What about the pony rides?' Laura asked. 'They were really popular last year.'

'Oh, Craig Wilson said that he's happy to bring his ponies in. But again, I guess I'm just a little bit nervous.'

Sophie spoke up. 'How about we put it to a vote, Jenny? It seems pretty harsh to drop all these things that have been a part of the garden party since I was a kid. And I know a lot of the primary school kids are looking forward to it, aren't they, Callie?'

'Yes, they've already started doing some drawings in class, and I know our three boys are really keen. If we make it less attractive to kids, there'll be a lot of disappointed families around.'

Jenny bit her lip and looked around the room. 'Well, I guess we should put it to discussion, and then we'll take a vote.'

Gladys sat up straight and pursed her lips. 'I'm afraid I agree with Jenny. It's a garden party. I don't even like the term "Spring Fair" because that makes it sound like a sideshow alley. This is a fundraiser for the RFDS, and I think we should just sell plants. In fact, I don't even think we should have afternoon tea or have raffles and the 100 Club.'

Jenny shook her head. 'No, Gladys, there will be afternoon tea. There always has been. I've already got the tables and chairs organised, and we've had lots of volunteers to make cakes.' She looked over at Jenna. 'Jenna is even closing the tearooms for the day, so we'll get more passing trade from the highway. She's kindly agreed to put up a banner directing people into town. Has it been delivered yet, Jenna?'

'The banner's ordered, and I'm expecting it to be delivered later in the week,' Jenna replied.

'You'll be right to put it up along your front fence on the highway?' Jenny asked.

'I will, Jenny. Amelia's Ben said he'll come and help put it up as soon as it's delivered.'

'He's just waiting for your call, Jenna,' Amelia said.

Callie leaned forward. 'Okay, I would like to move that we accept Craig's offer of the pony rides, have face painting, and include the clown. I think that will cater to most of the age groups. I don't think we need to have the jumping castle, though.'

There were lots of nods around the table. Gladys sat up straight and pursed her lips. 'It's a garden party, not a children's show,' she insisted.

Jenna said, 'But it's all about raising money for the RFDS, and if we don't have things for the kids, we're not going to get the parents to spend money.'

'You don't know this town as well as we do.' Gladys glared at Jenna.

'And yes, we know that the children like to be involved. It's also a good lesson for them,' Sophie said quietly.

Amelia added, 'I agree.'

The vote went ahead, and all but Gladys smiled when it was agreed to include the children's activities.

Once the meeting was over, Jenna stood to go back to the kitchen, but Amelia called her. 'Jenna? A favour?'

Jenna waited as the other women headed out to their cars. 'Sure, what's up?'

'I'll wait outside for you, Amelia,' Laura said. 'I've got plenty of time. Harry's in Charleville for the day.'

'Thanks, Laura. I'll only be a minute.'

'Are you okay, Amelia?' Jenna thought Amelia had looked a bit pale during the meeting. In contrast to her pale face, Sophie's cheeks were pink, but Amelia had looked a bit drawn.

'I'm fine. Bump's good.' She patted her tummy. 'I had a checkup yesterday and everything's on track. I'm just a bit stressed. We're picking my brother up at the aerodrome tomorrow, and I was hoping you could save a table for us for lunch. I think we'll come but I can ring you if we have to cancel.'

'Jenny thought that was him arriving before.'

'No, he's coming tomorrow.'

'Sure, not a problem. But why would you be stressed?

Don't you get on?'

'We used to, but things are pretty rocky in my family. Too detailed to go into now while Laura's waiting, but one day I'll tell you all about how I came to Augathella.'

'I'll look forward to it.' Jenna put her hand on Amelia's arm. 'And the table's not a problem, I'll keep it free for the day in case you want to stay longer.'

'Thank you. And if I pull faces at you when we're having lunch, come and rescue me!'

'I can do that.' Jenna chuckled.

As Amelia hurried out to the car park, Jenna shook her head. Of all the people to have family issues, bright and bubbly Amelia was the last person she would have expected to have a difficult family. She was such a sweet person. Her grandfather had a soft spot for Amelia, and Reg'd been chuffed that she'd been to visit him at the aged care facility a couple of times since he'd moved in.

If her friend needed rescuing tomorrow, Jenna would step right in. She had already taken a dislike to Amelia's brother and she hadn't even met him.

Chapter 4

Emily

Emily took more notice of the little town when she drove in after leaving the tearoom. Jenna had given her the address of her apartment block and told her to do a drive-by to see if it suited her. Emily didn't say that a tarpaulin under a tent would suit her at this stage. She was desperate; she needed to find somewhere to live quickly, and that would be the first problem solved. Then, she had to find somebody to look after Ophelia once she started at the school.

The town was a little bit busier than when she had driven in earlier. Two buses came around the corner as she stopped at the stop sign. Children waited in a line outside the primary school. As she did a recce along that street, they appeared well-behaved and were all in uniform. That was a plus. For a moment, she considered stopping at the school and going into the office to talk to the principal, but she realised it would be too hard with Ophelia. She'd have to wait until she had someone to look after her. It would be very unprofessional to turn up without an appointment, dragging along a little toddler. She and Mr Hamblion, the principal, had had a long conversation on the phone when he'd called to offer her the one-term contract.

She turned left at the end of the school street and went down two blocks of older-style houses. The grass in front of each was dry and brown, but the occasional green shoot was trying to push up towards the late spring sunshine. Most of the yards had small gardens, and an elderly lady on a walker waved and smiled at Emily as she drove slowly past. Calm descended on her like a blanket. She had chosen well, and if only she could get a sitter for Ophelia, everything would be fine. She had a good feeling about Jenna's place. Jenna had been friendly but reserved and hadn't asked a million questions about why Emily was here, what she was doing at the school, and most of all, where was her partner and Ophelia's father. Emily's chest tightened, and she pushed the thought away and blinked to stop any tears.

Augathella was going to be the right place as a temporary stop to get her head together. It couldn't be more different from Townsville. There were no balmy tropical breezes, palm trees, lush green grass, or children playing in the street outside her house. Most of all, there were no military helicopters going over as they did their daily exercises. Her breath caught and she cleared her throat before glancing over to the back. Ophelia was sitting contentedly in the baby seat, and Emily felt bad. She'd been ignoring her ever since they left the vintage tearooms.

'We are going to look at a new house for us, darling, just for a little while. Somewhere where you can play and be happy and somewhere Mummy can go to work and we'll find somebody really lovely, like a grandma, to look after you,' Emily said. In a town like this, with a mix of young people and retirees, there had to be someone who would be experienced in looking after children. Someone she could trust.

That was the next job. She slowed as she approached the third brick building along and, as Jenna had described, Emily was pleasantly surprised. Jenna's home was in a block of four units, a square brick building with a well-kept lawn greener than most of the others. The strata obviously paid for a gardener. At the edge of the lawn, there were a couple of flowering shrubs at the base of each set of steps. The units were set in a square, and the two front ones had steps back-to-back in the centre, going to front doors. Her only worry was who else lived in the units, and she grimaced.

Beggars can't be choosers, Emily told herself. She had to take this job; it appeared the probate money wasn't going to come through very soon. She closed her eyes and took a deep breath as she parked outside the units.

Chapter 5

Jenna

After everyone had left, Jenna quickly wiped down the benches, turned off the coffee machine, loaded the dishwasher, and switched it on. She checked the cool room to ensure it was at the right temperature and checked the back door was locked before she took off her apron, brushed her hair, and headed down to her car at the back of the house.

Emily had been an interesting person, but she wondered if she had done the right thing by offering her the spare room in her apartment. She had assured her that the baby wasn't noisy and that she would be at work all day, and the baby would be in care. A light bulb came on in Jenna's head. Ruth Mason, Fallon's mum, would be free now that Petie Cartwright was going to kindy five days a week.

Jenna smiled to herself as she locked the front door. It hadn't taken long for her to settle into the town, and know all about who was related to who, and who fitted where.

Very different to her life on the Gold Coast where she hadn't known the name of one person in her apartment block.

Ruth had come in for coffee earlier in the week with Fallon and Callie Cartwright, and she'd been saying how bored she was.

'I'm not a gardener, the house stays tidy, and I only go out to look after this little man, the two days that Fallon is working.' She tickled her grandson under the chin. 'I've been helping Jenny get her shop ready, but I still have too much time on my hands.'

On the spur of the moment, Jenna took a left into Hill Street on her way back to her apartment. She told Emily that she'd be home around three-thirty, so she still had time before she met her there.

She smiled as she pulled up outside the house. Ruth had obviously minded Ryan while Fallon was at their meeting.

Jenna knocked on the front door, and Ruth's footsteps hurried down the hall.

'Jenna, what a surprise. How lovely to see you. Come on in, love. Fallon and I have just had a cup of tea; Ryan's due to wake up soon. The little monkey's been playing all afternoon. The pot's still warm.'

'No, thanks. Just a quick visit. I just wanted to ask you something, Ruth.'

'Sure, love, come on in.'

Jenna followed Ruth down the hall. Fallon was sitting at the table, where a pot of tea in a bright yellow and red tea cosy sat in the centre. 'Hi again, Jenna. You survived the first committee meeting, and you handled Gladys Tingle like a pro.'

'She wasn't too bad. I was expecting worse.'

'Are you sure you don't want a cuppa?' Ruth asked.

'Thanks. I'm good. I've got somebody waiting at my apartment for me. I think I might have found someone to take Alana's room.'

'I'll have to get going, Mum.' Fallon pushed her chair back. 'I'll get Ryan and then leave you to talk to Jenna.'

'Don't rush on my account. I'll only be a minute.' Jenna stood beside the table.

'We'll be back tomorrow. I'm working again.'

Ruth beamed. 'I'll have Ryan all day. Fallon's been doing some helicopter mustering.' She pulled a face. 'I do like the idea of having my grandson to myself all day, but I would much prefer it if my daughter wasn't up in the air doing dangerous things.'

'Who are you mustering for?' Jenna asked.

'Craig Wilson's station. The other side of Braden and Callie's place. His regular guy is up in the Northern Territory, so he asked me to fill in for a couple of days.'

'Do you enjoy it?' Jenna didn't need to ask; she could see it on Fallon's face.

'I do. I've been looking forward to getting back in the air.'

'Sit down, Jenna,' Ruth said as Fallon headed up the hall.

Jenna shook her head. 'Thanks Ruth, but I can't stay long. Emily, the woman who came into the tearoom, is waiting for me to meet her at the apartment. She's starting to teach at the primary school after the holidays, Ruth, and she's got a little toddler. She's looking for someone to look after her a couple of days a week. I thought of you straight away.'

'That sounds wonderful. I'd love to meet her.'

'Fabulous. I'll let her know. But wait until you meet her and make sure you're a fit. She seems nice and the little girl was really well behaved.'

'I appreciate you thinking of me,' Ruth said with a smile.

'My pleasure. As long as I don't turn into a Gladys Tingle, sticking my nose in.'

Ruth chuckled as they walked to the front door. 'No chance of that, love. You're a local already.'

Chapter 6

Amelia - the next day

Amelia Riley grabbed her hat as a gust of wind carried in gritty dust to where they waited by Ben's work car. They were parked at the aerodrome just outside of town, awaiting their visitor.

Ben was around the back, checking one of the tyres because he suspected they'd got a flat as they left their house.

'There have been a lot of kids roaming around town in the last couple of weeks, and I've heard at the council some tyres have been slashed.' He came back around shaking his head. 'No, everything is okay. It must've just been an uneven surface on the road.'

'You worry too much,' Amelia said. 'The kids in town wouldn't do that.'

Ben put his arms out and pulled her against him and turned his back to the wind to protect his wife of four weeks. He put his finger under her chin and tipped her face up to look at him.

'Are you excited about your brother coming? You've been very quiet about it.'

Amelia bit her lip and hesitated. 'I sort of don't know. It's a bit nerve-wracking because so much has changed, and it's been so long since I've seen any of my family.'

Ben's hand squeezed her shoulder gently. 'I know you're disappointed that none of them turned up for the wedding.'

'Well, that was our choice to bring it forward because of this,' she tapped her tummy, 'but I was disappointed they didn't make any effort to come. Or even to let me know they weren't coming. Not even a card or a good wish. I'm really on the outer.'

'So why do you think your brother's coming now?'

Amelia hesitated again, not sure whether to tell Ben what she suspected Josh's mission was. She knew her family well. 'I think maybe he's at a bit of a loose end since he and Marnie split up.'

'His wife?'

'No, his girlfriend. I suspect she got sick of waiting for him to put her first. Josh is a bit like Dad. The station takes first place.'

Amelia had never been very forthcoming about her family to Ben, just that she'd moved away because her dad had been so hard. Another brother had moved away from Granite Springs at the same time and worked his own property just out of Darwin. Amelia had been surprised when Matt and Molly had got married. They had only both been nineteen, and she still remembered the argument when their father had exploded. 'She's pregnant, isn't she? She's trapped you into the marriage.'

Matt's eyes had been cold as he regarded their father. It had been the same week that Amelia had decided to pack up and leave, and she hadn't been home since.

'No, Dad,' Matt had said. 'We're getting married because we want to have a life together. We will have a family sometime, but that's not the reason that Molly and I are getting married. You can either give us your blessing, or not. It's not going to make a damn bit of difference to us.'

Amelia's enduring memory from that week was the tears that Mum had shed as two of her children had left home under difficult circumstances the same day. Circumstances totally caused by their father. Amelia had got a lift to Darwin with Matt, bought herself a van, and found a companion. Chilli Girl, the rescue dog.

Amelia had stayed very separate from the goings-on of

her family after that. As she travelled through the Northern Territory and down to Queensland, meeting Ben had been the best thing for her. For the first time in her life, she felt loved for herself. Fair enough, she knew Mum loved her, but Dad was such a tyrant. He virtually told her mother how to feel and what she could express. It was a very unhealthy relationship, and sometimes Amelia wondered how she turned out normal. Or at least she thought she was normal.

'So, a loose end, you reckon?'

'Yeah, I guess Joshua just wants to see his little sister.'

The wind dropped, and Amelia reached up and took her hat off. Ben smoothed her hair. 'You are happy, though, aren't you, sweetie?'

'Happy? That's a very poor word for how I'm feeling. I have the best husband in the world, and we've only got six weeks to go until little Bump is born.' She grinned up at the man she adored. 'Or big Bump, as you called him this morning. I didn't know how to take that. I didn't know if you were having a go at my size or admiring the size of your child.'

Ben pulled her as close as he could with the big "bump" between them.

'Ouch,' she said 'Bump is kicking again.'

'Do you know he wakes me up in the night? I can feel him kicking on my side of the bed.'

'Get used to it,' she said. 'There's going to be a lot of that.'

'But you are happy, aren't you, Amelia? I know it must be hard. I see Sophie with her family, and Callie and her new brood. I know Mum is looking out for you, but it's not the same as having your own mum around for your first baby, is it?'

'Ben Riley, don't be so stupid. I'm as happy as can be, and I love your mum. She's so excited too. Anyway, I still haven't given up hope that Mum will turn up for the birth. Maybe she's even coming with Josh today.'

The drone of an approaching aircraft reached them.

'Look, this must be Josh now.' Amelia's toes tingled with nerves as she wondered why her brother was coming now. He could've flown down from Darwin for their wedding last month. Jenny and Tom, her in-laws, had made a huge fuss of her. The Cartwright clan, as she started to think of them—Callie and Braden, and Sophie and Kent—even though Sophie was a Mason now—had made sure Ben and Amelia had the best wedding ever. Jenna had kindly given them the use of the tearooms, and it had been a small and intimate reception, but it had been the happiest day of Amelia's life.

She took a deep breath as the aircraft landed and another gust of wind puffed gritty red dirt towards them. Ben tucked his arm around her and blocked her from the wind. 'You don't want to be all dusty when your brother arrives.'

'Don't worry about it, sweetie. He's used to it.'

Her heart set up a rapid beat, and for a moment, Amelia felt faint with nerves. She clung to Ben.

'Are you okay?' he said.

'Yeah, just a bit nervous. It's been two years since I've seen any of my family. Who knows what's changed in that time? But don't worry. Josh is the normal one. It's the others who take after Dad, and that's why I got out. I really feel sorry for Mum being there with the rest of them. But Josh is a sweetie. We were the odd pair in the family, but Dad did have him under his thumb. I'm just so sad that he and Marnie aren't together anymore. But she got sick of waiting for him, I guess.'

Or putting up with Dad, she thought to herself.

They stood there quietly as a small Cessna reached the end of the runway, and turned in to taxi towards the hangar.

Amelia's mouth dried. How ridiculous was it that she was

so nervous about meeting her brother, one of her two brothers who she knew cared about her.

It seemed to take ages for the propellers to stop, and then the door opened, and her long, lanky brother jumped out of the plane. He walked across slowly, a bag slung over his shoulder, and Amelia couldn't stop herself from hurrying forward to meet him. Ben waited where they had been standing.

'Joshi,' she cried out as she opened her arms wide.

'Josh,' he said quietly, ignoring her open arms.

Amelia slowly put her arms by her side as her brother stood there staring at her, and didn't hold his arms out for a hug. Had she so easily forgotten how closed off her family had been in terms of showing physical affection? She folded her arms over her stomach.

'It's good to see you, *Josh*,' she said. 'I was so excited when you emailed to say that you were coming to visit. How long are you going to stay?' She kept looking at him as he stared back at her. His eyes dropped to her stomach and his mouth tightened. The silence lengthened until it became awkward.

'Well, that's you here safely then,' Amelia said briskly. 'Come over and meet Ben.'

'I'll just see to the aircraft first, and then I'll meet him.' Josh put his bag down on the ground beside Amelia's feet and turned to walk back to the aircraft.

She left the bag there and walked back to Ben, tears stinging her eyes. This wasn't the Josh she knew, the Josh who she had made mud pies with, and had midnight feasts with when they were growing up. The Josh who had ridden with her, and taught her how to crack a whip. They'd been very close as children and well into their teens until he'd gone out onto the property fulltime.

Now he seemed like a totally different person.

Ben held out his hands and took both hers in his, having seen that the initial meeting hadn't gone well. 'You okay, love?'

Amelia nodded and forced her voice to stay even. 'Yes, he just has to see to the plane.'

'Okay, well, I look forward to meeting him shortly,' Ben said. Amelia sensed the hidden worry behind his response.

Well, if Josh turned out like the rest of her brothers, that was his problem. She was not going to let him make her unhappy when she had so much to look forward to, and she'd get to the bottom of why he had come to visit if it was the last thing she did.

Chapter 7

Jenna

Jenna was thoughtful as she drove through town. As soon as Emily left, she'd head out and see Reg.

She was generally out at the tearooms by about seven-thirty each morning. She preferred to do the baking there, and sometimes she didn't get home until after five. She'd usually have a quick shower and head off to the aged care home to see Reg.

Her grandfather had settled into a new routine. He still wandered down to the pub in the morning for half an hour, and then suss out who was heading out of town. Then he would hitch a lift with them and spend a couple of hours out with her, sitting on the front porch at the tearooms while listening to any grey nomad or tourist who wanted a chat or some information about Augathella.

At the home, Jenna would sit with him before he had his dinner. They would talk about her day, and then either play cards, read the newspaper on her phone together, or watch the quiz shows that came on before the news. Some nights they would just sit there, and Reg would hold her hand and tell her about his life as a shearer and a stockman.

'Did I tell you about the time I spent up in Western Australia?' he'd asked her last night.

'No. I thought you'd only worked around here.'

Reg tapped his nose. 'There's a lot you don't know about me yet, lassie.'

'I'm looking forward to hearing it all.'

'There's one thing I want you to know.'

'What's that?'

'I haven't got a will or anything. There was no point. There still isn't, even though I've met your mum and you now. I haven't got anything much. When I'm gone, you'll find a shoebox in my wardrobe. In that shoebox is a little wooden box. What's in it is yours.'

Jenna had blinked away tears. 'Don't talk like that. You'll be around for years yet. You're going to give me away at my wedding when I get married.'

'Get married? Who's the lucky fella?'

She gave him a cheeky grin. 'I don't know. I'll tell you when I meet him.'

'Can't believe I got myself a daughter and a granddaughter,' he'd say each night when she left him.

'I can't believe I got myself a grandad,' Jenna said. 'Best grandad in the world, I think I've scored.'

On the way home, Jenna usually went to the pub for dinner or to pick up a takeaway and take it home. Other nights, she would catch up with the group of friends she had made in town. Kimberly from the school, Callie when she was in town, Fallon, and Amelia.

Before Alana left, they'd have dinner together one night a week. Jenna's life was busy, and she felt content. The only thing she wasn't sure about was Luke.

When she first met him on the afternoon of the opening of the tearooms a month ago, she thought he was a really nice-looking guy. They had dinner together at the pub as a group, and the group seemed to grow as more people found out that others were eating there that night. Luke walked her home, and Jenna felt the first glimmer of attraction. But that hadn't resurfaced. When he wasn't in town, she didn't miss him like she knew she would if she was attracted to him.

He was a really nice man, but there was no point in

thinking about a relationship because he came from Narrabri, which might as well have been in the next continent. It was too far to drive, and his managerial job was based in Narrabri, while she had a new business and her new life in Augathella.

On the occasions he came to visit, Jenna was friendly, and they developed a solid friendship. She always suspected that underneath it all, Luke would like more.

One night, they sat and talked about it, wondering what was wrong with being friends with benefits. Maybe that wasn't far away.

***

Jenna parked in the carport, walked up the front steps and unlocked the door of the apartment. When she'd driven in, she'd seen Emily waiting. Her car was parked on the road, one door up from the units. She hurried inside and did a double check to ensure everything was as it should be. She didn't spend much time in the unit now that Alana had left.

Anyway, as she looked around the house now, everything was in its place. She had done a quick vacuum through Alana's room last weekend after Alana had collected the last of her stuff. She had barely lived there in the last six weeks as she had moved in with Rory. Jenna looked in the bathroom and the kitchen and found everything in order. When she was done, she walked back to the front door.

Emily was walking up the front steps, carrying Ophelia. Jenna hadn't had much to do with babies, but she had never seen such a well-behaved child. Ophelia looked around with her big eyes, taking everything in, snuggled into Emily, but never made a peep.

Emily was another matter. Jenna trusted first impressions, and knew Emily was a good person. She might be quiet and a bit reticent, but she was kind, and a good mother. There seemed to be a mystery behind her sudden appearance in Augathella. A teacher with no place to stay, and no one to mind her child. Jenna suspected Emily was running from something, but it wasn't her place to pry.

Anyway, Emily might find the place too small for them to stay. Jenna opened the door and held it open for Emily to walk in, carrying the wide-eyed Ophelia.

'Come on in. Sorry, the place smells a bit musty, but it's closed up all day while I'm at the tearooms. And I'm used to the Gold Coast, so I'm still not game to leave the windows open all day. Everyone says it's safe here, but you never know.'

Emily said, 'That sounds reassuring, and please don't worry about it being musty. I can't smell anything.' She stood there and looked around, Ophelia sitting on her hip, reaching up and tangling her hands in Emily's long, fair curls. 'This is lovely, Jenna. It looks fairly new.'

Jenna replied, 'Yes, I believe these units are only a couple of years old. This one has two bedrooms, and there's a little room out the back. If you decide to take it, you can choose. We can have a living area each. You could put your television out there.'

Emily shook her head. 'No need for that. I don't have a television.'

Jenna asked, 'What about furniture?'

Emily responded with a frown. 'All I have is what's in my station wagon. I'll be doing some op shopping when I find somewhere.'

Jenna gestured to the living room. 'That's a sofa that I brought from the Gold Coast when I moved here. There's really nothing in the living room at the back, because I never use it. It's sort of like a family room.'

Emily asked about the spare bedroom. 'Does it have a bed?'

'No, but that living room sofa is a sofa bed. I'm quite happy to move that into the room if that suits you. Like I said,

I'm rarely here, and I have lots of other things to do once I finish at the tearooms, so I'll tell you about them later if you're interested. But we could certainly make that into a bed for you. As you can see there's no television out here. I've got a small one in my bedroom.'

'Okay,' Emily said slowly. 'I'm thinking.'

Jenna hesitated, but Emily kept talking. 'The first thing I have to do is find someone to look after missy here while I'm at school. I'm only working two days a week for the next term after the spring break next week, so I need someone quickly.'

'I hope you don't mind, but I had a bit of a brainwave after you left the tearoom this afternoon. One of my friends in town, Fallon, has a little boy, and her mum, Ruth, sometimes minds him. Ruth has also been looking after one of my other friend's little boys, but Petie's now full-time at kindy and ready to go to school next year. So, Ruth's at a bit of a loose end. Anyway, I hope you don't mind, but I stopped by on my way home and asked her if she was interested in more babysitting.'

Emily's eyes brightened, and she smiled. Jenna thought, not for the first time, what a beautiful young woman she was.

Emily responded hopefully. 'What did she say? I would be more than happy to talk to her.'

'Of course, it depends on how you find her and if you're a fit. And, of course, she needs to meet Ophelia. But between you and me, I think you'd get along very well. Ruth is lovely. And very experienced. Have a think about it.'

'I will.'

'I suppose before you look for a babysitter, you need to be sure you've got somewhere to live. Come on, I'll show you the bedroom in the back area. There's a second toilet at the back of the laundry, but we would have to share a bathroom.'

'That's okay. I can stay out of your way,' Emily replied.

Jenna added, 'That'll be pretty easy because I'm not here a lot of the time. As I said, I'm generally out and about most of the day and often in the evening. Come and have a look around.'

They wandered through the apartment, and Emily exclaimed with delight when Jenna showed her the little lawn area at the back. The space was divided by a low fence from the adjacent unit.

'Oh, a garden where we can sit out and Ophelia can play.' She bit her lip again and looked hesitantly at Jenna. 'What sort of rent would you be looking at, Jenna?'

'Well, the same as Alana was paying. If you're happy with that?'

'It depends on whether I can afford it or not. I can't pay a bond or anything until I get my first pay check at the school. Things have been a little tight since we left home.'

Jenna reassured her with a grin. 'Look, I don't require any bond. I can't imagine you're going to be any trouble. As long as you can promise no wild parties?'

Emily smiled back at her. 'No, I can't see that happening. The worst that could happen is if Ophelia got sick, she might spit up on the carpet or something, but I can buy some cleaning stuff to have just in case.'

Jenna nodded. 'Sounds like a plan. Alana was paying me a hundred dollars a week. How does that sound?'

'That's perfect.' Emily released a soft relieved sigh. 'As long as you're sure it's enough?'

'Yes, a hundred dollars a week is fair.'

'Thank you, Jenna. I accept. I wonder how soon I could meet Ruth?' Emily hitched Ophelia more comfortably onto her hip. 'It would be great to get everything organised. I had no idea it could happen so quickly, and work out so well.'

'That's the nature of this town, Emily. Everyone here is lovely and will make you feel very welcome. Now that we have your rental sorted, how would you like me to take you over to Ruth's house? You can meet her and see what you think.'

Emily asked, 'Oh really? You don't have anything else to do? It's not too late for Ruth?'

'How about this? I'll give her a call first, have a quick shower, then I'll help you bring your stuff in. After that, you can follow me over to Ruth's house, and then I'll go and visit my granddad.'

Emily nodded. 'That sounds good to me.'

'Then, how would you feel, or how would Ophelia feel, if I took you out to dinner and treated you to tea at the pub to welcome you to Augathella and my unit?'

Jenna was taken aback when she saw Emily's eyes fill with tears.

'Thank you, Jenna. You're very, very kind.' Emily shook her head. 'I might pass on dinner, but I'll certainly come to see Ruth with you.'

Jenna held out her hand to Emily and said, 'Welcome to your new home.'

Chapter 8

Amelia
Earlier that day

Amelia stood straight with Ben's arm around her waist as they waited for Josh to come back across the tarmac. Her stomach was in knots, and she knew it wasn't good for the baby, but she was still nervous. She had been settled in Augathella for over a year now, made so many friends, fallen in love with Ben, was about to become a mum, and had been a wife for the last four weeks.

The thought that her parents and brothers had made no effort to come down to her wedding, or even send their good wishes, or God forbid, a wedding present, was making her feel ill. She didn't really want anything from them if they hated what she had done that much.

Josh had been her biggest tormentor when they were growing up, but he had also been the brother to teach her how to ride and the one to give her a love of horses. And, if she was truthful, as much as she'd clashed with Joshua often in her later teen years, she missed him the most.

But he was the one Dad had told that Amelia was not getting any share of the property, and Josh had been the one to break it to her the night before she left. That had led to an almighty fight and lots of hurtful things said, but surely her family could accept that she was making her own life down here in Augathella.

Ben pulled her closer. 'Calm down, sweetheart, you're as tight as a bowstring. Are you feeling alright?'

'I'm sick in the tummy,' she said, 'but it's only nerves. I

can't understand why Josh has come down *after* the wedding. Why couldn't they have come for the wedding? If he can come now—'

'What did the email say?' Ben had been quite surprised when there hadn't even been a phone call from Amelia's family when she had told them that they were getting married. She hadn't been able to get through on the phone so she had left a message, and followed it up with an email.

'Josh emailed. He said he was in Darwin and he'd be arriving today. That was it. I don't know whether he's going to stay with us, or at the pub. I just don't know.' Amelia's voice broke for the first time.

'I know it makes you sad, sweetie, but we've got our own family now, and we have to make Bump our priority. I don't want you getting upset, and I'll be honest, if your brother upsets you, I'll tell him where to go.'

'No, let me handle it. If there's any chance of making peace with my family, I think this is the place to do it. This is where I can be firm. I don't care that they didn't want me working on the property. I know Dad's attitude was way out of date, and he doesn't think much of the female sex and our capability, but I still would like to have some contact with them. I don't want to be estranged. I feel sorry for Mum; she's the meat in the sandwich, but her first loyalty is to Dad, and I can understand that.'

'Okay, we'll take it step by step, and like I said, I've got your back. But if your brother says anything out of line, I'm going to say something.'

'Ben, please don't say anything until we talk about it, okay?'

'I'll think about it.'

'Promise?'

'Okay, sweetheart, I promise, but you know that I love you, and your welfare and your happiness are my priority.'

She stood and stared as Josh finished securing the aircraft and walked across the tarmac. Her eyes filled with tears as a wave of love and despair that she had lost her family filled her.

Josh looked a little bit older. The lines on his cheeks had started to deepen, and his skin was as rugged and tanned as always. But Josh had always been the best-looking of the family, and he still was. He even reminded her of Hugh Jackman sometimes, and she'd often teased him about that.

He stood in front of them, and nothing was said for a moment. Then he opened his arms. 'I'm sorry, Mellie.'

Tears flowed from Amelia's eyes as she stepped into her brother's hug. 'Oh, Josh, it's so good to see you. You had me worried before. I thought you were going to get in the plane and leave straight away.'

'And it's good to see you too. I'm sorry it's been so long.'

Amelia stayed in her brother's loving hug for a while and eventually pulled back, taking his hand. 'Joshi, this is Ben, my husband.'

Josh started to put his hand out for a handshake and paused midway, a frown on his face. 'Your husband?'

'Yes.'

'I didn't think you were getting married until November. I'm sure that's what Mum said.'

'No, we brought the date forward because,' she patted her tummy, 'we wanted to be married before the baby was born.'

'You're married?' His voice was strange. 'Already?'

'Yes, but you knew. What do you mean "already"?'

'Mum and Dad don't know. None of us knew. You could've let us know.'

Amelia drew herself up to her full height, even though she wasn't very tall. 'Could've let you know? I emailed. And I rang. And I left messages when no one would answer their phones.'

Chapter 9

Amelia

The atmosphere between Ben and Josh was quite chilly, and no matter how much Amelia tried to get them chatting, she had no success. Ben tried hard at first, but Josh's response was cold and fairly non-communicative, so Ben clammed up. After their initial handshake, they walked towards his work car. Josh went to get in the back.

'No, you sit up in the front. You can see more from there,' Amelia said.

'No, no, I'm fine. I'll get in the back. You need more room, sis.'

'I thought we might go and have some lunch first before we go back to our place,' Amelia said brightly. She was getting cross at the pair of them. If they didn't want to come, they could drop her there and they could butt heads at home.

'Whatever suits you,' Ben ventured into the conversation. 'The house is a bit of a mess at the moment, Josh. We're trying to get the painting done and the new carpet down before Bump's born.'

Amelia glanced in the rearview mirror and saw the hint of a smile on her brother's face, and she relaxed a little bit. Maybe Josh was nervous about meeting Ben.

'Where do you want to go, Amelia? To the pub or the tearoom?' her husband asked.

'I think it's a bit early for the pub. Let's go to the tearoom,' she said, not mentioning she'd already booked a table. 'That way we can either have a light meal or a full meal. Whatever you want.' She slid a glance to Josh knowing what a sweet tooth he had. 'Jenna makes the best cakes, Josh.'

'Sounds good to me.' The atmosphere had thawed a little.

As Ben drove through town and out towards the highway, Amelia half-turned in her seat. Josh was taking notice of the land around them. 'How's your work going?' she asked. 'Are you still freelancing as well as helping Dad?'

'It's okay, I suppose,' he said. 'A bit less these days. Dad is trying to give me more responsibility.' They exchanged a look, and Amelia knew her brother wasn't happy about that.

'Sounds like Dad,' she commented briefly. 'Are you still working for the same helicopter place?' she asked.

'No.'

Josh's tension had come back a little bit, and Amelia refused to let the worry take over as she turned back to the front. She put a hand on her stomach and focused on breathing evenly and deeply as Ben drove the last couple of kilometres out to the highway. He'd been quiet too.

'We're almost there,' she said. 'This is a new place in town, although I suppose it's not really in town. It's out of town. You'll meet Jenna, the girl who started it up. She only moved to town four months ago, and she's done an incredible job starting up this business. Town's becoming a lot more touristy too.' Amelia knew she was chatting for the sake of filling the silence. This was going to be a great visit if things didn't improve.

No one else spoke.

'It's a bit different from where we grew up, Josh,' she said. She caught his nod from the corner of her eye.

Ben drove into the half-full car park, and parked near the fence. Amelia went to get out, but she paused, knowing Ben would come around and help her. She still wasn't used to being almost twice her usual size.

Ellie, Jenna's young waitress, met them at the top of the

steps. Amelia spoke before she could say anything about a reserved table. 'Can we go over there, Ellie?'

Ellie caught her eye and nodded. 'Sure.'

Within minutes, they were sitting around the table on the veranda.

'Nice to be almost in the bush,' Josh said. 'Not a bad place here.'

'Our house is in a similar position,' Ben ventured.

Silence again. Amelia held back a sigh.

'Yes, it appealed to both of us. It's just up the road from Ben's parents' place. We're in the last street on the other side of town and we've got an uninterrupted view across the paddocks to the hills.'

'When it came on the market, we snapped it up,' Ben said.

Josh stared at Amelia for a long moment. 'A baby, Mellie?'

'Yes, Josh. A *husband* and a baby. Now, let's sort this out. What do you mean you didn't know we were married? Didn't Mum tell you?'

'Mum doesn't know either.'

'What? I rang and left several messages, and I emailed.' Amelia frowned.

'For the past two months, we've had no satellite. We've been totally out of touch. There was an early spring storm and it took out our satellite. Another lightning strike took out the transformer that services all the properties around us, and we've been running on generators for the past six weeks. Not only did it take out our dish but it took out all the satellite dishes within a hundred-kilometre radius, so our three neighbours are out too.'

'But surely you've been to town?' Ben asked.

Amelia looked at Ben and said, 'Town is Borroloola and it's three hundred and fifty kilometres away from Mum and

Dad's place.'

'No, we haven't been up there since before the storm. We had a downpour and a flood, and we couldn't get out and the road only cleared to the airstrip last week. I flew Mum to town last weekend and she's stocked up, ready for the wet season.'

'During the wet season, Ben, we used to get stuck there for up to six months at a time, and it was really bad. So, Mum's got a huge pantry and a huge cool room.' Amelia frowned at Josh. 'Surely you would have checked your phone messages when you got to town.'

Her brother looked sheepish. 'Would you believe we were so used to not having service, neither of us took our phones.'

'Is that the truth?'

Josh raised his voice. 'I am not a liar, Amelia.'

She looked past him. Jenna was standing at the coffee machine watching them and she raised her eyebrows at Amelia.

Amelia gave a slight shake of her head and turned back to her brother. 'So, you mean it wasn't a deliberate thing that none of the family came to our wedding?'

'I promise you, no one knew about it,' Joshua said. He shook his head slowly. 'I still can't believe my little sister is married and is having a baby. And no, we didn't know. Wait until Mum finds out. There'll be no stopping her. She misses you so much, Mellie.'

'Is the satellite working yet?'

'No, it's going to be another three weeks.'

Amelia bit her lip. 'How come you came by yourself? Why didn't Mum come with you?'

Joshua's expression turned serious. 'Mum hasn't been well. She talked about it when Dad told me to come, but she's had COVID, and she hasn't been good since she recovered.'

'Long COVID?' Amelia said, her eyes wide.

'No, she just ended up with a really bad cough afterward, and she's tired, but the last couple of weeks she's improved out of sight. She's even been back in the kitchen baking.'

'Are you sure she's alright?'

'Of course, I'm sure.'

'What did you say about Dad telling you to come? Is he alright?'

'Dad's as fit as a Mallee bull. Always has been, always will be. He's indestructible.'

'I don't know about indestructible, but I know he's immovable,' Amelia said with a grimace. 'And you didn't answer my question.'

Josh glanced over at Ben when he spoke for the first time.

'We knew you were engaged,' Josh said.

'We got engaged at our friends' Sophie and Kent's wedding.' Amelia looked affectionately at Ben. 'Ben got down on his knee beside a pot plant and proposed.'

Josh's eyes narrowed. 'And you're happy?'

'I think I have a fair idea of what's going on here,' Ben said. 'While Josh tells you the truth'—his tone held a threat—'I'll go and get some menus.'

He stood and Amelia bit her lip as she looked across the table at her brother. 'Josh?'

'That's why I came down here. I've got to be honest, Mum did get that email, the one telling her about you and Ben getting engaged and she shared the news.'

'And what did Dad say?'

Josh shrugged. 'Same as usual, I guess. He said he didn't have to worry about you anymore. Took a load off his shoulders. Said Ben could look after you.'

Amelia made a sound between a grumble and a laugh. 'Nothing has changed, then.'

'He's alright. He's just old-fashioned. You know him,

Amelia, you know what he's always been like.'

'I do, and he's lost two of his kids because of it. Mattie is over in Darwin, and I'm down here. If he had been a little bit more amenable to both of us or more reasonable, we would still be there helping out.' Her cheeks warmed as she looked across at Ben chatting to Jenna at the counter. 'But I'm pleased he did what he did because if I hadn't come down here, I wouldn't have met Ben.'

'He sent me down here, Mellie. To suss Ben out.'

Josh didn't realise that Ben had come back to the table and heard what he said.

Joshua looked from one to the other and smiled as Ben walked round the table and put his hand on Amelia's shoulder. 'You can go back and tell him I love my wife. Falling in love was the last thing I ever wanted to do, but when this feisty girl and her van turned up in town with a vicious dog—'

'Chilli Girl is not vicious,' Amelia said. She turned to Josh. 'I rescued her on the road not long after I left Darwin. You'll meet her when we go home. So, tell me, what are we going to do? How are we going to get in touch and tell Mum that we're already married and about the baby?'

'What about Matt?' Josh asked. 'Have you been talking to him? Does he know?'

'Yes, he knows. I called him at the same time I tried to call home.'

'Maybe he could drive over to the property from Darwin.'

Amelia stared at her brother as though he was crazy. 'Do you know how far that is?'

'Of course I know how far that is. You could always come home with me, Amelia. Tell them in person.'

She shook her head. 'I'm not going to risk getting stuck at the property when the baby is due.'

'How long have you got to go?'

'Five and a half weeks.' Her eyes filled with tears. 'At least I feel better now. I thought when I emailed and left a message for Mum that we were getting married and I was pregnant, I thought you'd all disowned me.'

'Don't be stupid,' Josh said.

'Surely in this day and age there's a way we can get in touch with them,' Ben said.

Josh and Amelia shook their heads at the same time.

'No, we're at the mercy of the weather, as well as the tyranny of distance,' Josh replied. He gestured outside. 'You think you're in the outback here? This is like a city compared to Granite Springs. Anyway, I'm starving, can we eat and then figure something out.'

Ben had put the laminated menus in the middle of the table and he picked one up and handed it to Josh. 'Go for it.'

By the tone of his voice, Amelia knew Ben wasn't very impressed with the first member of her family that he'd met. He reached over and squeezed her hand. 'What would you like for lunch, sweetheart?'

She shook her head. 'I'm not very hungry. Maybe just a pot of tea.'

Ben frowned at her, glared at Josh and headed to the counter.

'I guess you're ordering your own lunch, big brother.'

Chapter 10

Amelia

Once the ice thawed a little between Ben and her brother, conversation was civilised in the half-renovated kitchen of their sprawling home.

Amelia just sat back her in the chair at the red Laminex table that had been in the house when they bought it. She looked around; they were sitting in the kitchen instead of the living room because she was more comfortable on the kitchen chair. Ben chuckled every night when he pulled her out of the soft deep sofa that they had paid a fortune for.

Holes graced the plaster on the kitchen walls where they had pulled the original cupboards out, and taped-over electrical wires hung from every corner of the ceiling. It was a work in progress as was much of the rest of the house.

'Are you doing the work yourself, Ben?' Josh asked as Ben walked in from feeding Chilli Girl.

'As much as I can, but there's not a lot of time for the house at the moment. I've been working a fair bit of overtime at the shire.'

'Maybe I can earn my board this week and give you a hand? Happy to.'

Ben nodded, and Amelia was pleased to see that an olive branch had been offered.

Ben pulled out a chair, and Joshua put his hands on the table in front of him. His voice was gentle. 'Don't get cross, Mellie, but I think we need to clear the air.'

'We do,' she agreed.

'This is the last thing I ever would've expected you to do.

I thought you wanted to have a career as a stockwoman. Now look at you, hitched, having a baby, and making your own love nest.'

Ben made a snorting sound but left it to Amelia to answer.

'Yes, I'm pregnant, I'm married, and I'm making a home. Thank you very much, Joshua,' Amelia replied.

He grinned. There'd been no malice in his words, and Amelia knew it was just Joshua's way of getting to the point. He was direct.

Ben sensed that they would be better off alone, so he picked up his keys when he finished the coffee Amelia had made while he was out feeding Chilli. 'Braden called when I was out the back. He asked if I had the time to go out and have a look at something on his place this afternoon. Are you two right here by yourselves? You won't kill each other, will you?' Ben said with a grin.

'We're fine. We've been fighting for as long as I can remember and we've both survived,' Josh said.

'What's this "something" you've got to look at?' Amelia tipped her head to the side. She appreciated Ben's concern for her, and she knew that he must trust Josh if he was going out to give them space. 'You don't have to go, sweetheart. Perhaps it's a beer Braden wants you to look at?' Her smile was wide.

'No, seriously, Braden's putting in more dongas for the cattle crew and he wants me to check out the best location with regard to the water supply. I'm sure there'll be a beer involved at the end.' Ben turned to Joshua. 'I'm a building inspector in Charleville. I took some flex-leave to meet you, but I don't mind going out to help Braden.'

'What do you two want to do for dinner? How about we go out to the pub when you get back?' Amelia suggested.

Ben nodded. 'Sounds good to me. We'll take Josh out

and show him the sights of Augathella.'

'Well, it's certainly more cosmopolitan than our place,' Josh said.

Ben raised his eyebrows. 'Can't wait to visit one day.'

'And we will, Ben. Once the baby's born, and you get some leave from the Shire, we'll drive up and see Mum and Dad, because I think if I wait for them to come down here, I'll be waiting for a long time.'

'Oh, I don't know about that,' Josh said. 'Mum is keen to see you. She just wasn't sure how long you'd stay here. My sister's not the best communicator, Ben,' Josh explained. 'We didn't know you were a local here and my sister was putting roots down.'

'She is.' Ben bent down and kissed Amelia. 'I'll make a booking at the pub for dinner on the way through town.'

'Now, Josh,' Amelia said when the front door closed behind Ben. She waited until she heard his car back out of the car port. 'Tell me what you're really doing here.'

'I told you. I came to check out your fiancé, and then I rock up and find out you're already married.'

'Obviously the communication issue we've discovered. You could've saved yourself a trip. You could have taken your phone to town, or you could have called me from Darwin. None of it is my fault, Josh.

'Anyway, no matter how much you and Dad don't like that I'm here, and I'm married, and I'm pregnant, there won't be any changes. I love Ben; he's a good man, and we are going to make a good life together. You and the family have to accept that. I'm a big girl now, and capable of making my own life decisions.'

'He seems okay,' Josh finally said.

'He's more than okay. And I love him, and I love his parents. I've settled into this town, made some great friends, and I'm happy here.'

'I can tell. But what about not working with cattle and working on the land? That's all you ever wanted to do at home. Remember, you just wanted to be out there.'

'Well, that was really all I knew, wasn't it, Josh? I wanted what Dad wouldn't agree to but I found another path for my life.'

'Okay, I guess I can accept that.'

'You have to. Tell me, has Dad made it up with Matt?'

'No, we never hear from them.'

'I wish I was there to sort it out.'

Josh reached over and put his hand on Amelia's. 'You never change, Mellie. You always liked everyone to get along, and you always want to see everyone happy. I think it's the trait I love in you the most.'

Amelia's eyes pricked as she thought of the good times she'd had growing up at Granite Springs. 'Yep, I did like everyone to be happy.'

'And the old man really let you down, didn't he?'

'He surely did.'

'Mum was devastated when you took off and bought that van. The first time you sent a photo, I thought she was going to have a conniption.'

'Well, it worked out really well. I met some lovely people on the road, had some great experiences, and ended up in the best town in Australia.'

'Okay, sounds good to me.' Josh lifted his hand and covered his mouth as he yawned. 'Do you mind if I go and have a bit of a kip? What time is it now?'

'It's just after three. I'll show you the guest room. That was the second room we did up, after the nursery. I might go and have a rest, and then we'll take you out on the town tonight.' Amelia stood and gathered their cups and carried them over to the sink. She turned around, surprised to find her brother standing behind her.

Joshua reached out and pulled her into a hug. 'You know, I really have missed you, Mellie. We all have.'

Chapter 11

Jenna

Jenna sat on the double sofa in Ruth's family room and watched the interaction between Emily and Ruth. Ruth was such a lovely person; always smiling and happy. As soon as they walked in, she extended her arms for Ophelia to come and snuggle in with a giggle and a smile.

Emily's eyes had widened slightly, and then she smiled. 'Hello, Ruth, it's lovely to meet you, and you certainly have the touch.'

'What a gorgeous little girl,' Ruth said, holding out one hand to Emily and shaking it not in a masculine way, but with affection. 'It's lovely to meet you, Emily, and I'm so pleased you've come to town. I think you'll fit in very well at the school. And your timing couldn't have been better. Jenna probably told you that I've been babysitting on and off for the last year or so, and my last little man is about to start school full-time next year. He'll be at kindy full-time next term, so apart from helping out our daughter with her little boy a couple of days a week, I'll be at a loose end, so if you are happy with what you see here, I'll be happy to work out which days with you.'

'Thank you for welcoming me to your home, Ruth.'

Jenna looked up as Fallon came in carrying Ryan, wrapped in a towel

'I'm still here. I decided to give Ryan his tea and his bath. Saves our tank water at home.' She looked across at Emily. 'Hi, I'm Fallon. You must be Emily. Welcome to town.' She turned and looked at her mother and the toddler in her arms.

'What a gorgeous little girl.'

Ruth offered the ever-ready cup of tea and Jenna was surprised when Emily accepted.

'Thank you, just black, no sugar.'

Even though it was late in the afternoon and closer to dinner time, Ruth brought out a tray of homemade biscuits.

As far as Jenna knew, Emily hadn't eaten since she'd first arrived at the teashop. She'd had a couple of cups of coffee there, and hadn't eaten at the apartment. She almost looked fragile, and with her various comments about money, Jenna wondered whether she was saving money on not eating as she should. She'd keep an eye on that.

She walked to the door. 'I'm off to see Reg now. You're right to get in at home, Emily?'

Emily patted her pocket. 'Yes, I've still got the key.'

'And if you change your mind about dinner, I'd love to see you there.'

'Are you having dinner at the pub?' Fallon asked.

Jenna replied, 'Yes, I usually go there after I leave Reg. I guess I'm lazy. The last thing I feel like doing after being at the tearooms all day is cooking for myself.'

'Jon and I were thinking about going there tonight. That's why I gave Ryan his tea early. Jon needs to go to the rural store if he can get into town before it closes.'

'Sounds good. It would be nice to have a get together. Emily, think about coming for dinner because Callie and Braden are coming into town too, Jon said. Callie works at the primary school. Have you been there yet? Have you met anyone?'

Emily hesitated, and Jenna chimed in, repeating her earlier offer. 'Emily, if you'd like to come, I'd like to treat you to welcome you as my new tenant and to welcome you to town. Give it some thought. If you do decide to come, I'll be there about six.'

Jenna stood and went to carry her cup into the kitchen, but Ruth waved her away, saying, 'Leave it on the tray, sweetie. I'll sort that out.'

'We will see you at the pub, Ruth?' Jenna asked.

'No, I want to watch that music show on TV tonight. It's getting close to the finals.'

Jenna chuckled and headed out to her car.

Chapter 12

Emily

Emily was surprised by how comfortable she felt in Ruth's home. In fact, she was surprised at how comfortable she had felt since arriving in Augathella this morning. For some reason, it just felt right. Ophelia had been so well-behaved, not that she was usually anything else, and everyone had been so welcoming.

As she walked out the door after negotiating a very reasonable rate with Ruth for babysitting Ophelia, she held her arms out to the little girl.

'Mum, mum,' she yelled loudly. 'Din din?'

'If you'd like to go out for tea, I'm more than happy for you to leave Ophelia here for a couple of hours,' Ruth offered. 'It's almost six now.' Ruth took Emily's hand again. 'It's been so lovely to meet you, Emily. I hope you enjoy living in Augathella. Jenna is a sweetheart, and she'll make a great landlady.'

'I already feel as though she's more a friend,' Emily replied. 'I'm actually overwhelmed by the welcome I've had, and how everything has worked out in one day.'

'Well, if you want to finish off the day with dinner at the pub, the offer is there.'

Emily's eyes welled with tears. Maybe things are going to look up a bit, she thought to herself. Her welcome had been warm and comforting. Not one person had asked difficult questions or wanted to know her background or why she was here, and that made her feel safe.

'Thank you, Ruth. I will accept your kind offer. I'll take

Ophelia home and give her a bath and tea, and I'll get the porta cot.'

Ruth waved a hand. 'No need, love. There's a nursery with a cot and a bed in the spare room. And lots of toys for all ages.'

Emily had surprised herself. A week ago, a month ago, a year ago, going out in a group and leaving Ophelia behind would have been the last thing she considered.

The last thing she'd have been able to do.

##

Emily drove back the two streets to their new home and carried Ophelia inside. She held her daughter in one arm and went inside and sat her on the floor with a couple of toys. 'You stay there. I'll be back in a minute. I've just got to get our food out of the fridge, sweetie.'

Ophelia smiled at her and picked up her favourite toy, a little yellow car with one missing wheel.

It only took a couple of minutes for her to empty out the camp fridge. She smiled as she opened the fridge in the kitchen. Jenna had already cleared the bottom two shelves for her, as she said she would, and one of the drawers in the freezer was empty. She didn't have anything frozen to put in there yet. Once she had the food stored, Emily brought Ophelia into the kitchen and sat her on the floor, putting out more toys from her bag.

Emily smiled as she handed the toys over. They carried all their belongings with them in the car—she had no intention of ever going back to Townsville—their clothes and their bedding, and the food filled the back of the station wagon, but toys certainly made up the majority of their luggage.

She quickly peeled a potato and chopped off a piece of

pumpkin to prepare the mash for Ophelia's dinner. There was one piece of chicken left from last night, and she sliced it up into bite-sized pieces. Once the vegetables were cooked, she mashed them with some butter and milk. She sat at the table with Ophelia on her lap; her little girl was still too little to sit in a chair, and they didn't have any small chairs with them because there wasn't enough room in the station wagon. She'd have to think about it; perhaps if she had enough money to top the car up, she could drive down to Charleville and look at some op shops. Once the tank was full, she'd be using very little fuel in this small town.

Ophelia was well-behaved. She ate all of the food that Emily offered to her. After she was finished, Emily wiped her face and hands with a wet flannel washer. 'I think, if we're in luck, there is one little container of jelly and fruit left in our bag. Let's have a look, shall we?'

Ophelia started pointing as soon as Emily mentioned the jelly. Her daughter had a sweet tooth and had enjoyed the one biscuit that Emily allowed her to have at Ruth's house.

After she cleaned up in the kitchen, she carried Ophelia into the bathroom and ran a shallow bath. Ophelia splashed, and eventually Emily lifted her out, nuzzling her nose into her baby's warm, sweet-smelling skin.

She grimaced as she dried Ophelia, embarrassed to see how threadbare the towel was. It would be wonderful to get a pay packet, and be able to replace some of their linen.

'Yes, definitely a trip to the op shop tomorrow. There's nothing else we need to spend money on until my first pay. New towels, and maybe some new clothes for you.'

Ophelia was wide awake, giggling, and playful. 'Out,' she said, pointing to the door.

'Do you want to go outside, sweetie? We'll go out and have a quick look in the back garden before we go back to Ruth's.'

Emily carried her daughter out the back door and sat on the steps, her eyes fixed on the horizon. Her stomach growled, and she realised how hungry she was. She knew she had to eat more; she had to stay well to look after Ophelia, because if she got sick, there was nobody else.

Once the sun had slipped below the horizon and lit up the evening sky in a palette of apricots and mauves, Emily held Ophelia's hand and helped her walk up the back steps and through the door. Ophelia walked around the lounge and sat back down on the blanket where her toys were.

Emily walked across to her bag and took out her purse and opened it. The fuel docket from today fluttered to the floor, and she picked it up and put it safely in the back. She needed to keep track of her money because everything she did was in cash.

She opened the zipper at the back part of her wallet and pulled out the bundle of notes, counting what she had. She still had four hundred and fifty dollars left, which would fill the car up, buy food for the next couple of weeks, and once she'd paid two weeks rent to Jenna, it would leave her a little to spend at the op shop. Perhaps she could look for a small highchair, and when they finished here, she could take it back. She certainly had enough to buy a cheap meal at the hotel. Jenna's invitation had been kind, although she wouldn't let Jenna pay for her dinner.

Without thinking about what she was doing, she put the money safely back in the second part of her purse and slipped twenty-five dollars into the front section. She would go out for dinner, and have an entrée only. It would be good to meet people from the school before she started work.

Emily still wondered whether she had done the wrong thing taking this job and stopping here in Augathella; perhaps she should have just kept heading for South Australia. But the opportunity of having a term's work and getting some money behind her had been enticing. The only problem was, it was a lot closer to Narrabri than Townsville had been. However, there was no way she would go that way; she would stick to the far western highway.

For the first time in a long time, contentment stole over her as she sat there, watching her little girl playing happily with her toys.

Chapter 13

Jenna

Jenna was surprised but happy to see Emily walk through the side door of the pub; Emily stood hesitantly looking around.

'Emily,' she called. 'Over here.'

Emily looked over and Jenna gestured to the table where she was sitting with two other couples. Two young boys were bickering at the other end of the table, and the noise was so loud that one of the women turned around and said, 'If you boys don't stop squabbling, you will be sitting outside.' There was immediate silence, and to Emily's surprise, the boys settled down. Jenna stood up and walked over to stand beside Emily.

'Emily, this is Callie and Braden Cartwright, and Sophie and Ben Mason.' The men stood up and nodded to her, and the two women smiled their welcome.

'Welcome, Emily. I'm Callie. I believe you're joining us at the primary school after the holidays.'

'Yes, I am,' Emily said. 'It's nice to meet you all.' The man sitting beside Callie stood and came round, pulling out a chair for her.

'So, you've moved to Augathella to start work at our lovely school,' the other woman, Sophie, said.

'Yes,' Emily said, 'I've heard good things about the school.'

'Very different to when Braden, Kent, and I went there. It was only a two-teacher school back in the dark ages.' Sophie grinned. 'Braden and I are brother and sister; in case you were wondering.'

Emily's gaze dropped down to Sophie's stomach; she was obviously very pregnant and looked like she didn't have long to go. For the first time, she also noticed the double pram against the wall behind Callie. 'Yes, I'm looking forward to working there. When is your baby due?' she asked.

'Six weeks,' Sophie replied, 'but it feels like six months. This has been the longest pregnancy on earth.'

Callie laughed. 'For goodness' sake, Sophie, you were four months pregnant before you found out you were even having a baby.'

'You know me, Cal, I like to whinge,' Sophie said. But she was a pretty girl, and her smile was wide. Emily felt as welcome here as she was at Ruth's house, and by Jenna at both the cafe and in her apartment. The feeling of contentment that had settled in her through the day stayed with her. The conversation was fast, and she was happy enough to sit back and listen to the bantering between Sophie and Braden and their partners.

A little boy walked up to Emily. 'Hello, my name is Petie. What's your name?'

Emily said gently. 'Hello, Petie, I'm Emily.'

'That's a pretty name,' Petie said.

'Those two naughty boys down there are my brothers,' Petie explained. 'That's Rory and Nigel, and they are arguing again. Mummy said if they wake the twins up again, they are in big trouble. I know how to be quiet.'

Braden glanced down to the back end of the table and leaned over to Callie. 'Don't worry, love, I'm keeping an eye on them.'

'Twins?' Emily asked him with a smile.

'Yes, a big surprise for us when they made their appearance very quickly.' Braden leaned over the table as the noise in the bistro was getting louder. 'Jenna tells us you have a little girl. How old is she?'

'Eighteen months.'

'Shall we go and order?' Jenna interrupted. 'Before it gets too busy. I'm going to get some menus, Emily, and you can tell me what you'd like.'

Emily shook her head. 'No, I'll come with you. I'm not going to let you pay for my dinner. You've been way too kind to me today already. I should pay for your dinner.'

Jenna shook her head. 'No, it's my shout. You can buy me a drink if you like, though. I'll have a white wine.'

'Okay, thank you. Sounds good to me.'

'I'll go and get the drinks,' Kent said. He stood. 'A lemon squash for Callie and Sophie, a beer for Braden, and a wine for Jenna. What would you like Emily?'

'Just a squash for me too. Thank you, Kent.'

Braden walked to the bar with Kent, and Emily spoke to Callie. 'How old are your twins?'

'Just gone six months,' she replied. 'Petie, Nigel, and Rory are my stepsons, and now we have Meggie and Munro.'

'Twins would be a handful,' Emily said.

Callie nodded. 'You could say that, but I'm back at work one day a week, and Braden stays in with the twins that day.'

'He's a good dad to do that,' Emily said, and as soon as the words came out of her mouth, a wave of depression hit her. She sat rigid, wanting to flee the room, and go—

Where?

There was nowhere to go. Augathella was as good a place as any, but staying here too long would lead to questions; questions that she didn't want to answer. She closed her eyes and concentrated on listening to the sounds in the room as the clinical psychologist had taught her.

Don't get too close, she told herself.

Chapter 14

Jenna

Jenna smiled as she spotted Amelia walk in.

'Look. There's Amelia and Ben. Is everyone happy if we invite them to join us?'

Of course,' Sophie replied and the others nodded. 'That must be her brother who was coming to visit. She mentioned that at our meeting yesterday.'

Jenna glanced across at Emily, who seemed to have lost her colour in the last little while and hadn't spoken for a few minutes.

'Emily, are you okay?' Jenna asked. Emily nodded without speaking, and Jenna worried that someone might have said something to offend her. 'Is there something wrong?' she asked quietly.

Emily shook her head. 'Just a bit tired.'

'It won't be a late night,' Jenna said sympathetically. 'You've had a big drive today.'

'Okay, I'll give them a wave.' Sophie's voice interrupted their conversation. 'There are three spare chairs at the end of the table down beside the kids.'

Soon, Amelia and Ben had joined them. Amelia introduced her brother before they sat down. 'Everyone, this is Josh. Josh, this is Braden and Callie, and on the other side, Sophie and Kent, and this is Jenna. You'll remember her from lunch.'

She looked at Emily, and Jenna stepped in. 'Hi, guys.

Welcome, Josh. This is Emily, a new teacher at the school next term.'

Jenna glanced across at Emily as she nodded briefly to Amelia, Ben, and Josh, and then put her head down again. She was very pale, and Sophie looked at Jenna and raised her eyebrows.

Jenna gave her a slight nod to acknowledge her concern as Amelia's brother pulled out a chair beside Jenna.

'Okay if I sit here?' he asked.

Jenna nodded, and although she was more focused on Emily, she wondered what Amelia's brother was like.

So far, he'd seemed okay, although she had been aware of some tension at the table when they'd had lunch at the tearooms today.

As Josh settled at the table, and told Ben he'd like a beer when asked, Jenna kept one eye on Emily, but it was almost as though Emily was elsewhere in her thoughts, looking down and seemingly unaware of the room around her.

The conversation at the table ceased for a moment, and gradually, Emily looked up, becoming aware of the silence.

She smiled, but to Jenna it seemed forced, and gradually, some colour returned to her cheeks. 'Sorry if I zoned out for a minute. I am tired after the big drive today. It will be good to be settled.'

The conversations picked up again, and Jenna was pleased to see Emily respond to Sophie.

Josh turned to Jenna and asked, 'So, Jenna, tell me what you are doing in Augathella. Amelia said the tearooms belong to you. Nice lunch today. How long have you been here?'

Jenna replied, 'Not long, probably about three or four months now.'

'And are you liking living here?'

'I'm loving living here,' she said, 'It's a great little town. The business is going well, and I've made great friends.'

'Where are you from?' His voice was deep and as she met his gaze, a slow spark fired. She hadn't realised what a good-looking guy he was until she'd really looked at him.

'City. Country living is new to me. How about you?' His blue-eyed gaze held hers and it was hard to look away.

'I'm from a place called Granite Springs, where Amelia grew up. I don't know if she's mentioned it.'

Jenna had heard a little bit about Amelia's background and knew that she had left home because of some issues with her parents.

'That's up in the Northern Territory, isn't it?'

'It's pretty much on the border between Queensland and the Northern Territory at the base of the Gulf. We've got a big spread, and I work it with our dad.'

'I grew up in Brisbane, worked on the Gold Coast for a while, and came from there to here.'

'A bit of a change,' Josh said. 'But one for the better. Are you here to stay or is it just a business stop?'

'No, I think I'll most probably stay on. I'm really starting to like the town. But who can really say? Who knows what's around the corner?' she said.

'Ha, sounds like there's man on the scene,' he said with a grin.

Jenna burred up. 'Why would a man on the scene make a difference to whether I want to stay or go?'

He lifted both hands and put them up. 'Sorry, sorry, obviously a sensitive point.'

'No, not a sensitive point at all. Don't you think that a woman is able to decide what she wants to do, irrespective of whether a man is involved or not? For example, I'm settled here. I've got a good business going, so if I went to the Gold Coast and I met someone I wanted to have a future with, I'd expect *him* to follow me here. I don't see why the woman always has to follow the man.'

'I'm sorry, I didn't mean to step on your toes.'

'And how about any relationship up there with you?' He'd really pushed Jenna's buttons. 'Is that why you're staying at Granite Springs, because you've met the love of your life there?'

'I'm way too busy for that sort of thing in my life.' A glimmer of temper laced his voice. 'Dad and I run almost half a million acres; it keeps us pretty busy.'

Jenna shrugged.

Josh shook his head slowly. 'Look, I don't know how we got into this conversation, but I don't understand what we were arguing about.'

'We're not arguing. We are having a discussion. Excuse me, I need to speak to Sophie.'

***

Joshua watched Jenna walk around the table. She was a very pretty woman with a determined step and he let his gaze take her in as she stood behind Sophie and put her hand on her shoulder. As she did, she looked back at Josh, whose eyes were still on her. Despite their lively conversation—almost an argument—attraction surged as he'd sat beside her. Josh had actually noticed Jenna as soon as they'd walked in. She had presence, her smile was happy and she held herself confidently. Plus, she was a very attractive woman.

He wasn't going to look away, and she held his gaze as if they were sharing the same thoughts. She seemed interested and determined in what she was doing, and he couldn't help but admire her. It didn't hurt that she had beautiful eyes, a lovely shade of green. A tingle ran down his back and from that moment, his heart raced as a connection established. Josh had never felt this way before.

He sat there for a moment until he looked away, then glanced up to the end of the table, where Ben had his arm around Amelia, and their heads were touching. He had come here to check if Ben was the right person for Amelia, on Dad's instructions of course, and he wondered why he had so readily agreed.

They were happy, but even if Amelia had chosen someone else, it had nothing to do with him or Dad. His sister had always known what she wanted and had gone for it. It was just a shame that Dad held such old-fashioned values about a woman's place.

Josh was proud of Amelia for sticking to her guns and leaving home. It looked like she had found herself a good home and, from what he had observed so far, a good man who obviously loved her.

Just to make sure, he'd stay a couple of weeks. While he was here, he'd have a look around because he had often thought of buying some land for himself. He liked the look of the land he'd seen as he'd flown in.

Where did he fit into the property with Dad? He was uncomfortable with the family dynamic Dad had created over the past few years. Amelia and Matt had gone, and as for his other brothers, they seemed quite happy, married, and settled in houses a hundred kilometres away from the main house, looking after their sections of the station. They rarely came back to the main homestead. Dad's three-monthly meetings were about the only time they saw Peter and Robert.

Josh sat back and looked at the happy interaction around him, his eyes occasionally straying to Jenna as she worked her way along the table and spoke to everyone. This was something that was totally out of his experience. Families and the rare social occasions had never held this warmth or happiness.

Josh folded his arms and leaned back in his chair. He was in his early thirties and still living in the same house with his parents; he had never lived anywhere else.

Ben had told him that Braden had quite a spread a few

kilometres out of Augathella. He'd have a talk with him and see if anything was on the market. It wouldn't hurt to have something down here; it would be close to Amelia for visits, and he could put a manager on the place.

And more importantly, it would be mine, he thought.

Chapter 15

Joshua

Josh was still in Augathella a week later. He had been out to Braden Cartwright's property a few times and had been really interested to see the way they did things out here. He and Braden had really hit it off, and Josh was enjoying sitting out there having a beer with him this afternoon. The weather was starting to warm up now.

'I'll have to start getting things done before the heat arrives. I've fallen behind over the past six months since the twins arrived, and now that Callie's gone back to work, there doesn't seem to be enough days in the week. How warm does it get up your way?'

'We're a lot warmer than this through the day, even in the winter,' Josh said, thinking of the hot days and cool nights he'd left at home. 'I'm used to the heat in the summer, having grown up with it. It's when it's wet and we're flooded in, can't get out to the cattle, that's a problem. We've had unseasonable floods this winter, and that's caused a myriad of problems too. Couldn't even get to the airstrip. We lost our satellite relay and because of that it caused a few problems between Amelia and me. I came down here to suss Ben out before they got married,' he said with a grin. 'And when I turned up here, not only are they already married but they're having a baby,' he added.

'You didn't know?' Braden asked.

'No, and my parents don't know either, so I'll be telling them when I go back. Amelia would prefer to tell them face-to-face now that she's learned what happened with the satellite and the phones, but it's impossible. She can't travel. Maybe when I go up, I can talk Mum into coming down here,' Josh explained.

'Don't worry yourself about Ben. He's a good bloke. I've known him all my life, and he'll look after your sister.'

'Yes, I'm starting to figure that out myself. I really like the country down here, and the people,' Josh admitted.

'It might tempt you to move down here,' Braden said.

'Actually, that's what I've been sussing out. I'm looking for some land just to diversify a bit and be a bit independent. You know, something of my own instead of the family stuff. Do you know of anything for sale at the moment?'

'I know a couple of places coming up. I don't know how much land you're looking at or how much you want to spend, but I can introduce you to some people,' Brayden offered.

'Sounds good. I'll give you my email, and we'll keep in touch,' Josh said as Braden's two oldest boys walked into the shed.

'Mum said dinner's ready,' one of the boys announced.

'I'll get going,' Josh said.

'No, come on in. Callie said that she was hoping you'd stay. She's cooked enough.' Braden replied.

'Thanks, Braden, you've made me very welcome,' Josh said.

'It's the country. You should know how things are done,' Braden responded.

Josh shook his head. 'It's very different where we are. No local pub to go to, no one lives within two hundred kilometres of us. A totally different way of life.'

'I can sort of understand now why Amelia is happy here,' Josh mused. 'She loved the place as much as I do, but Dad wouldn't have her out on the cattle. Now she's living in town and seems as happy as anything.'

'She did some work for me before she and Ben first

hooked up. In fact, she met Ben out here one day when that dog of hers bit Ben.' Braden chuckled.

'Yeah, I've heard the story about Chilli Girl,' Josh said with a smile.

'Don't worry, she's happy. Come on, we'll see what Callie's cooked up for us,' Braden suggested.

Chapter 16

Jenna

The next night

'Thanks for coming out with me, Jenna,' Josh said.

Jenna nodded. 'I enjoy eating out at the pub. Saves me cooking.'

'I thought it would give Ben and Amelia some space. I've been in the house with them a week now, and it's not a real big place.'

'So, it wasn't the attraction of my company?' Her eyes met Josh's squarely.

'Yes, it was. I enjoyed spending time with you at the pub the other night, so I thought if the two of us had some time together, we could have a chat. Get to know each other.'

'What did you want to have a chat about?'

'Get to know you? Find out a bit more about the town, the people in it, and how much you like it.'

'I like it.'

'Amelia said she worked for you for a while.'

'Yes, she helped me when we were starting out and during the grand opening; we had it a couple of months ago.'

'What about Ben? Do you know him very well?'

Disappointment flooded though Jenna. She'd been really excited when Josh had got her number from Amelia and called her a couple of days ago to ask her out.

'Is that why you asked me out? To snoop around about your new brother-in-law? That's pretty low.'

'If I'm honest, yes, I do want to know more about Ben. I

like him, but my sister is important to me. I want to go home knowing she's happy.'

Jenna folded her arms. 'Ask her.'

'I have. But to be honest, that's not the reason I asked you out.'

'Well, even if I did know Ben very well, I wouldn't feel comfortable talking about him. But luckily for me, I don't know him very well, so I won't be telling any secrets. But I can tell you he's highly regarded in the community, and that's all I'll say. Now, perhaps we can order, eat, and I can go home.'

'Oh, come on, Jen. Don't be like that.'

'Like what? I feel like I've been made use of, to be taken out for dinner so you can find out the gossip about your brother-in-law. I think that's a pretty low act, Joshua.'

Josh leaned back in his chair, ran his hand through his hair.

Despite her anger, Jenna still appreciated how good looking he was, and other than the Ben stuff, she found his company enjoyable. Josh was interesting, and she'd enjoyed listening to his stories about where he and Amelia had grown up. In fact, more than enjoyable, she really had felt that spark that was missing with Luke, and that's why she'd been so cross when she thought he had only asked her out to pry about Ben.

'Okay, truce.' Their eyes met and held, and a warm quiver shot down her back. 'Tell me some more about where you live. I thought Augathella was isolated and small, but it sounds like you have a totally different lifestyle up there.'

'We do, but tell me some more about you. I've been talking about home since we got here. What about you? You grew up in the city, you said.'

'Yes, Brisbane. Then when I moved to the Gold Coast I got into real estate, and that filled in a few years. I got jaded. I bought an old house and started a business out here.'

'But what did you do in real estate? It's a bit different to making cups of tea for tourists.'

'Hey, it's more than that.' Jenna leaned forward, and her arm brushed Josh's. Heat ran up her arm and she looked down at his skin with surprise. Desire followed quickly, and her cheeks warmed as her thoughts turned in that direction. 'I'm quite an entrepreneur and businesswoman if you must know.' She forced a chuckle as her gaze stayed on Josh and she tried to ignore the feelings that were running rampant in her body.

Josh nodded and smiled at her. 'I can see that. I've heard nothing but positive comments about your venture out there. Apparently, it's the talk of the district.'

'I'm pretty happy out there. And I don't know if Amelia's mentioned it, but the upside to coming to town was that I discovered that my grandfather, who I hadn't known about, was living out here.'

'Go on, really?'

'Yeah, really.'

'And it was just a coincidence that you encountered him?'

'It was meant to be, I guess, if you believe in that sort of thing. Have you ever been to the pub in the morning?' she asked.

Josh grinned. 'No, why would I be at the pub before lunch? A bit early for a beer.'

'Have you driven past?'

'Yeah, I probably have if I think about it.'

'Well, my grandad sits in the chair at the door from opening time. He's a local identity.'

'You're talking about Reg.'

'Yep, Reg is my grandad.'

'I was walking down the street yesterday to go to the

butcher for Amelia, and he called me from across the road, waylaid me, wanted to know who I was, what I was doing in town, who I was related to and how long I was staying. We had quite a good chat. When I told him where I came from, he made me pull up another chair, and we chatted for about half an hour. When he heard I was from the north, he told me about some trips he'd done when he was young. He told me about his new daughter and granddaughter, but I didn't know it was you. He's quite the character.'

A warm feeling suffused Jenna's chest. 'He is a sweetie.'

'He told me they call him Reg, the fella from Augathella. Love it.' Josh reached across the table and took Jenna's hand. 'Pretty special to discover your family.'

'Should we go and order now?' she said as that damn blush rose up into her cheeks again. Her whole body was on fire.

'Would you like another wine?' Josh asked.

Jenna looked at her glass and nodded. 'Why not? I'm walking home.'

The rest of the evening was very pleasant, and she had quickly forgiven Josh for his interrogation about Ben.

As they stepped out of the pub, it was bright outside. The full moon had risen, and the beautiful, fat yellow orb hung low over the paddocks to the east.

'Beautiful, isn't it?' she said as Josh took her hand.

'Sure is. You should see it up our way, The Milky Way sky is absolutely incredible.'

They were quiet as they walked down the street to her front gate, and Jenna turned to him when they stopped outside.

For the first time in a week, she regretted that Emily and Ophelia were sharing her apartment. She would have invited Josh in for a coffee, but didn't want to disturb them. She didn't want the night to end. It was a new feeling for her, and one that she was going to examine later.

'Thank you so much for taking me out, Josh. I ended up enjoying the night.'

'So did I. Maybe we can do it again before I leave.'

'Sounds like a plan.'

He reached down and kissed her cheek, smiled, and went to turn away.

Jenna put her hand to her cheek, but before she could think, Josh turned around and put his arms around her.

'Is it okay if I kiss you good night properly?'

Her eyes were wide as she nodded, and the full moon was soon blotted out by Josh's head as Jenna was thoroughly kissed goodnight. His lips were warm on hers, and softer than she'd imagined. It had been a long time since she had been kissed like that. Actually, she had never been kissed like that before. And she didn't want it to end. Josh's hands were on her waist and her skin was burning there too.

'See you tomorrow?' he whispered as he lifted his head.

'Yes, please.'

'What time do you open?'

'I get there about seven-thirty if you'd like an early breakfast.'

'See you in the morning.'

Josh was whistling happily as he walked back to the corner.

Jenna stood with her hand on her lips until he disappeared. At last, she knew what the spark was everyone was talking about. It had taken a while to experience, but wow.

Chapter 17

Emily

The first week that Emily had shared the unit with Jenna had gone by very quickly for her. Jenna had been extra busy at the tearoom and had left before Emily was awake the last three days. On the rare occasion that they were in the house at the same time, Jenna hadn't stopped smiling.

Emily had been to the primary school on the last day of term, and Callie had taken her under her wing. She had also taken Ophelia to Ruth's place on two mornings to give Ophelia a chance to settle. She'd been a bit put out that her little girl had waved her off from Ruth's arms as Emily backed out of the driveway.

Ophelia had been settled when she picked her up. 'Happy as anything. I don't think she even missed me,' Emily said to Ruth.

'And school was good?' Ruth asked. 'What you were hoping for?'

'Yes, it was. Even better, the principal asked me if I could do three days because someone else dropped out, but I said I couldn't commit until I checked with you.'

'I'd love to, and if it clashes with Ryan's days, Fallon can drop him here because she has to come into the aerodrome.'

'Thank you, Ruth. It will help me get a bit more money together before I move on,' Emily had said.

***

Jenna

On Saturday morning, Emily decided to take a trip down to Charleville to do some shopping. Jenna waved them off;

she was having a late start today as Ellie was going to open up for her. Josh wasn't coming for breakfast as he had the last three mornings, and was going to spend the morning with Amelia. She had got so used to his company; she was really going to miss him when he left next week.

She frowned. Josh lived so far away, there was no chance of a relationship. It wasn't as though they could catch up on weekends. It was going to hurt because Jenna knew she'd fallen hard and fast.

She made herself a cup of tea and took it back to bed and felt decadent as she snoozed until about 8:30. A knock on the door surprised her; who could be knocking at the door at this time of the morning?

Her heart leapt. Maybe it was Josh.

And Emily was gone for the morning. She pulled her robe over her summer pyjamas for decency's sake, fluffed up her hair, and peered out the living room window and hurried to the door, excited anticipation fizzing through her veins.

It wasn't Josh.

Mum and Dad's car was parked out front.

She opened the door with a smile. 'You're early, Mum.'

Her mother stood on the small front landing by herself. Jenna glanced over to the car. There was no sign of her father. Jenna frowned as Mum put her hand up to Jenna's cheek and stared at her.

'What's wrong, Mum? There's something wrong, isn't there?'

Her mother nodded mutely.

Jenna stepped back and held the door open as her mother walked inside. She stiffened, as her mother's arms went around her.

'Mum, what is it? Tell me. Is Dad okay?'

Her mother's voice was muffled, and she finally stepped back and looked at Jenna, tears rolling down her face. 'Dad's fine. He stayed at the aged care facility.'

Jenna kept staring at her, wondering what was wrong, and then she knew. 'It's Reg. Is he sick? I'll just get changed. Just wait for me, Mum.'

'There's no rush, sweetie. Your grandfather passed away through the night in his sleep.'

Tears sprang to Jenna's eyes. 'Oh, Mum. No. Not Reg. I can't believe it.'

Curling her fingers, she pushed the heels of her hands against her eyes to stop the tears. Stars filled her vision as she pressed hard, and Mum reached for her as she swayed. She buried her face into Mum's shoulder and they cried together.

Finally, Mum moved back a little and ran her hand over Jenna's hair. 'I know you won't want to work this morning. Do you think you should get Ellie to stay for the day and get one of the other girls in for the afternoon to help?'

'I will. I couldn't go to work now. I just couldn't. I'll spend the day with you.'

'Do you want to come to the home to see him? He's still there.'

'Yes, Mum, I do,' Jenna said, shock making her shiver as she let go of her mother. 'I'll just take a quick shower.'

'I'll put the kettle on. I need a hot drink,' Mum said.

Jenna was quick in the shower, and a few minutes later, she was dressed. Mum had a teabag in a cup waiting for her, and they sat at the table together, both talking and occasionally crying.

'I still can't believe it, Mum, but I guess I should have been more prepared. He was old, wasn't he?'

'It'll be a shock to a lot of people, sweetie. He was just such an institution in this town. But we've got to look at the happy times we found with him. If you hadn't moved here, we would never have known about him, and we would never have had those couple of months with him.'

'I guess you're right, Mum. But even though we didn't know him long, I loved him.'

The day was spent at the home, seeing Dr. Harry and making arrangements with the funeral chapel down at Charleville to come up.

Together, she and Mum cleaned out his small cupboard. As Reg had told her a few weeks ago, he had very little.

Like he'd said, there was a shoebox on the shelf.

'He told me this was here only a short while ago. He said there was a box in there that he wanted me to have.'

'I know, he told me too that he wanted you to have it.'

Tears rolled down Mum's face as she folded Reg's other pair of pyjamas. 'We'll look later.'

'Do you think he knew his time was close, Mum?'

'I think he did. He got your dad to take him down to the solicitor in Charleville last week.'

'He told me he didn't have a will, because he had nothing, but now that he had you and me, he had everything.'

'That's why he went down with Dad.'

By the time Jenna got home at three-thirty she was totally drained. She'd call Josh later and meet him somewhere. As much as she wanted to have an early night and think about her time with her grandfather, she wanted to see Josh. She needed Josh.

As she stood at the kitchen window looking out over the dry lawn, the shock started to wear off and sadness set in.

Augathella without Reg wouldn't be the same, and for the first time, Jenna wondered if she did want to stay here. Mum and Dad would start travelling again, and everyone else here had their own families to be with.

Tears seeped from the corner of her eyes and she brushed them away angrily, before she smiled for a moment, imagining Reg saying, 'Chin up, lassie.'

She boiled the kettle; it wouldn't be long before Emily

was home, and she always appreciated a cup of tea.

A car pulled up outside, and she flicked the kettle back on to bring it to the boil, then walked to the door. She didn't want to frighten Emily, who wouldn't be expecting her to be home yet, although she would have seen her car in the carport. She opened the door for her, and stopped in surprise as Luke bounded up the front steps. She stared mutely and her eyes filled with tears.

'What are you doing here?' She shook her head as tears rolled down her face,

'Jenna, are you okay?' Luke stepped forward and put his arms around her. 'It's okay. When you can get your breath, tell me what's wrong.'

She leaned into his shoulder, sobbing.

The sound of another car turning into the driveway made her lift her head, and she stepped back as Emily drove into the other side of the carport.

'Come inside, Luke. I'll make a cup of tea.' She forced a smile through her tears. 'It's all I seem to do lately. Make cups of tea for comfort. I had some bad news this morning. I haven't been to work. My grandad passed away through the night, and my parents and I have been dealing with it all day.'

'I'm so sorry to hear that. Sit down, and I'll make the tea.'

'Make a pot, please. It's on the sink, just waiting to be warmed. The tea leaves are in the caddy on the shelf above the kettle. You have to meet Emily. She and her little girl are sharing the apartment with me now that Alana's moved out.'

***

Emily hesitated as she went around to the back door to lift Ophelia out of the car. She smiled as two arms reached up to her. 'Mama. Jenna play?' Ophelia asked with a big smile.

Ophelia had fallen in love with Jenna. They spent a lot of time playing on the living room floor before Jenna left with Josh for dinner each night. Emily appreciated the help as she cooked Ophelia's dinner. She wasn't sure why Jenna was home, and she wondered who'd been hugging her on the porch as she'd driven in. The man was too tall for Josh.

Emily bit her lip. Surely, Jenna would have known that she was coming home now, so she wasn't going to walk in on anything.

Hopefully.

With a shrug, she lifted Ophelia out and reached for her bag that was next to the baby seat.

They walked slowly across to the front steps, Ophelia pointing at the different flowers and saying, 'Blue, yellow, pink.'

'You're such a clever girl,' Emily said. They had both settled into Augathella so well. Emily was even considering perhaps accepting work after Christmas if there was work available at the school.

They walked slowly up the front stairs, and the front door was still open, but Emily stood there and tapped on the door before they went inside. 'Jenna, it's me. You're home early.'

'We're in the kitchen, Em. Come on in.' Her voice sounded strained. Emily put her bag on the sofa in the living room as she carried Ophelia into the kitchen.

Her eyes widened when she saw Jenna's red- rimmed eyes and puffy eyelids.

'Jenna, is everything okay?' She went to take a step forward and realised the man she'd seen was standing at the fridge.

She turned her head and stifled a horrified gasp. The blood left her head and her head spun so much, she bent and put Ophelia on the floor. Unusually, she started to grizzle, sensing the tension in the room.

Luke? How could Luke Elliott be here in Jenna's kitchen? How had he found where she was?

Emily blinked and forced herself to look again. She wasn't wrong. She had to swallow to stop herself gagging. As she turned to the window trying desperately to compose herself, her fingers closed around the car keys, in case she had to make a quick escape.

'It's okay, Emily. My grandad died this morning. I haven't been to work.' Jenna put her hands over her eyes and wasn't looking at either Emily or Luke as their eyes met.

Luke blanched and his mouth dropped open.

'Oh, and this is a friend of mine, Luke.'

Emily turned away slowly, Ophelia hanging onto her leg. She didn't know what to do. She didn't know what to say. She didn't know whether to let on to Jenna that she knew Luke Elliott. Luke must have seen the uncertainty on her face before she turned away, and he held out his hand.

'Hello, Emily, is it? It's nice to meet you.'

Emily just nodded as Luke stared at Ophelia, and then back at her. His expression held grief.

Chapter 18

Emily

'I'll just go and bath Ophelia,' Emily said.

'I'll be going out shortly,' Jenna said. 'I'm sorry Luke, I'm busy tonight. I should be home later, but would you be right if I wasn't, Emily?'

'We'll be fine, but you take care.' Emily left Luke and Jenna in the living room.

If she had the house to herself, that would be much better. Being Friday night, she had the weekend ahead, and maybe she had some big decisions to make. What was Luke doing here? It appeared that he knew Jenna well. Was it just a coincidence that he'd turned up in the town she was in? Jenna had never mentioned Luke.

She trawled through her thoughts, through all those memories, both happy and sad, and then pushed them away, realising how stupid she was being. Luke was a good man but he knew too much of her past.

Emily didn't want anybody to know where she was. She didn't want anyone to know what had happened. It was hard enough here with all these damn pilots around. Fallon was a helicopter pilot, and Josh, Amelia's brother, flew both helicopters and planes. It was the last thing she needed to think about.

Those days were in the past, and she needed to move on. She needed to get over it. She needed to find somewhere where she and Ophelia could start a new life, a place where she could get a job, suitable daycare, and earn enough money to make a good life for them. Tears welled up in her eyes, and she brushed them away angrily. Ophelia started splashing in the bathwater, and Emily blinked. She'd been so wrapped up in her thoughts that she couldn't remember undressing her little girl and putting her in the water. How dreadful. What if she'd slipped, and she hadn't been paying attention? But when she looked down, she realised that her hand was on Ophelia's little bare back, and she was splashing in the water and grinning up at her mummy.

'I do love you so much, little one,' she said. 'We're going to be alright, aren't we? We are.'

She'd often wondered if Luke would come looking for her. It weighed on her, an explanation. He and Troy had been really good mates when they'd all been at high school, and she was sure that he would know about the accident. But she was also sure that he wouldn't know all of the horrible details that came afterwards.

The details that meant Troy's life insurance hadn't come through, and the small estate he'd left behind was still caught up in the throes of the legal machine. When it did come through, it probably wouldn't be enough for them to start anew. Neither of them had had any family, and that was what had brought her and Troy together in the first place. If only she had known what his state of mind was, and what he was hiding. If only she had known that she would be a widow at twenty-seven.

She looked down at her precious little girl looking up at her, and realised that even if she had known, she wouldn't have given away the chance to have her beautiful child.

'Emily Jansen, you just have to toughen up and get on with life,' she murmured.

If Luke Elliott came to see her, she would deal with it then.

Chapter 18

Jenna

When Luke left, Emily was still in the bathroom with Ophelia, and Jenna knew he could tell by looking at her what she was thinking.

'I think you know, Luke, it's nice to have you as a friend, but that's all we can ever be. I've met somebody else, and I realise now what I should have been feeling with you. But please, let's stay friends.'

Luke's eyes were hooded as he nodded. He spoke quietly, 'Of course. But can you tell me about Emily. Where is she from?'

Jenna shrugged. 'I don't know much; she's only been in town for ten days or so. She's starting work at the primary school after the holidays. Why do you ask?'

Luke shook his head, 'I was just curious. Does she have a new partner?'

'A new partner?' Jenna frowned.

Luke shook his head. 'Sorry I meant a partner."

'I don't know. As far as I know, it's just her and Ophelia.'

Luke leaned over and brushed his lips over her cheek. 'I wish you all the best. Take care of yourself, Jenna, won't you?'

'I will, Luke.'

As soon as Luke had gone, Emily came out of the bathroom. Jenna had a shower and washed her hair, letting the steaming hot water run over her face, soothing some of the soreness around her eyes and easing her sadness a little bit. She didn't know whether to ring Joshua or go around to

Amelia and Ben's house. The word was probably getting around town now about Reg, and it was going to be hard to talk to anybody she ran into, her grief was so raw. All Jenna knew was that she wanted Josh to be holding her.

The depth of her feelings amazed her; how could she have such strong feelings for him after knowing him for little more than a week? It was like one of those movies that used to make her shake her head in disbelief. She had read about people meeting and falling for each other straight away, and she knew what she was feeling was real. She'd had several other semi-relationships over the years, and she'd never had this intensity of feeling before. The problem was they had to sort out what was going to happen because she knew that Josh felt the same way about her; he didn't have to tell her; she just knew.

Jenna scrubbed her face with the washer, rinsed her hair, and when she was out of the shower and dried, she rubbed moisturiser around her puffy eyes. She wound her wet hair up into a roll on the back of her head and walked to her room with a towel around her. She chose a pair of jeans and a long-sleeved T-shirt because it was still a little bit cool at night.

Emily was sitting in the kitchen, feeding Ophelia her vegetables, when Jenna came out of her room. Emily stood and put Ophelia on her hip, and with her other arm, she reached out and hugged Jenna.

'I'm so sorry to hear about your granddad, Jenna.'

'Thank you. I'm still getting used to the news, but I'm okay. Emily, can I be honest with you?'

Emily was surprised, and her eyes widened; she looked around the room as if looking for someone.

'Luke's gone?' she asked.

Jenna replied, 'Yes. He's gone.'

'Where do you know him from, Jenna?'

Jenna found it interesting that both Luke and Emma were

so interested in each other, having just met. 'Oh, he's a pilot friend; he flies in here for work. Braden and Kent brought him along to the opening of the tearooms. He works out with Braden, Kent, and Jon on their properties. We have a bit of a friendship, that's all it was.'

'Ah, I see.'

'Why do you ask?' Even though Jenna was emotional, she picked up the tension between Luke and Emily.

'Oh, no reason, just interested. Anyway, what were you going to say to me? You said you wanted to be honest with me.'

'I won't be home tonight, Emily.'

'You said that before. You do whatever you have to do. I'm sure your mum and dad will need your company.'

Jenna shrugged. 'It's not Mum and Dad. I'm going to spend the night with Josh. I need . . . I need time with him.'

Emily's smile was sad. She patted Jenna's shoulder. 'If you know what you need, Jen, you go for it. We should all do that. One day, when you're feeling less sad, I'll tell you my story.'

'I'll look forward to it.'

Emily reached out and hugged her.

'Thanks, Emily. Have a good night, won't you?'

Emily smiled. 'And you have the best night ever, Jenna.'

Chapter 19

Emily

Emily knew that Luke would come; she was sure of it. As sure as the sun would rise in the morning and set in the afternoon. She knew that Luke would want to help her; he wouldn't let her go, even though she had made the dreadful mistake of letting him go.

Ophelia was asleep, and Emily was sitting in the living room with the lights out when there was a soft knock on the door. She'd showered, put on one of her best dresses, and waited for him to arrive.

She opened the door, and Luke walked in without speaking. Slowly, his hands reached out to her, and she stepped into his embrace. Having her face on his shoulder, with his arms holding her tightly, filled her with a peace that she hadn't felt for more than three years.

'I've been looking for you for a long time, Emily. It was hard to find you. They said you moved away as soon as Troy died.'

'I did,' she said softly.

'I couldn't find you. Where did you go?'

'I went to a little town called Ravenshoe on the Atherton Tablelands. There's a small cottage hospital there. I had enough money to rent a little house, and when I gave birth to Ophelia, we stayed there for six months.'

'What are you doing in Augathella?'

'I'm on the way to my new life. Maybe South Australia. I don't know where. I wanted to get as far away from Townsville as I could and away from Narrabri, too.'

'That makes me sad to hear. Why would you want to get

away from Narrabri?'

'Too many memories, Luke. Too many memories of bad choices. That's where I made the mistake of marrying Troy.'

He stared at her, his eyes sad.

'Don't look at me like that. I know it was a mistake. I should've chosen you. You should know. If only I'd known what he was really like.'

'Did he ever hurt you, Emily?'

'Not physically, but he had a very sharp tongue. When he found out I was pregnant, things changed for the worse.'

'Tell me about the crash.'

She lifted her eyes, stepped back, and stared at him. She knew straight away that he suspected what really happened.

'I can't.'

'It was suicide, wasn't it?'

She nodded slowly. 'It was, Luke. I've come to terms with it now, and I can't take any responsibility for it. Troy had mental health issues. The thought that he killed others with his selfishness is something I can't forget.'

'He had a good reason to be disturbed, Emily. I don't know if you knew about his childhood background before you moved to Narrabri when we were in high school.'

'No, his parents were both dead by the time I moved to town. When we were married, I used to hear him calling out for his mother in the night.'

'I'll tell you about it one day,' he said.

She nodded. 'Maybe.'

'Do you think I'm going to let you go now that I've finally found you? I can't believe that you're here. I walked in, and I thought I was seeing the vision that I've been wanting to see for over two years now.'

'I thought you were with Jenna for a moment, and pain ripped through me.'

'I only came here because Jenna and I have struck up a

friendship.'

'She told me you were only friends. I wondered, though, when I saw you hugging her on the veranda.'

'She'd just told me about her grandfather's death. She's a good person. And then, when I walked into the kitchen, I saw you.'

'I didn't know what to do,' she said.

He smiled. 'I know you so well, Emily.'

'I know, Luke.' She sighed. 'But I'm not good enough for you. I will never forgive myself for leaving you.'

'I know, Emily. But I also know how charismatic Troy could be when he wanted something. And when he saw that we were falling in love, he wanted you.'

Tears filled Emily's eyes as she looked up at Luke.

'I never gave up looking. I knew that it wouldn't last with Troy. I knew he would tire of you, but I never dreamed that his demons would catch up with him like they did.' Luke smoothed her hair back from her face. 'We need to talk, and we need to talk about the future. Can I ask you to do that with me? When the time is right? When you feel comfortable?'

The peace that had fallen over Emily when she was sitting there, waiting for Luke to come, grew, and the lightness of her being was a totally new feeling for her.

'We can talk about it, but not now. I've got commitments here for the next ten weeks. I won't be going anywhere in that time.'

'I can live with that,' he said. 'I have to visit here a lot over the next few months. I've just taken over the supervision of the cattle sales on another three properties. In fact, I could probably get a room at the pub and stay here for a month or so now.'

Emily smiled and reached her hand up to his face. 'That will give us a lot of time to talk.'

'It will, Emily.' His arms wrapped around her, and her

head rested on his shoulder. Something had led her to this little town for a reason, and she knew she had come home in more ways than one.

Chapter 20

Jenna

When Jenna opened the little wooden box that night, her world shifted. She stared down at the tiny pink diamond, and then she cried again as she read Reg's spidery writing.

His note was short. 'I found this diamond on the ground many years ago in the north. Take it and live the life you want to, my darling girl.'

She sat for a long time before she left home and walked to Amelia and Ben's house.

The lights were on as Jenna walked up the front path, Chilli Girl beside her. Before she could knock on the door, it opened, and Josh stepped out, closing the door quietly behind him. His arms wrapped around her, and he held her tightly. 'I'm so sorry, Jen. I just heard the news from Ben.'

'It's been an awful day. My tears have gone,' she said. 'I don't think I can cry anymore.'

They stood there quietly, their heads together, Josh holding her close. 'I've been thinking about us today, about lots of things, even before I heard the news. I don't want to leave, Jenna. I don't think I can leave you.'

Her eyes met his, and her smile was tremulous. 'You're certainly not going to go and leave me, Joshua Foley.'

'I'm not.'

'Because wherever you're going, I'm going with you.'

'Where to?'

'To Darwin, Granite Springs, wherever you're going, I'm going with you.'

'What about your tearoom?'

'That's not important to me. Finding my grandfather so late in life and then losing him so quickly has taught me a very good lesson. When you love somebody, you spend time with them, you don't put other things first, not your career, a business, or anything. I want to come with you.'

Josh's face lit up with the biggest smile Jenna had seen yet. 'You know people are going to think we're crazy, being with each other for only ten days.'

'I don't care what people think, Josh. *I* think I'm crazy. I know Mum and Dad are going to think I'm crazy. But you know what? I don't care. I want to come with you.'

'I want you to come with me too, but I never would have asked you,' he said.

'You know, there's something else I want to ask you.' Jenna looped her arms around Josh's neck.

'Something else? Nothing could be better than telling me you're coming with me.'

'Maybe not quite so early in the night, but later on, when the bistro is empty, how would you like to go to the hotel?'

His face brightened. 'You mean stay the night at the pub?'

She nodded. 'Yes, please.'

'I think that's the best idea I've heard for a long time,' he said.

Josh pulled her close, and her lips met his. Jenna's grief eased as happiness consumed her.

Chapter 21

Two weeks later

The last day of spring in the small town of Augathella marked the culmination of a big week for the town. On Monday, local identity, Reg, known affectionately as the Augathella Fella had been farewelled in a moving service at the local church and then interred in the local cemetery.

On the same day, Emily Jansen started her new career at the primary school after happily leaving Ophelia at Ruth's house.

During the preceding two weeks, the town gossips had been interested in the time that Luke, the manager from Dwyer Holdings, had spent in Emily's company.

On Wednesday, there was a ceremony at the hotel when a brass plaque was fixed to the wall above the chair that Reg had claimed for many years. Jenna and her parents had been chuffed when the mayor had come up from Charleville for the ceremony.

On Thursday, Jenna's parents stood at the aerodrome and farewelled their daughter as she left town in Joshua Foley's plane. Josh promised they would be back within the month because he was going home to tell his dad that he'd bought a property adjacent to Braden Cartwright's station. Jenna had argued, saying he didn't have to leave Granite Springs just for her, but Josh insisted.

'It's what I want, Jenna,' he'd said, 'and I want to see you still running Jenna's Vintage Tea Rooms. For a while at least.'

Ellie was looking after the tearooms in Jenna's absence.

Saturday, the day of the Spring Fair, dawned bright and clear.

Gladys Tingle shook her head as they stood in Jenny Riley's garden on Saturday morning. 'I don't know what's happening in this town, but I see young girls coming here and taking up with young chaps straight away.'

Beryl replied, 'You're just jealous, Gladys.'

Gladys retorted, 'I've never told you that I had a bit of a fling a lot of years ago with Reg. Now that he's passed, I can tell. You didn't know that, did you?'

'Get out of here. You're making that up,' Beryl said.

'That'll give you something to think about.' Glady's smile was smug.

On this beautiful spring Saturday, Jenny Riley's RFDS Spring Fair was a huge success. Children ran happily up and down between the avenues of roses as they moved from the clowns to the pony rides and the face painting. The crowds came from faraway places like Tambo, Charleville, and even Cunnamulla. They partook of delicious cakes that Jenna had spent two weeks making before she'd flown north with Josh. The highlight of the day was when Doctor Harry and his fiancée, Laura, were seen heading for the hospital when Amelia Riley and Sophie Mason went into labour within minutes of each other.

***

Callie and Braden parked outside Ruth's house when they left the fair. Ruth had offered to mind the boys while they went to the hospital to visit Sophie. Jon and Fallon were there, too, and Fallon insisted that Callie leave the twins as well.

'The more the merrier,' she said. 'Give Sophie and Kent our love,' she called after them as they hurried back to the car.

As they parked at the hospital, Jenny and Tom Riley followed them into the car park.

Callie waited until they were out of the car. 'News?' she

asked.

'A baby boy, twenty minutes ago. Ben just called and told us to come straight up. Sophie?' Jenny asked.

'A baby girl, twenty minutes ago. Kent just called.'

'Oh, my goodness, Harry and Laura have been busy. I'm so pleased they decided to stay in town.'

Callie and Braden walked quietly down the corridor, and Laura met them at the nurse's station.

'Just a very quick visit to say hello to your new niece. She still has to be weighed and checked over.'

'Is everything okay?' Braden asked. 'Is Sophie alright?'

'Yes, Mum and bub . . . and Dad are doing well.'

Callie's eyes pricked with tears as she watched Braden hurry across the room and kiss his sister's cheek. She could hear the tears thick in his throat as he spoke. 'Well done, sis, I love you.'

'I'm a real mum now,' Sophie said.

'You've always been a real mum,' Braden said as he hugged her.

Books 4-7 of the Augathella Short and Sweets series are available individually and will be in a boxed set at the end of 2024.

An Augathella Christmas
An Augathella Wedding
An Augathella Easter
An Augathella Masquerade Ball

OTHER BOOKS from ANNIE

Daughters of the Darling
From Across the Sea
Over the River (2024)
Porter Sisters Series
Kakadu Sunset
Daintree
Diamond Sky
Hidden Valley
Larapinta
Kakadu Dawn

Pentecost Island Series
Pippa
Eliza
Nell
Tamsin
Evie
Cherry
Odessa
Sienna
Tess
Isla

The Augathella Girls Series
Outback Roads
Outback Sky
Outback Escape
Outback Wind
Outback Dawn
Outback Moonlight
Outback Dust
Outback Hope

Augathella Short and Sweet Series

An Augathella Surprise
An Augathella Baby
An Augathella Spring
An Augathella Christmas
An Augathella Wedding
An Augathella Easter
An Augathella Masquerade Ball

Sunshine Coast Series

Waiting for Ana
The Trouble with Jack
Healing His Heart
Sunshine Coast Boxed Set

The Richards Brothers Series

The Trouble with Paradise
Marry in Haste
Outback Sunrise
Richards Brothers Boxed Set

Bondi Beach Love Series

Beach House
Beach Music
Beach Walk
Beach Dreams
The House on the Hill

Second Chance Bay Series

Her Outback Playboy
Her Outback Protector
Her Outback Haven
Her Outback Paradise
The McDougalls of Second Chance Bay Boxed Set

Love Across Time Series
Come Back to Me
Follow Me
Finding Home
The Threads that Bind
Love Across Time 1-4 Boxed Set

Bindarra Creek
Worth the Wait
Full Circle
Secrets of River Cottage
A Clever Christmas
A Place to Belong

Others
Whitsunday Dawn
Undara
Osprey Reef
East of Alice
Four Seasons Short and Sweet
Follow the Sun
Ten Days in Paradise
Deadly Secrets
Adventures in Time
Silver Valley Witch
The Emerald Necklace
A Clever Christmas
Christmas with the Boss
Her Christmas Star

About the Author

Annie lives in Australia, on the beautiful north coast of New South Wales. She sits in her writing chair and looks out over the tranquil Pacific Ocean.

She writes contemporary romance and loves telling stories that always have a happily ever after. She lives with her very own hero of many years and they share their home with Barney, the ragdoll puss, who hides when the four grandchildren come to visit.

Stay up to date with her latest releases at her website: http://www.annieseaton.net

Awards

2023: Winner of the long contemporary RUBY award for Larapinta

Finalist for the NZ KORU Award 2018 and 2020.

Winner ...Best Established Author of the Year 2017 AUSROM

Longlisted for the Sisters in Crime Davitt Awards 2016, 2017, 2018, 2019

Finalist in Book of the Year, Long Romance, RWA Ruby Awards 2016 Kakadu Sunset

Winner ...Best Established Author of the Year 2015 AUSROM

Winner ...Author of the Year 2014 AUSROM
Best Established Author, Ausrom Readers' Choice 2017